SCARS OF THE BROKEN

Published by:

Grand Mal Press

Forestdale, MA

www.grandmalpress.com

Copyright 2016, Ryan C. Thomas

Library of Congress Cataloging-in-Publication Data

Grand Mal Press/Thomas, Ryan C.

p. cm

Cover art by Grand Mal Press

www.grandmalpress.com

FIRST EDITION

Thank you to the many people who helped this book become a reality—Craig Wade and Brian DeLaney; Andrew Lennon; the San Diego horror writers crew—Anthony Trevino, David Agranoff, Bryan Killian, Robert Essig, and Miguel Rodriguez; Kyle Lybek and Leigh Haig for their generous editing help, and my amazing wife, Tera, who sacrifices much to allow me to write.

SCARS OF THE BROKEN

by
Ryan C. Thomas

GRAND MAL
P R E S S

For Tera, my superheroine

Chapter 1

I didn't know if it was a record that Guinness would consider, but I'd been in Berlin exactly one hour before I found myself nose-deep in a psychotic girl's crotch while she pressed a switchblade to my balls.

Mind you, I've never been good with girls. Throughout my thirty years they've laughed at me, thrown drinks in my face, called me nerd and dork and every variation of loser I can think of. One actually hit me with her purse. Like she was an old woman and I was a thief. That happened in a bar a couple years ago. She thought I said she smelled shitty instead of pretty. Truth be told she smelled like a petting zoo. Owning twelve cats will do that to you. Purses hurt, by the way. They've got buckles and zippers and shit that knows exactly where the bridge of your nose is.

But the thing about girls hitting you—it doesn't hurt as bad as girls rejecting you. Trust me, I've been rejected by girls all my life, so I know. That's a pain that sits in your heart, not on your flesh. Only thing you can do, if you can find the strength, is stay positive. As my buddy Tooth used to say, don't sweat rejection, dude, there's more pussy in the sea.

He wasn't much for metaphors.

But to his credit, if he ever *did* see pussy in the sea, like just a lone vagina floating in the waves, all gray and pruned, he would have fucked it. The guy had a work ethic.

Despite all my bad luck with girls, however, I'd never had one shoulder-throw me to the ground simply for asking if she knew where James Peter Fountai—

That's as far as I got before *wham!* My head hit so hard I saw stars.

Her free hand closed around my throat and squeezed. "Who are you?"

"Roger," I mumbled, my chin rubbing against her jeans in an area that I normally associated with happy thoughts. That I could see the outline of her underwear and was getting an erection was something I would deal with later at therapy. If I lived.

"Roger who? Why are you here? What do you want? Answer me!"

I felt the dagger tip slip through my own jeans, felt my testicles try to retreat all the way up into my chest. "Huntington. James Peter Fountain invited me. For the *Star Wars* prequels to have never been made."

She looked up at the large muscular man leaning against the wall next to us. "The fuck is he talking about?"

Muscle Man wore an army green sweater and sunglasses. His knuckles were raw and bloody and his black jeans were torn at the knees. Recent scrapes and cuts stitched across his cheeks. He'd seen some kind of action in the last hour. Probably out murdering more Americans asking for directions. "I dunno," he said, "I thought the prequels were pretty good. That annoying pidgin-talking alien was a cock, but the red-faced guy, he was pretty bad ass. And I liked all the trade federation robots. What was it they said? 'Roger Roger?'"

"Kill me now," I mumbled.

"I heard that," Switchblade Girl replied. "And if you don't get real serious real fucking quick, I will plunge this knife up into the nub you call a dick and let you bleed out in front of me."

"I told you. James Peter Fountain asked me to come here. I swear to you, I'm not lying."

"Here?"

"Yes, here, this apartment in East Berlin. I've got a piece of paper in my pocket with this address written on it. He told it to me over the phone when I got to the airport. He said someone would be waiting for me. I assumed it would be him."

She looked up at her cohort, eased up her grip on my neck. "Oh fuck. This is the guy?"

Muscle Man detached himself from the wall and leaned over me, his face upside down in my view. "You mean to tell us you're the guy that kills killers? The stone cold fucking murdering crazy bastard that cuts baddies' heads off? You?"

I swallowed. My Adam's apple hurt. "I paint too."

Slowly, Switchblade Girl rolled off of me, removing her knife from my groin. She flicked it closed, stuffed it in the inside pocket of her brown leather jacket. "I'm sorry, I thought you were some-one else. 'Roger,' you said?" She offered her hand to me and I took it, letting her help me get up. Her palms were hot and her fingers were soft and I was aware, after I made it to my feet, that her eyes were now drawn down to the bulge in my pants.

Muscle Man said, "Knives give him a hard on. Definitely a serial killer."

I turned away from her, embarrassed. Not that I should have been, considering she'd just tried to castrate me. I should have been furious, screaming at her, demanding some form of reparation. But some things just come to me innately, and trying to not look foolish in front of women is one of them. I gave myself a quick push down and faced her again. "Yes, my name's Roger. And I'm still very confused as to what is going on here. Is this Fountain's place or not? Where is he?"

"Not here," she said, moving now to the small kitchen where she opened a pantry and took out three cans of soda. She returned and offered me one, threw the other to Muscle Man. "Katrin," she said.

"Who's that?" I asked.

"Me, ya cock."

"Right." I turned to Muscle Man. "And you are…?"

"Not gay, so don't get any ideas."

Echoes of Tooth. That tough guy attitude showcased for self-preservation. I knew this guy better than he thought and I had no trouble calling him on his shit, even if he could kick my ass. "No worries," I told him, "I don't like flabby tits on men."

He puffed up his chest. "But you'd like 'em if they was dicks."

I was confused. "Tit dicks?"

"Tit dicks you'd like to suck, I bet. Boom." He cocked his head. "This is getting weird. Be a lot easier if I just punch you, yeah?"

"He's fucking with you," Katrin said, patting the shoulder of my broken arm. It was in a padded sling but it still hurt. "He's Craig. You get used to him. Well, maybe not the smell. What's with the arm?"

"Cannibals. Long story."

I saw my suitcase on its side near the door, where it had fallen out of my hands when Katrin took me down. I snatched it up and set it on a chair beside a small table. For the first time, I was able to take in the apartment, which was bigger than most houses I'd been in. More of a massive loft when you got down to it. I surmised that several adjoining apartments had had their walls knocked down to

create one conjoined space. What appeared to be a series of bed-
rooms was across from the large living room furnished with three
couches and a giant flat screen television. A bathroom was behind
me, and next to the kitchen was a dining area.

Windows ran around most of the main living space, looking
down onto a bustling city street. From where I stood I could see a
dozen shops lining the street below us. It was a grand view of East
Berlin. Mostly small eateries and liquor stores and delis. There were
a lot of people out walking, plenty of them on cell phones, just like
back in America. The occasional taxi went by, followed by sedans
and delivery trucks. It almost looked like parts of New York City,
without the trash, bums, and religious zealots waving signs on the
street corners.

The one stark difference was the line of buildings off in the
distance to the south. Large concrete blocks, every one of them
the same. I'd seen pictures of them in magazines and books about
the Cold War. Housing blocs. Cold, depressing, designed to stifle
free thought. Stick some bars on the windows and they'd look just
like prisons. Instead of tearing them down, the people of Berlin
had transformed them into supermarkets and restaurants and
megastores. I knew this because I could see the neon signs on them
even from this distance. The new world and the old world comin-
gling for the sake of commerce.

Just beyond them were the gold horsemen of the Brandenburg
Gate. I could only see a snippet of it, but what I saw was pretty
amazing. I'd have to go check it out the first chance I got.

"You're early," Craig said. "We weren't expecting you till later in
the day."

"My ticket was upgraded. They put me on an earlier flight. Wish
I knew how."

"Early?" Katrin asked. "I heard you were supposed to be here
weeks ago."

I held up my arm to punctuate my injury. "Doctors frowned
on me not healing up. Yeah. So between this and the idiotic questions the detectives in California wanted to keep asking me, I had
to push things back a bit. So . . . Fountain is coming back?" I asked.
"Or do I just hang out here and stitch up my scrotum?"

"He's back in an hour," Katrin said. "And I suppose I'm sorry about the knife thing. We've had some people skulking around. A couple men in suits showed up here the other day. They took pictures of us then left. It was weird."

"Took pictures of you? Like, just came in and snapped off...pictures?"

"Like I said. It was fucking weird. So yeah, we're a little on edge."

What had I gotten myself into? "Well I don't have a camera, just clothes. Fountain gave me the combination for the keypad. If he'd told me I was entering a ninja den I would have knocked louder."

"Didn't hear you knock at all," Craig said, tossing his empty soda can into the trash. "Maybe try using some muscle next time, mate. We build our structures strong over here."

"Yeah, well, I guess I'm sorry I just walked in. Considering you're on high alert. I take it you have no idea what they wanted? The picture takers, that is."

Katrin took a seat on the couch across from the television and started flipping channels. "Fuck no. And that's what concerns us. There's nothing here worth a damn, and Craig and I got nothing major on our records that should raise heads. But they snapped a half-dozen pics, swept some kinda wand thingy into the room, then turned and jogged off before Craig could get himself outta bed."

"It was early. Sue me," Craig said. "By the time I got down to the street they were in a car and gone."

Letting go of the fact they each had records, I wondered briefly if Katrin and Craig were a couple. But judging by the way he took a seat clear across the room from her, I was banking more on them being roommates. "Put on the game," he said.

"Fuck off," Katrin replied. "And go clean yourself. You're getting blood on shit." Craig huffed and she settled on something that looked like a crime drama, only I couldn't be sure because I had only studied my *Learn German in an Hour* ebook for about five minutes, right up to the part where it said most Germans speak fluent English.

She put the remote under her and glared at Craig as if to say, try and get it. He rolled his eyes and took out his phone, started fussing with it.

I cleared my throat, not quite sure what else to do.

She looked over the back of the couch at me. "That noise for me?"

"What? No. I just—"

"I'm not the Entertainment, you know. Either pull up a seat and chill out or go unpack. That bedroom over there is vacant. You might as well take it. There's Wi-Fi in the apartment but James has rules against us giving out the password. You'll have to wait for him to arrive to get it from him. If you're hungry there's meats and cheese in the fridge. Make a sandwich or go to the deli on the corner and get a sausage or something. Beyond that stay quiet because I'm watching this."

"You're watching shit," Craig said, fingering one of the cuts on his cheek.

Then something happened. Katrin sort of…changed. The look she gave Craig was so focused I swear I felt the hair on my arm stand up. Her eyes narrowed and her lips grew thin. Craig gulped and shook his head. "Stop looking at me," he said, then stood up and went to a room off the living room. Had to be his bedroom judging by the way he slammed the door and turned on a stereo loud enough to shake the walls. There was a screech a second later as he plugged in headphones (or so I assumed) and the apartment was quiet again.

I had no idea what that was all about and I wasn't about to ask. If she was serious about Fountain coming back in an hour, I'd just wait it out on my own, in my new room. Or I could go hail a cab and get a ride back to the airport. Fuck this place. Fountain hadn't told me I'd be staying in a loony bin with two nutjobs and I was already hearing that voice in my head that said I should run away. Not Skinny Man's voice, thankfully, which had grown quiet these late few weeks, just that voice of reason that keeps us all alive. Call it your gut, call it intuition, it was warning me that living here was going to be hell on Earth.

I brought my stuff into the empty bedroom and sat on the bed. The room was bare, save for a painting of a stone monastery on the wall. Maybe it was a real church, maybe it was made up, I didn't know. I scanned my phone for any messages from Fountain or my parents but there was nothing. I'd sworn off social media after the episode with the cannibals in San Diego because I was getting too many weird messages from sickos wanting details about my ordeal. So I currently had no one to engage with.

Except Tooth, who I swear I could hear somewhere in the room, chuckling. I knew it was just my screwed-up mind playing tricks again, just like when I heard Skinny Man, but I wanted so badly to believe he was real and could hear me. I needed a real friend. "This place kind of sucks," I said.

Dude, Katrin is totally hot. Tooth's voice sounded like it was in front of me now. *Go talk to her. Maybe say something insulting so she sits on your face again. Most action you've seen in months.*

"She was trying to stab my taint. She doesn't want to talk to me."

God, you're being such a pussy. She knew what she was doing, and I could tell when she saw your pathetic lightsaber at half-mast she was proud of herself. Girls like to know they can give you a boner, man. Don't you know anything?

"I'm not going to talk to her. I'm not gonna talk to anyone until Fountain gets here and tells me what the flying fuck this is all about."

I could almost kind of see Tooth now, which happened whenever my mind was really working overtime. He leaned against the dresser and fussed with his hat. *Fine, be a wuss. You like it here, in Berlin? Remember those Nazi fucks we kicked the shit out of that time? Must be tons of 'em here, right?*

"I don't think Germany is like that anymore, Tooth. Seems to me they're trying real hard to not be associated with that stuff anymore. Everyone I've met is polite. Well, except for the two people in the other room, one of whom is clearly British and one of whom was only defending herself against a strange man in her apartment so I can't blame her too much."

You're losing me.

"I'm saying there're no Nazis here. Let it go."

How can there not be? Wasn't that long ago. People out there . . . it was like, their grandfathers and shit.

"And our grandfather's made black people use separate bathrooms. And our great grandfathers kept them in cages and whipped them if they didn't pick cotton. Times change, you know, and new generations do their best to atone for their ancestors' atrocities."

Fine, there's no Nazis. But you know what is here?

"Your dick cheese. Stinking up my new bedroom."

Well yes, but I'm talking about beer, you cumstain. You're in the fucking motherland and I'm so jealous I wanna punch you in the head. Get off your ass and go ask Katrin to take you somewhere to get a German beer. A real German beer. Not that Berline Weiss shit your read about in your travel book. I'm talking the good shit. Then, you get her good and drunk, bring her back here, and burrow into her chasm. C'mon, man, at least let me live vicariously through you. Go ask her.

I unzipped my suitcase and rifled through it for my phone charger. "I'm not asking her. She clearly doesn't like me and I do not want to get on her bad side."

Same old Roger. Still afraid of girls. Jesus.

"Fuck you, Tooth. I'm not afraid of girls, or anyone else for that matter. I just don't see the point of pissing off my roommate. You wanna bang Katrin so bad, you go talk to her. I'm not asking her so let it go."

There was a new voice behind me: "Who're you talking to?"

I looked up, saw Katrin standing in the doorway to my room. She had the remote control in one hand and her soda in the other.

"No one," I said, embarrassed that she'd caught me having one of my conversations with a dead person. "Just talking to myself."

She looked me up and down, scanned the room, then took another step in and looked at all the walls. Like she could smell something but couldn't tell where it was coming from. "Well, tell your other self to keep it down and tell him I'm not in the mood for beer now. James called and said he's coming to get you. He'll be here in a couple minutes. Says you're going out so grab a jacket and be ready."

She turned and left the room. I could feel my jaw hanging open as I searched around for Tooth. His image was gone, as was his voice. I sat on the bed and stared blankly into the air before me.

How the hell had she known Tooth suggested I ask her to get a beer?

Chapter 2

I waited out on the street where the air was warm and smelled mostly of concrete. I watched a young mom pushing her baby in a stroller, bopping her head to her iPod headphones. Some teens in hoodies brushed past me as if I was an annoyance. Didn't matter what country you lived in, teens had attitude either way.

Fountain pulled up in a black sedan, and when I got in the passenger seat he leaned over and shook my hand. "You made it."

"I did."

He noted my arm. "Still hurt?"

"It's better. I can move it now. Still gets sore if I sleep on it wrong."

"You meet Katrin and Craig? They didn't scare you, did they?"

"No. I'm used to having knives thrust into my balls."

"She's a fireplug, that one. I found her in a coffee shop some years ago."

"Was she lost?"

He chuckled. "No, she worked there. For about ten minutes. Got fired after I ordered from her."

"What'd she do, stir your coffee with a machete?"

"She punched her boss in the face. But I caught the way he patted her backside after she rang me up. My guess is he deserved it."

We turned down some side streets. I tried to keep an eye out, memorize the lay of the land, in case I had to venture out on my own. Hoenstrasse, then Vinterstrasse, then we were riding alongside a wide channel of water that ran through the middle of the city. Stone walking bridges arced over it at varying intervals so pedestrians could get from side to side. Cars had to go the long way around.

"So you bought her freedom?"

"I gave her a job. Like you. Which is why we're going to talk. How is your arm, by the way? And the other...wounds? When I left you you looked like you'd lost a fight with a rhino."

"I'm healing. It still hurts when I do this." I smiled. An old Vaudeville joke.

"Then don't do that. No need to smile here anyway. People are too focused. Hell, it's a focused city."

"So what, like, Germans are angry or something?"

Now he smiled. It was genuine. "No, they're quite happy. Events you're thinking of are long over. Atonements have been made."

"Have they?"

"By some. By most. It's a generation thing. These days Berlin is about commerce, tourism, same as America."

I saw signs pointing to the Holocaust Memorial, another for Checkpoint Charlie. "Looks like they cashed in on it, anyway."

Fountain's smile became a frown. "Now you're being too American. Knock it off, Roger. You might not like what happened here before you were even born, but don't point fingers unless you want to listen to how the world views the Gulf Wars. Berlin is the Mecca of Europe now. It's beautiful, and progressive, as you will come to see."

"Fair enough. Actually, I could give a shit about politics. Only elections I care about these days are for who's running the Jean Grey School of Mutants."

"I'm afraid you've lost me."

"That makes two of us. Where are we?"

He pulled up to the curb outside of a quaint restaurant that resembled something you might find in the North end of Boston. Small sign by the door, dark paint, candles inside. Nothing that said delicacies could be found inside. A local COIK establishment. Which no doubt meant it was expensive. "I thought you might like to eat."

We made our way up a short walk, opened the thick oak door and entered a room that smelled like wildflowers. Fountain shook the maître d's hand, asked about his wife. They knew each other, obviously, which might explain why we were escorted past other customers waiting for their tables to a private seat near the back, under a big painting of the river we'd seen on the way here. "Is that the Spree?" I asked. I'd read about it in my five minutes of German studies on the plane.

"It is. Mesmerizing, is it not? You should walk along it someday, check out the museums. Maybe get a tour of the Reichstag. Or head to the island."

The waiter came back and Fountain ordered in German. I didn't make out any of it. The waiter said something back, then left. "I got you something special," Fountain said.

"A beer. I hope. I hear it's good here."

"I ordered wine. A Pfalz Riesling. You'll like it. Have you traveled much before?"

"No. And not to be rude, but, I'm still waiting to find out what I'm doing here. You could've called me if you just wanted to know how little of the world I've seen."

Fountain steepled his fingers. "But you've seen plenty of life. I looked at the most recent stories of Marshall Aldritch's death online. Seems like even in the face of overwhelming evidence most people refuse to believe he did what he did. That must drive you mad."

"He and his followers burned beyond recognition. Fuck 'em."

"Fair enough." He paused. "Your friend, is she okay?"

"No. Of course not. But I haven't spoken to her since I left."

"My prayers go out to her."

The wine arrived and we sipped it. It was simultaneously bitter and fruity, with hints of vanilla, and I had to admit it was damned good, not to mention very strong. I felt my face go flush with the first sip.

"This is good," I said.

"You're not an oenophile. I can tell. But I'll teach you what you need to know. In time."

"I'm sure you will."

A minute later some appetizers arrived that I couldn't place. All I know was they came with tiny forks, and I'm not refined enough for tiny forks.

"Just try them," Fountain said.

So I did. And they were good. Firm bits of something unknown covered in a white sauce.

"It's skate. You know, like manta ray." Fountain popped a bit into his mouth and chewed.

I ate a few more pieces, washed it all down with wine. German food wasn't as bad as I thought it might be. We filled up the next couple minutes reminiscing about the mansion in San Diego, mostly discussing how the press put so many spins on what the police had found that no one really knew the true story except me, Victoria, and Fountain.

Finally, an entrée of seared pigeon arrived. The meat was rare in the middle, pink at the edges, all of it dusted in giant crystals of sea salt. It was accompanied by a generous salad. "They eat pigeon here?"

"It's farm-raised. Try it. It's good."

I shrugged. Why not, I thought. You kill enough people in your life rare bird seems almost boring by contrast. What was the worst that could happen? I die of some bird parasite? There are worse ways to go, I know.

I took a bite. It was beyond good. It was amazing. I wolfed it down, and polished off another glass of wine.

"How are you feeling?" he asked.

I looked at my wine glass. "What's that mean? You didn't poison me did you, Dr. No?"

"Of course not. I just want to know if you're okay to take a walk. We'll leave the car here."

"Walk where?"

"I'll show you. If you're willing to follow."

"Sure," I said, snatching up the last of the pigeon. "You've been such a romantic so far, I guess I should put out."

"You are—what do the kids call it?—snarky…at times."

"I'm just joking. Sorry, I've been listening to Tooth a lot lately. He gets snarky."

"The boy who died next to you in New Hampshire? Your friend? You hear him?"

"Only when I'm off my meds. Or getting drunk. Lead the way."

• • •

Instead of using the front door, we went out the back, which dumped us onto a city street lined with small evergreens. White lights were strung through them as if it were Christmas. It looked nice.

"This way," Fountain said, and turned right, heading down the block, past some posters promoting a local dance club.

I caught up with him, noticed he was scanning the streets like a paranoid drug addict.

"So this is weird," I said. "Leaving our wine, not paying the bill."

"There's a small basement bar up here. Sometimes it has musicians playing, sometimes it's just a jukebox. It's out of place for this street, which means it's a commodity. You don't mind crowds do you?"

"Yes."

"I figured. But you'll survive."

We crossed the street, headed into a small hotel called the Lux Moderne. Fountain led the way past the concierge desk to an elevator that took us down a floor underground. From there we had to make our way to the end of a hallway that culminated in a black door. We pushed it open. Inside was the bar he'd mentioned.

A bouncer carded us and I feared my California driver's license wasn't going to cut the mustard but the guy barely glanced at it before he waved us in. We took seats at a small table near a small, empty stage. There was no live music tonight, just the jukebox, and that was playing some reggae song I'd never heard. I couldn't tell if they were singing in German or English or Swiss for all I knew. The beat was okay, so I bopped my head a bit, realized I looked like a jackass, and cut it out. As soon as I stopped, a waitress came by and asked if we wanted a beer.

"Bring me whatever is good," I said, to which she rattled off every beer they had. "An amber?" I pleaded, not remembering anything she'd said. At last she nodded.

"I'll have a chardonnay," Fountain said.

The man liked his wine, I guessed.

The bar was fairly empty. Besides me and Fountain, about fifteen people sat at the U-shaped bar or tables. Too early for the party crowd?

"We were being followed," he said, checking the room over.

I glanced about as well, but couldn't tell who I was supposed to be suspicious of.

"By who?" I asked. Everyone suddenly looked like an extortionist.

"Interpol."

"Say what now?"

"Don't worry. I think we're safe. They were parked outside the restaurant, probably pointing a microphone at us."

"For what? Tell me you didn't fly me here to land me in a German prison."

"Hardly. Here, look at this." He slid his cell phone across the table to me. "Play the video. Don't let anyone see it."

If it's gay porn, just run, Tooth whispered in my ear. *Unless he wants to pay you to play Lick the Red Baron. Then it's just a job and no one likes their job anyway so you might as well go with it. Money is money.*

As usual, I shook my head till the voices were gone and hit play. It showed a woman hogtied to a hitching post in a dark room. She was naked, covered in blood, and crying so hard she was choking. I hit pause.

"What the fuck is this?"

"It's been edited. Only thirty seconds. Please, just watch."

I resumed playing it. It got worse. A blade appeared, like a butcher knife, but bigger, held by a hairy fist. The girl's eyes went wide and the blade drew down her cheek, slicing her open. I shuddered and hit pause, tossed the phone back to him.

"I don't want to watch this. It's sick."

"But you knew what this was all about, you coming here to Berlin."

"I knew you had some team of mystics that was supposed to help me control my so-called fate constantly ending up in shitty situations. That's how you sold this to me."

"No, I said you had a gift and that evil abounded and—"

"Yeah yeah yeah. I remember. Doesn't mean I believed it all." Our drinks finally arrived and I took a long gulp of my beer.

"Then I'll play it." He held it up and hit play. I could tell if I didn't watch it now he'd just make me watch it later, so I gave in. The blade drew down the woman's face, opened up her cheeks. Blood ran down into her mouth. Then the blade went to her eye, and shoved in. I winced and the video stopped.

"Jesus. So, okay," I said, "this is the evil you speak of. I get it. I take it this goes on for a while?"

"Oh yes."

"Does she die?"

"After several days, yes."

I felt nauseous, depressed. It never got easier, seeing that kind of stuff. "And how is Interpol involved?"

Fountain put his phone away and sipped his wine. The reggae song stopped and a Kenny Loggins song came on. Imagine that. Halfway around the world to hear the same crappy music I avoided at home. Okay, who am I kidding, I liked Kenny Loggins. I just couldn't admit it to anyone else.

Fountain shook his head. "Like I told you in California, Roger, there are some things the law can't solve. But that doesn't mean that *we* didn't try. Years ago, my associates and I—"

"The religious cult that funds you that you won't tell me about?"

He rubbed the crucifix on his chest. "The one and same. Yes, years ago we went to the police. We had evidence, however circumstantial, of slave rings, murder for hire, more. They didn't care."

"They never do." Well, except for good ole Teddy back in New Hampshire, but he was an anomaly these days.

"All it did was pique their interest in me and my friends. They followed us, perhaps assuming we were the ones engaged in evil activities."

"And?"

"And they now know we get involved. I'd like to think they just believe we're vigilantes. Which is illegal. That they don't like how we've skirted their laws, doled out a more proper justice to those who deserve it. That would be what I hope. Either way, they're always looking at me and my team."

I remembered Katrin saying they'd had some visitors at the apartment. "They think you're involved?"

"I think…they watch too many movies. They think killers prefer the attention, that sometimes they tip off the police themselves. Ergo, if I tip off the police, I must be the one doing the killings."

"And the slave rings you mentioned, the hired killers, what happened?"

"The families that were selling their children have been dealt with. The assassins moved away and we lost them. For now."

"Dealt with how?"

"They are gone."

"Where? Miami, Alaska, a shallow grave?"

"Some yes. Some no. Some in their own personal hell. Our methods fit the crime, however they can."

"You…kill?"

"I didn't say that. I said we have methods."

"You said you make people go away. How am I misreading this?"

"You act shocked yet you have killed more than most. And yet I don't judge you at all. You've done a service."

"Yeah, I'm thinking of teaching a course at the college."

I stared at Fountain. Truth be told, I knew very little of him, beyond what he'd told me, which wasn't much. What if it was all a ruse? What if he *was* some kind of whack job killer? It made no sense in the end, but I had to question it, didn't I?

"The person holding the knife on that video. Who is he? Someone you know?"

"No. I wish it was. Then we could find him and stop him. No, we have no idea who he is."

"Or where he is, right? I mean, why take up the chase? He could be on the moon for all you know."

"No, he's here, in Berlin."

"How do you know?"

"Because he showed himself to me."

"So you *do* know who he is. Have a police artist sketch him, hang up posters."

"I didn't see his face. He was hiding his head under a sweatshirt hood."

"But you're sure it was him?"

"He flashed a scalpel, pointed it at me. I know his hand. That sounds weird, I realize, but I've watched that video enough times. Watched that woman die from his knife, noted the way his fingers squeeze it. Trust me, I know that hand."

"Did you chase him?"

"Of course. But I'm old and he's skilled. He slips away like a ghost. I don't know how he does it."

"When was this?"

"Months ago. I haven't seen him since. He's waiting to show himself again though, that much I know, but for what I cannot say."

"It all sounds hinky to me. Why taunt you?"

"He's turning the game around. He's flatlined on kidnapping and torturing women. He wants a bigger game. He wants to hunt the hunter, put an end to our organization."

"So he knows you're onto him?"

"What do you think?"

I didn't know what to think, to be honest. It all felt off. "So you saw a guy in a sweatshirt. Was there anything else to go on? Did he wear crazy shoes or have a limp or anything?"

"Just that he's fast. He uses disguises. He has unlimited funds, or so we suspect."

"More rich psychos. Great."

"Our research suggests he sells his videos on the black market. But we can't trace the money. He's tech savvy."

I finished my beer in one long gulp, banged the empty glass on the table just loud enough to get the server's attention. She looked up and came over. The way she moved would make a fourteen-year-old boy feel funny in his pants. Me, I just had a quick image of us fucking in the cockpit of the Millennium Falcon. She took my pint glass and winked as she sauntered back to the bar.

"Focus, Roger."

"Sorry. I have a dream I've yet to attain. So I have to admit I'm lost. You flew me here to be a part of 'your team'—"

"Making quotation marks in the air doesn't make it less of a team."

"But it's more fun. Moving on. You fly me here to join your team, show me a video of a girl maybe getting her eye cut out, by a killer who is now chasing *you,* and you expect me to do…what? Let him hunt me? Stop him? Teach him how a good depth-of-field lens can make all the difference in a home video? Meanwhile, the world's biggest police force has you under watch. This is nuts. What am I doing here?"

The server returned with another beer. I started to imagine what she'd look like in a Catwoman costume, then my brain flipped over on itself and I started to imagine her getting her eye cut out. Dammit.

"You're fulfilling your destiny," Fountain said.

"Wait. Why are we *here?* I get they're following you but what does it matter to not be in the restaurant? Why not just let them see you chasing this nutjob and tell them who he is?"

"First, this is Europe, Roger. The rules of law enforcement are different here. And so is the technology. They can see what's on our phone if they're close enough to us. They have ways. But here—" he swept his hands at the room. "We're underground here."

I remembered Katrin mentioning the men who had come to the apartment waving a wand. Could that have been some kind of spy technology detecting for data signals from computers?

"Second, as I've said they don't believe us. And even if they did, there's more at stake here than just stopping a madman.

"Such as?"

"We think there might be others involved. The police will stop at the one arrest. We need more than that."

"So now what?"

"So now you know how we operate." At this, he slid a wad of cash across the table to me. "It's five hundred Euros. To help you settle in. Don't spend it all on beer."

I picked it up and put it in my pocket like a cloak-and-dagger pro. "I'm still hungry," I said.

"Me too. Finish your drink and we'll go back and eat. And no more talk of this tonight."

The waitress appeared with our check. Fountain tossed some money on top of it and told her to keep the change. To my utter shock she then handed me a piece of paper and said, "I don't normally do this, but could I buy you a drink sometime? Not here, of course."

"Excuse me," I said…like an asshole. I looked at the paper and saw it was a phone number and a name. "Me?"

She looked down, a bit embarrassed. "Yes. I just read your comic. *Lena 12*. I read all four in the series. I recognized you."

"Recognized me how? My picture's not on it."

"I googled you. I wanted to see what else you'd done. I wasn't sure it was you, with the arm sling and all, but the hat, the scar above your eye…you created *Lena 12*, right?"

My stomach did a somersault. I looked at the paper again, said her name in my head: Christa. "How the hell…?"

"I pirated it, I admit. It's not in stores here. So the least I can do is buy you a drink."

"It's not in stores anywhere. How the hell did you even know about it?"

"I was on an artist website. I want to be a painter. Serving drinks sucks. Someone there mentioned it so I found it online. I really liked it. But if you don't want to… I didn't mean to assume…"

Now I wondered if her earlier smiles were more than just obligatory fakes to get tips.

"No. I mean yes. Sure, let's get a drink," I said, and put the paper in my pocket. Tooth had once told me never to give my number back to a girl asking me out, that it was better to make them crazy and leave them wondering if you were gonna call. Tooth was the worst Love Doctor in the world, but he did get girls in his day. Of course, this was the first time this had ever happened so I gave her my number and she wrote it down.

She thanked Fountain for the tip and left, looking back at me once and smiling, genuinely this time.

"See," Fountain said, "it's destiny you're here."

• • •

We finished our meal back at the restaurant, got some dessert and made small talk. None of the other customers seemed to notice we'd even left. Fountain mentioned the best places to get produce and see a movie, encouraged me to check out some museums, experience some nightlife. I sheepishly asked him about getting a job, to which he replied I had one. I assumed that's what the five hundred Euros was for, and so I left it at that.

When we exited the restaurant I checked for strange vans or black cars, then realized I had no idea what Interpol would use as a surveillance vehicle if they were following us. For all I knew the two women walking their dogs at the end of the block could be undercover agents.

Before Fountain dropped me off at the apartment, he handed me a piece of paper. A website address was written on it.

"This will fill in the blanks," he said. "I will call in a couple of days."

"Where are you going?"

"I have some people to see. I can't include you or the others. I'm sorry."

I got out of the car, felt the money in my pocket, wondered

what time it was and whether I should call Mom and Dad or wait till morning. With my hand still on the open car door, I asked, "This is real, huh? And you really think I can do this? Make some kind of difference with this guy on the video?"

"We all have a purpose, Roger."

With that, he drove off.

Chapter 3

Katrin was still up watching TV when I entered, and to my surprise she didn't try to cut my balls off.

But the night was still young.

Craig heard me shut the door and came out of his room. He looked pasty and sweaty, like a man who'd just eaten a jar of jalapeños and realized there wasn't a bathroom around for miles.

"How'd your date go, mate? You put out?"

"I think I was solicited." I pulled out the wad of cash, then regretted it. I had one roommate who thought she was Zorro and another who looked like he'd been out running with wolves; I gave it a couple of hours before they murdered me in my sleep and took my pay.

"Got your allowance from James, did ya? You know it means he gets to put his finger in your bum on Tuesdays. You read the contract, right?"

I knew he was joking, but it didn't make me feel any better.

"Relax," Katrin said, "we all get an allowance. It doesn't make you special."

"I didn't say it did," I replied.

"Did he take you to get pigeon?" Craig asked. "Fucking weird, you ask me."

I nodded. "I thought it was good."

"You were followed by those cops, we think."

I nodded again. "How'd you know?"

"We saw a car take off after you when you left. It's a white Mercedes, in case you're wondering."

"You're scaring him," Katrin said. "Let him settle in first."

Craig rolled his eyes. "*I'm* scaring him? You're the one tried to cut his knob off."

Katrin shrugged, as if to say it was an honest mistake and she was done dwelling on it. I knew it would mean nothing to tell her I was going to dwell on it for a while.

"It's not there now," Craig said. "The car, I mean. I don't care where your dick is."

"Well . . . thank God for that." I headed to my room and began unpacking my bags, wondering how I was going to make this my home with police skulking about and me not even knowing the real story why. It was bad enough this city was foreign to me, that it was proving to be dangerous off the bat was almost debilitating.

It was starting to sink in that my life was really changing, becoming something I never could have imagined. I mean, I'd read enough comic books in my day to entertain the notion that supernatural powers really did exist, I just never thought they'd find their way to me. Never thought they'd lead me here for some insane destiny, as Fountain put it.

And that got me thinking on God again, the one entity that may or may not even exist, but that may or may not be the sole reason my life had become the freak show it was. I liked to think I had a scientific mind, and I could explain to religious zealots why the sky was blue and where the planets came from and what types of life probably existed on Europa based on specimens found on Earth, but I couldn't explain how Tooth's voice felt so real in my ears, or why Skinny Man hadn't rolled my number or why Fountain's gun had locked up when he tried to shoot me. It was all so damned confusing and the last thing I wanted to believe was that I'd been chosen by an almighty being. For one, I sure as shit wasn't worthy, and two, there were still so many easily explained reasons for all of this, as outlandish as they might seem. Mere coincidence explained a lot of it. And as for Tooth's continued blabbering in my ear, and my visions of him in times of trouble, well, the human brain stores familiar information and during times of stress those synapses can fire off and make us see those images in our mind, tricking us into thinking they're real. Such is the basis for schizophrenia. And no one believes there are really invisible people talking to schizophrenics. It's just brain malfunction. Arthur Conan Doyle based Sherlock Holmes's prowess on the belief that when you eliminate the impossible, whatever is left, no matter how bizarre, is the correct answer. So I knew it was all just that, my mind playing tricks.

On the other hand…there's a lot to be said for Occam's razor. Maybe Tooth *was* a ghost following me around. How the hell did I know?

I removed my laptop from my suitcase and plugged it in. Thankfully the room was already equipped with adapter plugs. Fountain was a well-prepared guy. I punched in the Wi-Fi password

Fountain had mentioned to me while we were in the bar, but it was-n't letting me log in.

I ducked my head out of the bedroom and found Katrin star-ing at me.

"I think I'm spelling the password wrong or something."

She rambled off to me which letters needed to be capitalized, then went back to her show. I lingered for a second on her profile. She was indeed cute. The kind of cute where she could shave her head and still give guys boners in the bars. For the first time I no-ticed the tiny anchor tattoo behind her ear, the way her thin upper lip made her look a little pouty.

I gave up being a creep and sat on my bed, turned the com-puter on and waited till I could get Google up and running. Then I typed in the URL on the piece of paper Fountain had given me. It led me to a viral video site, and specifically to a video marked HARDCORE EXECUTION.

"You should know," Katrin said, now standing in my doorway, "before you watch that, you have a choice." She came in and sat on the bed next to me. Her leg touched mine and I felt weird. "I didn't know I had the choice. Craig, well, he would have watched it either way, because he's Craig. But I just want to be fair. James isn't always fair."

"Not fair how?" I asked.

"His demons drive him. Too far sometimes. And he has secrets he's unwilling to reveal. But this much I know about him: he does-n't lie. So if he tells you he sees greatness in you, he sees it, and he believes it's right. But that doesn't mean it's fair to drag you in. See what I'm saying? So if you watch that, there's no getting it out of your head. Forever."

"You know what it is?" I asked.

"We all do," Craig said. He was in the doorway now too. I had-n't heard him enter.

Jesus, the two of them were like ninjas.

"And she's right," he continued. "But you ask me, watching that shit is all that matters in this world. I gotta take a shit."

"He's so refined, ain't he?" Katrin said, cracking a smile for the first time. "It's your choice. I'll leave you to it. And oh, hey, next time you wanna just stare at me all creepy in my own home like some kind of rapist, I'll slice you from asshole to ear. Got me?"

She sauntered away and I snuck a peek at her ass. Sue me.

I hit play on the video, and my world changed forever.

Chapter 4

It was the same woman in the video Fountain had shown me at the bar. Only she wasn't beaten yet. Just bound and gagged and naked. Not the kind of naked you jack off to, though. Her tits were sagging and swaying, her body hunched over giving her rolls as she heaved and cried. She was dirty, and lightly bruised around her stomach. She was down on her knees, on some kind of cement floor, her neck and arms tied to that hitching post contraption. I'd seen similar things in dungeon porn videos, but this looked like it was built by someone with as much carpentry skills as a two-year-old.

Then the man appeared with his knife and I knew what was coming and why Fountain had not shown me this video in the bar. She was going to die. I knew that much. And I knew that I could watch it all if I wanted to. That was the point. That's why it was up on this site. Same as you could watch any number of execution videos on the web—Saddam Hussein being hanged, Daniel Pearl being beheaded, any number of people committing suicide. Sites like this one thrived on attracting the sick and demented who viewed it as entertainment. Me, I found nothing intriguing about such things.

I scrubbed forward and sort of watched it in fast forward, averting my eyes when the blood was too much. The man cut her stomach open. I fast forwarded. Now her intestines were out, splayed across her knees. Still she cried. I fast forwarded. Now one eyeball was gone, which I already knew was going to happen but was still unprepared for. A giant black hole filled the space where it had been. She was screaming, her face was drenched in blood. I felt nauseous. I slid the timeline bar to the last minute. She was gone. Just a mutilated body on the ground. It looked like someone dropped ground beef in a big pile. I hit stop. There was no need to rewatch this. It was vile.

I was about to close the laptop and go scrub my eyes when I noticed there were comments on the webpage underneath the video. People were saying it was gross, sick, and wondering who the guy was in the video. And then there were the others, proclaiming it a work of art, something totally awesome. A few people said they'd watched it over and over. One guy wrote that he liked how much she cried while she died.

My nausea turned into misanthropy.

And then I saw the links at the bottom leading to more videos. All uploaded by the same username: Little Angel.

Yeah, Fountain was right, something inside me was compelling me to look. I had to know that this was the same guy.

I clicked on them and saw they were definitely similar. Women tied to hitching posts, crying. One or two of them were guys, but mostly they were girls. A couple of them looked young, maybe in their early teens. It was the same hand and the same blade in each video. The same fucking guy.

There were no distinct markings on his hand. I could just tell it was the same guy. The same gnarled knuckles and hair patterns on the fingers. I understood why Fountain said he knew that hand so well.

I selected another video at random. An older woman, perhaps in her fifties, her hair mostly gray. Her body was starting to wrinkle, and she looked up to the sky with pleading eyes, as if wondering where God was and why no one was saving her. The man walked farther into the frame than usual, exposing the right side of his lower back and buttocks. He was naked. But unlike Skinny Man, who'd masturbated with delight as he killed Tooth, this was no doubt just to avoid getting evidence on his clothing.

His arm extended with the knife and he sliced her lips off, threw them aside like he was trimming the fat off a steak. I held back bile from rising in my throat. Next he sawed down over the bridge of her nose and took it clean off her face. Blood erupted in a wave of red and spilled down her chin and breasts. I jumped forward in the video, twenty minutes according to the scroll bar. She was still alive but she was missing her ears, her eyes, and a chunk of her scalp. She looked like a wailing skeleton. Her chest had been split open and her breasts were lying on the floor near her feet.

I jumped ahead another ten minutes. She was still alive. But she was missing an arm.

Another ten minutes. Now, finally, she lay on the ground gasping for air, like a fish in a boat, her face barely human.

He was no longer holding a knife. Now he had a hammer.

He methodically stuck the claw end of it into one of her empty eye sockets and yanked down like he was trying to pull nails out of her head. Her skull cracked out over her forehead, and her face started to come off. I could see she was dead now, but he kept yanking. Then he started cracking at her skull, turning the hammer and smashing it down to break up the bone, and when he had a hole big enough he stuck his hand into her face cavity and yanked out a glob of brain. He threw it on the floor and walked away.

The camera spun toward a small table, on which he had placed three wallet-sized pictures. One of a family—a mother, father and daughter. The mother was the dead woman in the video. The other two pictures were of just the father, no doubt her husband, and the girl, no doubt her daughter. And then the video ended.

I ran to the bathroom and threw up.

Chapter 5

"I warned you," Katrin said. She stood above me as I sagged down next to the toilet.

"It's beyond sick," I said, wiping my mouth. "Oh Jesus, I'll never unsee that."

"I believe that is the point. But you've seen worse, or so I've heard."

"Yeah but…those moments are fuzzy and only come to me in dreams. Sometimes. But this… You watched it? You and Craig?"

"We both watched them. We watched them all. When James came to me. He asked me to watch them, every minute of them. And so I did. That's why we're here."

"How many? How many are there?"

"Twenty-two that we've found. There are probably more, but we don't know."

"And they're just online like that? Just available for everyone to watch?"

She swiped down on the toilet paper roll and let it unravel in her hand. Then she handed me the wad. "You puked down your neck there."

I took the wad of paper and stood up, looked in the mirror and wiped the vomit off my neck. "How are they just online like that?" I asked again.

"You can find anything online these days. Just type cucumber in a search engine and you find cucumbers up the wazoo. Literally. See what I'm saying?"

I went back into the bedroom and sat on the bed. It was getting late but now more than ever I wanted to call home. I wondered if my parents would be up. Probably not.

Katrin stared at me, like she was sizing me up. "I'm going to bed. James wants Craig and me to show you around tomorrow. So get some sleep. Or not. Up to you."

She left, shut the door behind her. My eyes went to the laptop and I couldn't help but see the images of the vivisected women in my head.

You'd better sack it up, Rog, Tooth said, *you're looking like a fruitcake in front of that chick. You've seen worse than what's on that video and you*

*know it. Besides, if you keep dwelling on it you won't be able to get your dick
up when Ilsa finally wants to go she-wolf on your cock.*

"I don't know that I care about sex right now, Tooth."

*Doctor, we're losing him! Quick, 200 CCs of anti-gayboy juice! Stat! No,
fuck that, we're gonna need to go big for this. Get me Natalie Portman in a
metal bikini and a packet of horny goat weed! Quick!*

"Carrie Fisher wears the metal bikini."

*No shit, Sherlock, I've seen the movies too. But episode six was made over
thirty years ago. Do you   Carrie Fisher here naked or Natalie Portman?*

"I dunno, I kind of ended up with a thing for Hermione. Can
we get her?"

*That's it. I'm done. I don't do sword and sorcery. You wanna fuck Hob-
bits, you do it alone. I'm going out to drink*

The voices stopped at that point. I like to think I pissed him
off, but my guess is my brain just got tired and those synapses took
a break from firing off random schizophrenic thoughts. I lay in bed
for a while, thinking of those videos. It was pretty hard to fall asleep.

Chapter 6

The next morning, Craig and Katrin took me to a breakfast café a few blocks from the apartment. I decided to take my arm out of the sling for the first time in weeks in an effort to avoid people staring at me. I let it hang a little loose by my side, ignoring the stiffness. It would still need time to heal completely, but at least I was inconspicuous again.

At the café, people reclined in chairs along the curb and sipped mimosas like they were at a resort in the Bahamas. Katrin explained that brunch was kind of a big deal here, and that if you wanted a good seat you had to arrive early. But since we were going shopping, we could just grab food and go.

We took the U-Bahn out to Mitte and emerged from the tunnel into a more rural looking landscape, complete with houses and parks and some mom and pop stores.

"Where are we going?" I asked.

"It's flea market day," Craig said. "All the shit you never wanted packed into one massive field chock full of the most annoying people you'll ever meet. It's fun."

We cut across the street and found ourselves in front of a giant park completely covered in tents and food vendor trucks. There were so many people I thought I must be at a music festival. "Holy cripes," I said.

"Arkonaplatz," Katrin said. "Mostly junk, but some treasures. Depends on what your fancy is."

We pushed our way into the throng of people and I found myself immediately lost in a maze as I stared at everything from electronics to clothing to children's toys, all heaped up in bins and on hangers and in piles and generally just splayed everywhere. Women argued in German over jewelry and men haggled over soccer shirts. Kids ran about like wild hyenas and dogs skirted my legs looking for scraps as their owners chased after them.

I found myself getting shoved into a tent run by an older lady who had several storage trunks full of piles and piles of knick knacks. An ugly sort of troll doll sat atop one pile and I thought it looked kind of creepy and cool so I picked it up.

"What's this?" I asked her.

"Ah yes, the Sandman," the woman said. "You remember it."

"The Neil Gaiman comic?"

"No," Katrin said, sidling up to me and trying to avoid getting knocked over by enthusiastic shoppers, "the demon who comes and blows sand in your face to put you to sleep."

"Oh, yeah, we have those stories in the States. Don't usually see him as a troll, though. More of a monster."

"Before the Wall fell, this area . . . the children didn't have much. But every night this little guy would come on TV and sing them to sleep. They called him the Sandman. He's a cute little communist, isn't he?"

"I just think he looks cool." I flipped the doll over and found the price. Fifteen euros, which made it… "Are you kidding me? For a little doll? It's stained and ratty."

"The price of nostalgia, right?"

"I guess I can't argue. I paid fifty bucks for an Aquaman doll once. But it was an original Mego."

"I wish I knew what that meant."

The lady in charge of the tent waved at me. "Hi. You buying or not?"

I put the doll back. "No. Sorry. Unless you have a mint one, in the package. "

She huffed and went to attend to other customers.

Just then Craig popped his head in between Katrin and me. "I found him. This way."

Katrin grabbed my shoulder and hauled me off through the crowd. "Keep up," she barked.

I struggled not to trip over so many people cutting in front of me, once almost losing sight of Katrin and Craig as they took a left between two red tents, then around a food truck selling sausages, and then down another long row of tents before we emerged into an area of the field that was open. Here, kids kicked soccer balls back and forth and teens played on cell phones and couples ate ice cream and generally just watched the business of the marketplace as if it were a sitcom.

They both moved quickly up a hill, past some remnants of the Berlin Wall and I couldn't help but stop and stare at the large cement slabs, now covered in graffiti, and marvel at how they were just tall enough to not be scalable, but short enough to feel like you had a chance. What a cruel joke. I stood against one, even as people took pictures of them, and raised my arms. Yeah, still about four feet to go to the top. How maddening it must have been to live like that.

"Roger! The fuck, man, come on!" Craig was a ways off waving for me.

I detached myself from the wall and sprinted after him, now moving toward an area jam-packed with food vendors and cars parked on grass. And then, somehow, we ended up circling back to the flea market, only on the far side of it now. "Who are we looking for," I asked, "the fucking Flash? What's the hurry?"

"This way," Katrin said, and motioned me toward a sheet-metal shed that looked like it came apart as a kit. Inside, they were selling hand-made furniture and other random decor. A young man in a flannel shirt was shaking hands with a happy customer carrying out a small rocking chair.

Craig walked up to the guy in the flannel and put a hand on his shoulder. "Hi, Michael."

Michael's eyes went a bit wide. "You should have called."

"We're showing a new friend around, figured we'd kill two birds with one stone. What do you have for us?"

"Were you followed?"

"We cut a wide berth. Didn't see anyone."

To be safe, or so I assumed, Michael scanned the crowd outside his little roll-away shed. Nothing seemed to catch his eye so he pulled out his cell phone and clicked through it. "Ok, here, I found this. It's traced back to Argentina."

Craig took the phone and showed it to Katrin. I looked over her shoulder and saw a vid capture of a woman, bound and gagged like in the videos I'd watched last night. Under the image was an IP address.

"We'll add it to the list," she said.

"What list?" I asked.

Suddenly Michael lunged forward and grabbed my shirt, spun me around and threw me down to my back. He got in my face. His crucifix, dangling on a gold chain, brushed against my nose. "Who the fuck are you?" he growled.

I instinctively grabbed his hands, tried to get my thumbs under his fingers and twist. The sonofabitch was stronger than he looked. "Is this a customary greeting in Berlin? Being tackled and harassed? Because it seems to be happening to me a lot. I'm cool with it and all, I just want to know the rules. Like, can I tackle anyone who says hi, or does it need to be Saturday or something?"

"What's he talking about?" Michael growled, twisting my shirt into a knot near my throat.

"Get the fuck off him, Michael," Katrin said, grabbing him and pulling him off me.

I stood up and brushed myself off, my heart racing, ready for a fight. It took a few seconds before I was able to calm down.

"Roger's with us," Craig said. "He's vouched for by Fountain. Can we get back to the matter at hand. You're sure this is legit. This IP stamp?"

Michael took a deep breath, composed himself. "My boys don't make mistakes. Tell you this though, it was a tough trace. That signal got all sorts of rerouted before they could find its origin. But yes, Argentina. Speaking of which…" Michael held out his hand, palm up.

Craig nodded at me. "Pay him."

"What?" I said, caught off guard. "Why me? What am I even paying for?"

"Information, son," Michael said.

"Well listen, Dad, I don't usually pay people who get in my face like that. In fact, you should pay me for a new shirt."

Michael shrugged. "I had to make sure you were okay, you know? No hard feelings. Now pay me."

I looked at Craig. "You pay him. This is *my* money."

"It's company money," Karin said. "You'll learn."

I huffed, peeled twenty euros off my stack, because it was the lowest denomination I had, and slapped it in his palm as hard as I could. I'm sure it hurt me more than him.

"What do I look like," Michael said, "a charity organization?" He flexed his palm for more.

The nerve of this guy. I gave him twenty more euros. I didn't slap it down this time, my hand still pulsing. "Take it or leave it," I said. At least that sounded tough, so I felt a little better about myself again.

He smiled and put it in his pocket. "Thanks. Now, one more tid-bit," he said. "I went above and beyond for you guys, as usual. Had some friends actually trace the service provider of the IP address for you. It was being billed to an apartment owned by a Rita Nunez. She's in her 50s. Lovely lady, likes pasta and reruns of *Seinfeld*."

"You take her out to dinner or something?" Craig asked.

"My friends called her, pretended to be a survey. People will tell you anything you tell 'em it's a survey and they could win money at the end."

"You? Giving people money?" I said. "That's a joke."

"Your friend Roger here is a comedian. I like 'im. Anyway, she lives alone, never married, no kids, no boyfriend. Must be a hef-fer—"

"Nice," Katrin said. "Chivalry ain't dead."

"Chivalry is just extended foreplay, Katrin, and in this day and age, who has the fucking time. Back to my point…my guess is your videographer piggybacked Ms. Nunez's Internet and then took off."

"They log Mac addresses," I said, thinking, that's right, dick, I know something about computers too.

"That they do, Money Man. But it means shit if the guy de-stroys the computer when he's done, which I'm betting the house on that he did. These days, you can get a workable laptop with WiFi card for one hundred euros from any pawn shop. They aren't keep-ing records of that shit. He dumps the laptop, and he's a ghost."

"But he was in Argentina," Katrin said. "Which makes twelve countries we've tagged him in. He gets around, doesn't he."

"But he's definitely here in Berlin?" I asked.

Craig nodded. "So sayeth the Fountain."

"Okay, you paid, I played," Michael said, "we're all square now. So it's time for you to go. I have customers coming. Go. Go!"

I could hear Tooth telling me to crack this jerkoff in the mouth, maybe grab the gold chain and cross around his neck and shove it down his throat, but I weighed the desire to get arrested and ass raped in a German prison against, oh, pretty much everything else in the universe, and decided to just leave quietly.

"Nice friend," I whispered to Craig. "Where'd you find him? The douchebag farm? Wait, I can do better than that. The . . . uh…"

"Can't remember. A bar somewhere a while back. Introduced

himself and told me Fountain was his friend. I didn't believe him but I didn't care after he bought me a half-dozen pints. Never let it be said alcohol doesn't have benefits."

"How's he know Fountain?"

"Fountain knows people. It just works that way."

"Does he ever lighten up, that guy?"

"Michael? If he likes you, he likes you. If he doesn't....he doesn't."

We made our way back toward the crowds, pretended to shop for a little bit. Katrin followed me over to a tent selling books in German. I picked one up, tried to guess the story from the woman on the cover. She was holding a gun and there were lightning bolts behind her. It could have been any cheap dime novel back in the States.

"It sucks," she said. "I read it. A vampire detective that never grows old. She learns one of her past lovers has been murdered by some bad vampires and goes and kills them. And there's a ton of sex scenes that'll make you laugh out loud. I think that's why it was really popular. All stuff like, 'He thrust his pulsing lance into her velvety scabbard.' That about sums it up. It was all the rage in Europe when I was little. Are you okay? When Michael grabbed you...your eyes went a little crazy."

I put the book down, picked up another. A Stephen King novel I'd already read. "I don't like feeling restrained," I said. "Sorry, didn't mean to ruin the meeting with your friend. Who's a douchebag by the way."

"From the farm?"

"I said I could do better."

"Relax. We don't like him much either, but he helps. I apologize for him doing that. Next time you may as well hit him."

"He's bigger than me. I tend to not like that."

"Yes, but the first shot generally wins. Trust me."

"That why you threw me to the floor? Taking the first shot?"

She chuckled, and I can't deny it lightened the mood. I could see a bit of a snaggle tooth in her smile, and it somehow made her seem innocent. Like a child who had hated going to the dentist and figured out a way to avoid it.

"Something like that," she said. "I might still do it again, too, so don't piss me off. But you seem okay."

She walked away and I stood there wondering if she meant I was an okay guy, or just feeling better after my potential fight with Michael. Dammit. Girls, why can't they ever just say what they mean?

Craig came by with a sausage on a stick, ate it, then jammed the stick in his arm till he drew blood. He let it run down his arm as he looked at me. "Sharp stick," he said. "C'mon, we're leaving this flesh feast."

I said a prayer for my sanity, and we caught the U-Bahn into the heart of the city.

• • •

We got off in Kreuzberg, which reminded me of Boston's south side. The buildings were sagging and paint was peeling off their fronts but they were filled with tiny art galleries and coffee shops and bakeries and all sorts of anti-establishment commerce. Despite this, the clientele ran the gamut from street rats to nouveau riche. Teenagers in hoodies and beanies skateboarded by us while wannabe models strolled by hefting canvas bags with Fendi and Dolce & Gabana logos stenciled on them.

"C'mon, this way," Katrin said, leading us to the end of the block, and then down another block, under the balconies of graffiti-covered apartment buildings. The cobblestone sidewalks were packed with hipster shoppers and oblivious idiots talking on cell phones. We stopped in front of a building with a red door and large picture windows covered in posters of cartoon characters. I read the sign on the door. FUTURE GRAPHIX COMIC SHOP.

"No fucking way," I said.

Katrin beamed at me. "We heard you like this stuff, and I want to say sorry for pulling my blade on you."

"They better have porn in here or something," Craig said.

Inside the racks were filled with thousands of comics I'd never heard of. The covers were different than American fare, more artsy, like those retro wine posters you see in shitty home décor stores. Yet somehow they looked classy on these books, driving home the idea that comics could be so much more than just stories about grown men in colored tights.

"Apology accepted?" Katrin asked.

"Hell yeah," I said, pulling a comic off the rack. I opened it up and saw it was in German. Shit, I wondered if I'd be able to read any of these.

She pulled it from my hands and put it back. "They have ones in English too. Just look around."

While I let my inner geek go on a treasure hunt, I heard Craig trying to pick up the girl behind the counter. "Hey, my wanker roommates are rubbing their knobs on this shit but I prefer the real deal. When do you get off? Fancy a pint? Got a boyfriend?"

"You asked those in the wrong order," she said.

"No, I didn't," Craig said. "'Cause if you do have a boyfriend, he ain't invited anyway, I just wanted to know if you was gonna need a good excuse. You tell him you need a girls night out, and you're meeting your friends at a poetry reading, and he's not invited. And he says, 'No worry I hate poetry anyway,' and you and I meet up and get pissed. Yeah?"

I glanced back to see how this was gonna play out and fuck me if the girl wasn't smiling. Jesus, that kind of shit actually works on some chicks.

She said, "Alright yeah. What's your name?"

And I tuned out after that because it just depressed me. Sure, I'd been in Berlin one day and met a girl, but she'd approached me, not the other way around. Because I still had problems talking to girls. Roger Huntington would never have game. I'd come to accept it as my reality.

Suddenly there was a comic in my face, a man on the cover holding a gun, cats milling around his feet. One of the cats was smoking.

"This is a good one," Katrin said. "And this one here." She handed me another. This one with a giant crab on the front being attacked by fighter jets.

"Hey, Roger Roger," Craig said, slamming his hand on my shoulder. "Time to go. I feel my balls falling off in here. Let's get some food, yeah?"

"I'm still looking."

"Look later, ya ponce. You live in this city now. Come back any time you want. If I don't eat now I'm gonna be a bitch to be around all day. Tell 'im, Katrin."

"It's true," she said. "He's a bitch."

I sighed. "Fine."

So I paid for the two comics Katrin suggested and we left and found ourselves at a burger joint that served pretty good double cheeseburgers.

Chapter 7

That night, about five minutes after Craig left to go meet Comic Store Girl at a bar, Katrin barged in my room and stabbed a finger at me. "C'mon, we're following him."

"For real?"

"Yes, I want to spy on his date."

I couldn't decide if her desire to snoop was born out of jealousy or simply because she wanted to fuck with him. But, screw it, I thought, I had nothing better to do.

The interior of the place they'd chosen for their date was a mishmash of wood, leather and steel that looked like a Tolkien Orc vomited on the walls. The crowd was thirty-something which meant the music was low enough that nobody had to yell to be heard. Score one for us aging folks.

Katrin and I slid up to the bar and ordered a couple of beers, slyly looking over our shoulders at Craig and the comic store girl; she was laughing hysterically at whatever Craig was saying.

"You do this a lot," I asked Katrin, "follow him around and stalk him?"

"Why not. He's so fucking annoying and sometimes this is the only way I can get back at him."

"How is this getting back at him?"

She took out her phone and laid it on the bar. "Because when that girl slaps him, I'll be ready with my camera."

I looked at Comic Book Girl again. She was still laughing, and I doubted there was much Craig could do short of spitting on her that would turn her off at this point. I'd seen girls act like this enough times. She was into Craig, and she wanted him and the sooner they both got drunk and left the happier she'd be.

"I dunno, she looks like she's enjoying herself."

"She's miserable," Katrin said, refusing to look me in the eye now. Most likely because she knew I was right.

A couple of seconds lingered by in silence, which made me antsy, so I said, "Fountain hasn't filled me in on much. I mean, I don't even know what you guys do?"

She turned in her stool and faced me. I couldn't help but notice her knee touched mine and she kept it there. Were people less concerned about personal space in Berlin? Not that I minded.

"I work for James. That's what I do. And James, he shows me sick shit like this video killer. And I do my best to help him make the world a better place."

"Why you? I mean…I know what he thinks about me. But what about you? How'd you get on his radar?"

"You wouldn't believe me. No one ever does."

I chuckled. "You sound like you borrowed that line from a bad movie. Allow me to respond in kind: Try me."

"I don't feel like it. It's not like it's even something I enjoy talking about."

"Maybe you just need a good listener. I can do that much. And I don't judge. So you have nothing to lose."

"What're you, a fucking counselor all of a sudden?"

"No. Sorry. I'm overstepping my bounds. I don't know why I do that sometimes. My best friend used to say I was shit with social interaction. Then my life went to hell and it got even worse."

"No, you're fine. Sorry I snapped. We all have our sordid histories, you know? But when a girl says she doesn't want to talk, it's not a clue that we want to do the opposite. It means we don't want to talk."

"But when I ask if something's wrong and you say 'fine' it certainly does mean the opposite."

"I'm not that kind of girl. I say what I mean. "

"Fine."

She cracked a smile. Yay for me, I thought. At least I had a modicum of game.

"Just don't get too pushy with women here," she said. "This isn't America. Pickup lines don't work. You gotta be real."

"Well check this out," I said, pulling out the paper with Christa's phone number on it. "I already got digits. And she came onto *me*!"

"Don't say 'digits.' And no shit? Good for you. You call her yet?"

That's when I felt an arm go around my neck. "Roger Roger! You're here!" Craig yanked me toward him and hugged me hard enough to nearly break my neck. I couldn't tell if it was out of camaraderie or if he was fucking with me. "You followed Katrin here, no doubt, as she continues her attempt to capture me crashing and burning in public. But alas, she never will, because I'm the fucking maddest bloke in Europe, and the birds know it. So suck it, Katrin. And now that you two are here, come join us for a drink, yeah? Stop being dickheads at the bar. You look like leftovers from a 90s teen angst music video. C'mon. I wanna hear about this bird whose number you got."

Craig dragged me to the table he was sharing with Comic Book Girl and sat me down. He slid in next to his date, and Katrin reluctantly sat down next to me.

"Roger met a girl!" Craig said, filling in Comic Book Girl, who pretended to care. "Call her up, man, let's get a double date going. What do you say, Brittany?"

"Sounds brilliant," Brittany said. "We'll make a night of it." Her fake caring was bordering on mockery now.

Craig punched me in the shoulder and damn it hurt. But I pretended not to feel it. "Yeah, okay," I said, and pulled out my cell phone. After a quick two minutes, during which Craig made lewd noises in the background as I bumbled out an invitation, Christa agreed to meet us. I hung up and looked at Katrin, couldn't tell if she was annoyed or not with her sudden fifth-wheel status. I kind of think she liked it, though; it made her judge and jury of not just one but two girls, and if there was one thing I knew girls loved, it was judging other girls.

• • •

Christa showed up a half hour later wearing a slinky black dress. It was so tight it looked like someone painted it on her body. Both Craig and Katrin's jaws dropped a little when they saw her. Not that Brittany wasn't damned good looking, but Christa looked like she'd peeled herself out of a high-class fashion magazine.

"Roger must have some big feet," Craig said.

"I just loved his comic book," Christa replied, "and I couldn't believe it when he came into my bar. He's such a great artist."

"I know he's great at some things, but art might not be one of them. Give him a gun though…"

"He's messing around," I said, "I don't own a gun. I do, however, have the need for a local art store. I didn't bring my paints with me. Maybe you could show me one?"

"I so could," Christa replied. "There's a ton of good places. Oh my God that's so awesome, that I get to see you at work."

"Great, a bona fide starfucker in our midst," Katrin whispered at just the perfect level to make everyone uncomfortable. That level where you heard it, but you're not sure anyone else heard it, so you don't say anything in hopes it'll just go away. But secretly, you sort of know everyone heard it. And so the table just goes quiet for a second.

Thankfully, Craig came to the rescue. "Shots! Right, ya fuckers, who wants shots?"

Hands went up all around.

It took Craig a minute to get back with the shots, which we all downed with smiles on our faces. Now things were starting to loosen up. Once Brittany found out Christa liked comic art the two of them became inseparable, although Brittany spent the conversation inching closer to Craig, until she was practically in his lap, at which point he started licking her ear.

"Well this is as much fun as a heavy period," Katrin said. She stood up and moved to the bar, where she sat down next to a guy in a thick red sweater.

"She's a moody bird," Craig said to me, "you'll either get used to it or ignore it. I kind of do both."

"How do you all know each other, anyway?" Christa asked.

"We don't," Craig answered. "Not really. I know Roger is a madman, and Christa a femme fatale, and I'm wanted in a dozen countries, but mostly we just met. But it's fine, because we're all just out for some blood, like the young and wild are apt to be."

Both girls giggled, but I didn't. Mostly because I didn't know how much of that was true. I still had no idea what Katrin and Craig were about. Other'n I knew Craig was about getting some tail and Katrin was about... I looked at the bar, saw her take Red Sweater by the hand and walk him slowly out the door, not bothering to look back at us.

It would be another hour before we all left, and I had forgotten all about what Craig had said by then, because when I got back to the apartment and crawled in bed, Christa crawled in with me.

• • •

The sex was wild and crazy and European. Her tongue went into places on my body I didn't know existed. She moaned like a wolf baying at the moon. She used muscles I was unaware girls had. At one point I was sure her head spun around 360 degrees. By the time we were done I had a clear understanding of how demonic circus clowns make love. To say it made me feel like a god is an understatement. I felt like I'd aced the most important test life can throw at you. Twice.

"Three times!" she said. "Holy shit!"

Okay, three times.

"Time for more," she said, rolling on top of me. Her breath was a wall of whiskey, but then so was mine.

When I slid into her, I could hear Katrin in the other room moaning as well. I stared at Christa's face as she bounced up and down on top of me, but I saw Katrin there instead. And the louder Katrin moaned in her room, the more Christa's face transformed.

Jesus, I thought, here I am with the hottest chick I've ever been with, and I'm thinking of the girl who tried to knife me. What's wrong with me?

To make matters worse, a few minutes later I heard Katrin crying, followed by a male voice asking if she was all right. Then Katrin yelled, and I heard her bedroom door open, footsteps, and then the front door shutting.

Christa rolled off me, slick with sweat and other juices, and put her arm around me. "Will you draw me pictures? Pictures of us doing what we just did? I want to capture that moment forever."

"Sure," I said, still hearing Katrin crying. I couldn't help it after that, I had to check on her, so I stood up and threw on my jeans, moved out into the living room. I could hear Katrin behind her door. I was hesitant to bother her, because like Craig said, I barely knew her, but I have a little issue with girls crying, especially if they're in pain.

Lightly, I tapped my knuckles on her door, ignoring the pain this caused to my wounded arm. "You okay?" I whispered. Her crying went silent, and I figured I must have embarrassed her, but as I turned to leave her door opened and she stood there in a tank top and underwear. I tried not to stare, even though I wanted to very badly.

"What?" Her mouth was a tight line. Her nostrils flared. She was a second away from garroting me.

"Did that asshole hurt you?"

"No. I asked him to leave. And he was actually a gentleman about it."

"Are you okay?"

"We're all okay, Roger, that's why we're here. Now please leave me alone."

She shut the door and I stood there confused and annoyed. Why couldn't girls ever just say what they were thinking?

Christa fucks like a minx, Tooth said, *but damn me if Katrin didn't have some sweet cleft going on in her downstairs area. You should try to make nicey nice with it again sometime.*

"Fuck off, Tooth. It's called respect. Get outta my head before you make me mad. In fact, just leave me alone for a while."

"Why? What did I do?" It was Christa. She had snuck up on me, wearing nothing but a long T-shirt of mine.

"Sorry," I said, "not you. Someone else."

"Who? Craig?"

"No one real."

She cocked her head. "Do you always talk to yourself?"

"I talk to a lot of people. It's kind of a long story."

"Well, come back to bed and tell me, I've got time for you." She took my hand and led me back to the room, and when we got in bed we kissed some more and I decided to talk about some of my favorite artists instead. Before I could get to the differences between Jim Lee and David Aja, she was snoring.

Somewhere around 3AM I woke up and rolled over to cuddle Christa. Only she wasn't there. I moved my hand around and felt something wet in the bed. It was tacky and got all over my arm and chest. I turned on the light on the nightstand and yelled, "FUCK!"

There was blood all over my pillow. A lot of blood.

Christa's blood.

• • •

I made it back to Katrin's room in about half a second, unaware I was still naked. When she opened the door she found me panting and chanting Christa's name, all while my dick was swinging like a pendulum.

"Seriously? This is how you make a move? Fucking Americans."

"No," I said, waving the pillow, just about the same time she saw the blood on my chest. "This is hers! She's gone!"

"The fuck?" Katrin threw open her door, pushed past me and ducked her head into my room. She came back out a second later and just stood there looking at me, at the blood, thankfully ignoring my nether region. "What the fuck is going on?"

"I woke up and I found this on my pillow. It's real. It's hers. It's fresh." I swung the pillow to punctuate my points.

"Why the fuck are you waving it around!"

"I don't know! I'm freaked out!"

"Oh my God!"

"I'm a little panicked here," I said.

"Ya think? Where is she? What happened?"

"How the fuck do I know? That's why I came to you."

"To give me a bloody pillow?!"

"Well, no. I mean . . . "

"Call her, idiot!"

"Yeah. Right. Here, hold this." I tossed her the pillow and raced to my cell phone. Before I could even dial I saw a new text. YOU CAN STITCH HER UP IF YOU CAN FIND HER. NO PO-LICE! I WORK QUICKLY. TONIGHT. HURRY. There was an address under it but I didn't recognize it, having only been a local for all of 48 hours.

Without thinking, I called her number. It rang and rang and went to her voicemail. So I texted back, WHO IS THIS? I gave it a second but got no reply.

"What're you doing?" Katrin asked.

"Look at this." I showed her the phone.

"This is madness." She thrust the phone back at me.

"This address . . . "

"I know where this is," she said. "It's outside the city. Jesus Christ, either she's playing some real sick fucking joke or—"

"Someone was inside the apartment. Fuck, they were inside

my room!"

"This text is an hour old. How the hell did you sleep through this?"

"I dunno. I didn't drink more than usual. But I feel pretty fuzzy now, in fact. Like maybe…"

"You think you were drugged? In Berlin? I doubt it."

"Maybe not drugged, but something. A fucking Tylenol PM, or something. I'm telling you, I feel it in my head."

"Well get your head awake and put some fucking pants on while I call James. Now!"

• • •

I threw on jeans and a shirt, made sure I had my phone and wallet. Done with that, I rushed outside to where Katrin was pacing on the curb, her phone to her ear. "He's not answering. Dammit. He does this when he has to meet with them."

"Who's 'them?'"

"People in the shadows, you know. James says he needs to see them and then boom he's off the grid for a day or two. We'll have to take the U-Bahn and catch a cab. I'm calling Craig now, seeing what he knows."

I started to ask her how Craig was going to help but she held up a finger and shushed me. Craig didn't answer either so she left him a message and told him to meet us. Then she was grabbing me and whisking me toward the U-Bahn station. We paid the fare and took the train to the outskirts of the city. I nervously tapped my foot the whole way, trying in vain to remember anything after the sex that might tell me who had broken in.

I read the text over and over as we sped down the rails, especially the part where it said they were working quickly. I had no idea who this person was, or how they'd gotten in my room, or why they'd targeted Christa, but I was far too jaded these days to suspect it was some weird random act of violence. This was the killer Fountain had spoken of. It had to be. Or someone connected to those crimes at least.

"These people who came to the apartment the other day, what did they look like?"

"They were Interpol," Katrin replied. "The usual. Black suits. Shoulder holsters. Haircuts that made them look like literal dickheads."

"But they didn't even interview you. They just…what'd you say? Waved a wand around?"

She nodded. "They scanned the room for computer signals. Probably looking for passwords so they could go read our emails or something. I don't think they got anything."

"But that's not legal. Don't they need warrants?"

"Probably. But this is the age of terrorism. They called it necessary measures. And look, to be honest, I say they were Interpol but maybe they were something else. You guys have your Men in Black, your Will Smith movies, in America. We have things like that here too. I don't know who they were. But I know they watch us. They watch James. And they have friends in high places."

"One of them had to be the person who came in tonight. Don't you think? Came in and took Christa."

"It's possible, but I'm not sure. Why show up, run off, then come back? They had to know we'd be on guard."

"Yeah but we weren't. I slept through someone taking a girl out of my bed, for fuck's sake."

"If you were drugged, it would have been at the bar. But would you have been able to get home and have your fun? Most sleep aids kick in after thirty minutes. You were up for at least an hour. It seems unlikely."

I snapped my fingers. "Shit! The guy you sent home. Who the fuck was he?"

"He was a cheap fuck. I regretted it. And it wasn't him. He was too dumb."

I glared at her, challenging her psychoanalytical skills. She got the hint and pulled out her phone.

"Fine, I'll call him." She dialed his number, demanded to know where he was. He said he was at his apartment, gave her the address, and asked if she wanted to come over. "No. But thanks. Another time." After she hung up she turned to me. "He's clean. And besides, his DNA would be all over."

"That's why he did it. Because he can say he was invited over so his DNA would be in the apartment."

"You read too many comics, Roger. We both know what's going on here. This is about getting to James through you. This is about the man in the videos."

I took out my phone. "What's the number for the police here? Is it 999 or what?"

"110. But the text said not to call. He'll kill her."

"I'm calling anyway." The phone rang and someone answered in German. "English?" I asked, and they spoke back in English, without much of an accent. I had to hand it to the German school system here for teaching an entire nation to be bilingual. I got halfway through explaining what was going on when Katrin grabbed my phone out of my hand and disconnected the call.

"What'd you do that for!"

"He will kill her, Roger. Trust me. We've been chasing this guy for a while. If you want to see this girl alive then we go it alone. That's why James brought us together."

"I don't have fuck-all of a clue why James Peter Fountain brought us together other than he thinks he's fucking Nick Fury or something. Which he's not. He's a bit of a nutjob, if you ask me. I don't even know if I believe half of what he says."

"Then why are you here?"

I thought about that one for a second, came up with the same answer I always came up with. "Because what if he's not crazy?"

"There you go. Now stay off the phone and think about what you remember from tonight."

"I already tried. I can't think of anything."

"Try harder. Do it."

I closed my eyes and thought back. Tried to remember who we'd seen at the bar, or who I might have seen outside the apartment when we'd gotten home, but nothing came to mind. The bar was just a bar, full of people I didn't take notice of, and there'd been no one on the street outside our place. "Nothing," I said. "I didn't think to be on the lookout. Fountain said this guy was a ghost."

"Yeah, well, he just figured out how to haunt us."

I shiver ran down my spine. "He was in my fucking room."

Chapter 8

We got off the train a few minutes later and hailed a cab. Katrin gave the driver the address and he swiveled his head around as if to ask if we were crazy. She spoke back to him in German and the best I could translate it as was *I know, now just drive.* At least that's what I got from the way the driver huffed and stepped on the gas.

We were a couple of miles into an industrial zone that may as well have been the decaying set of an apocalypse movie when I got another text. YOU'RE LATE. TOO BAD. YOU CAN WATCH THE RERUNS LATER.

"Sonofa…" I texted back. YOU HURT HER, YOU DIE. Then I tried calling again, praying the guy would answer and just talk to me, reveal himself, but he didn't.

"Fuck!" I slammed my phone down on the seat, causing the driver to jump.

"Almost there," Katrin said, "just a few more blocks."

As I stared out the window I saw the streets get more and more desolate. We turned down Gunterstrasse, then made a right on Apfelstrasse. I tried to remember the names, just in case, though I didn't know what they translated to.

The cab pulled to a stop and Katrin paid the guy, said, "Don't leave," and we got out. It took two seconds for the guy to leave.

"Great," I said.

"I figured as much. This is not a good area. C'mon, here's the address. It's that building there."

"How'd you know this area?"

"I wasn't always a *tugendbold*."

"Say what?"

"Figure it out."

We crossed the street and found ourselves in front of an empty, three-story office complex. A sign hung out front proclaiming it was for lease. I knew this because the English was under the German. That's when my phone blinked again and I got another text. LOG ONTO THE WI-FI.

I clicked through my settings and found the only open Wi-Fi signal, which was weak, only one bar, meaning it could be any of the four or five buildings around us as well. Didn't matter though, because my phone rang, and it was asking me to answer a video call. I tapped the answer icon and watched Christa's face swim into view.

"Christa! Where are you?"

"Roger, I—"

Wham! A fist came out of nowhere and punched her in the face. Her head snapped back and her eyes rolled up. She went silent as blood ran out of her nostrils.

"No!" I screamed, racing toward the building in front of me. Katrin had been watching with me and saw what happened, and she got to the door before me. It was unlocked and we threw ourselves into a dark hallway. On the phone, the picture zoomed out and I could see Christa from her shoulders up now. Whoever was holding the phone put it down in such a way that it remained on her. I could see a rope was pulled tight around her chest but beyond that I couldn't gauge her entire situation.

We walked fast, not sure of where we were going, just throwing open doors as we went and looking in rooms, using the lights on our phones to chase away shadows. Most of the rooms were empty, abandoned, nothing more than a couple forgotten desks and chairs so caked in dust they looked like sand castles. There'd been businesses in here once, but for whatever reason they'd left the building.

On the phone, Christa's eyes seemed to focus again and she moaned. And that's when the hand came back, wielding a scalpel. The blade went to her mouth. The kidnapper's other hand squeezed her face, pursing her lips. Christa tried to squirm but the muscular hand held her fast. The tiny blade went through her lips like a blowtorch through ice, shearing them clean off. Blood arced out like someone stepping on a squeezable ketchup bottle. Christa wailed and the fist came out again and punched her under the eye, splitting open her cheek.

"Stop it!" I yelled. "Tell me where you are, you piece of shit!"

Katrin threw open the last door in the hallway and found the room empty. There was nothing left but an elevator and stairs. I frantically hit the elevator call button but it didn't light up. I'd figured as much but had to try.

Katrin and I raced up the stairs and stopped on the second-floor landing.

"Three floors," she said. "He's probably on the top. Buys him more time."

"Or he wants us to think that. Fuck."

"We could split up?"

"No. He'll want that too. We need to do this together. Second floor, then third. Quickly."

We moved out into the second-floor hallway. I could still hear Christa's screams in my ears, could still see her lips coming off. Right then it hit me, the same as it hit me when I'd seen Jamie tied to Skinny Man's floor, as when I'd seen the woman get eaten alive in Marshall Aldritch's mansion. She wasn't going to make it. That was the point, right? To drive us crazy. To let us know we couldn't save her.

Or was I wrong? Was this guy more about the thrill of the chase? The same thrill people got from having sex in public. Getting caught was the drug. The chance of being found out begat adrenaline. He was the mouse and we were the cats and he was loving every minute of it.

Maybe. Maybe not. Fuck, he was in my head. Why did they always get in my head?

It's not that hard, pussyboy.

Skinny Man's voice. Shit, I so did not need this right now.

When are you just gonna admit you wanna jerk off to all the blood.

"Get out get out get out," I said, shaking my head till I felt dizzy.

I waited for his response. There was nothing. He was gone.

I heard Christa crying loudly, only this time it wasn't in my head. I checked the phone again, trying so hard not to look at her, to look instead at anything in the background that might tell me where she was. But I saw nothing. Just a faded gray wall and what might or might not be a leftover dry erase board.

The scalpel came up again. The free hand grabbed the top of her head. The scalpel slipped effortlessly into her eye. Her sobs went guttural.

"Oh Jesus," I said, feeling the wind go out from my stomach. I stopped and involuntarily doubled over. Not from pain. From anguish. From exhaustion. From the goddamn realization Fountain had been right. That this shit was always going to find me no matter where I went.

"Don't look," Katrin said. "Just turn it off. Turn it off!" She reached over and grabbed the phone from me, disconnected the call, stuck the phone in her pocket. She slapped me in the face. "Snap out of it! Wake up! She'll die if we don't hurry. Run, you on the left, me on the right. Go!"

I pulled myself together and we each took a side of the hallway and opened doors. If they were locked, we kicked them open. It hurt my heel like hell but the wood was old and the locks buckled out of the jambs with one or two blows.

All the rooms were empty.

"Fucker. He *is* on the top floor," I said.

As we raced up the next set of stairs I could hear my phone buzzing in Katrin's pocket. She glanced at me as if to say don't even think about it. I took the stairs two at a time and reached the top floor with a stitch in my side. Katrin blew past me and flung open the fire door. The top hallway was near black, and felt hotter. Or maybe it was just my body temperature reaching its maximum boiling point.

Then I heard a sound behind me, footsteps coming up the stairs.

"He's coming," I whispered. "Find a weapon."

I looked for one, but there was nothing around me worth using. No old axe in a fire safety box. No abandoned lead pipes. Not even a big rock. So I positioned myself to the right of the door in the hall.

"When he comes out, go for his eyes and throat," I said.

Krista whipped out her knife and flicked open the blade. Was she going to kill him? Did I care? Fuck no.

I heard the footfalls stop behind the stairwell door. Then I saw the knob turn. The door opened and a shadow emerged. I swung with all my might, caught the bastard in the mouth, my hand flaring up in white hot pain. I came around with my other fist but felt nothing but air because he ducked. When he stood up I jumped back, confused as hell.

It was Craig. "Hello to you too," he said, blood running from his lips.

"Why didn't you answer?" Krista demanded.

"I was sleeping. Sue me. I'm here now, and you two make a lot of noise, you know that?"

"They've got Christa," I said, rubbing my knuckles. "He's fucking butchering her right now. I don't care about noise."

Craig touched his bloody mouth, looked at me like he might rip my throat out.

"Not here," Katrin said, closing the door opposite us. "Everyone split up."

I grabbed the doorknob next to me and pushed. The room inside was empty, covered in dust and some discarded candy wrappers, and I could only tell because there was a wan work light going in the corner. "There's power up here," I said.

Maybe it explained the heat. Maybe not.

Craig was coming out of the room ahead of me. He looked at me and shook his head no.

Katrin was two doors down on her side, still coming up empty. I was beyond panic now, realizing we only had a couple more doors left and that Christa was no doubt suffering unimaginable torture.

I kicked open a door. Moved on. Kicked open another.

And then I found her. Three doors from the end. I opened the door and fell to my knees.

She was everywhere.

Her head was in the middle of the floor. Her arms and legs were in the corners. I saw fingers here and there, and an ear. A breast was near my knee and a foot was under the window. The rest was just chunks of meat, organs, intestines, what have you, laying in red blobs all willy nilly. It was like she'd exploded, only I knew the truth. She'd been cut to pieces and left for the cockroaches.

Up against the wall was a small TV on an old metal stand. On the TV a video was playing. A video of Christa being sliced up with medical instruments. The bastard hadn't been calling and showing us the murder in real time; he'd already completed it and videotaped it. That's what he'd been showing me on my phone. A recording of a recording. He'd had no intention of giving us a fighting chance.

I heard Katrin come up behind me and gasp. She left the room and I could hear her fumbling with my phone. Then there was a ring in the room. It was Christa's phone, and I could see how the killer had placed it in front of the TV to give us the best show.

Two things went through my mind right then. One: it was my

fault she'd died. Two: the killer had to have just left. He'd called me from here, positioned Christa's phone, been watching us in the building somehow.

"He can't be far," Craig said, thinking the same thing. And with that, he took off.

I followed and we met up in the stairs. Together we half jumped/half ran down them, all the way to the first floor. Somewhere above me I heard Katrin scream, not out of fear or pain, but out of anger, a screeching NOOOOOO that was sure to wake people as far as Dusseldorf.

Craig was fast, almost too fast to keep up with, which only pushed me harder. In less than a minute we were outside, out on the curb spinning in circles, looking at every shadow and waiting for it to move. But none of them did.

"Fuck!" he yelled.

"Where'd he go?"

Craig didn't answer, just huffed, his bloody lips now going puffy. And right then a big part of me just wanted to go back to bed, to just say fuck it all, and go to bed forever. But life is like a big dumb dog, waiting for you to walk in your house carrying some priceless vase. It jumps right at your nuts all happy-go-lucky just wanting to be pet and doesn't think twice about slobbering on your face as it knocks all that fragility to the ground, shattering it into a million sparkling shards of uselessness. Life is a good dog. A big, dumb, smelly good dog you just can't bring yourself to kick because it's just too stupid to know any better.

That's why that group of German gangbangers came around the corner right then. Because life is always glad you're home.

● ● ●

Craig muttered, "Bloody hell." He already knew where this was going. He was a seasoned vet when it came to hooligans. "Bloody fuck balls hell."

There were five of them, all bigger than me, all in jeans and hooded sweatshirts. The one out in front was bald and had a slight limp.

I kept my head forward, but my eyes glanced sideways at them as they came. Two of them were carrying retractable batons. This was so not what I needed right now. Not while I knew the killer was still in the area.

"Oy, you two," said the bald guy. "You in the wrong part of town, yeah? Oy, *arschloch*, I'm talking at you."

"Maybe they's police," said the little one with green sneakers.

"They ain't police. Ain't fat enough, yeah? And this one's got blood on 'im."

Baldy pointed to me, and I saw that I did, in fact, have some of Christa's blood on me. Standing in the dim moonlight it wasn't easy to see, but this guy was clearly a seasoned nighttime criminal and probably knew every shade of blood that existed. He'd probably knife a Vulcan just to see new shades of it.

"Did you see a guy running out of here," I asked, thinking this idiot might actually be able to help, "probably covered in way more blood than us?"

"Told you they was police," said Green Sneakers.

"Show us badges then," said Baldy.

Craig huffed, stepped right up to them. "For fuck's sake we ain't got time for this. If you're gonna mug us, fine, get to it, but answer my friend's question first. Did you see a man running away from this building in the last couple minutes?"

One of the guys in the back of the group spoke up. "No. Ain't seen no one."

"Will you shut up, Karl," Baldy scolded. "We ain't here to help 'em locate missing persons. We're here because everyone knows this is the Havoc Brotherhood's terrain. And they ain't police, so don't help 'em out."

"Well he was being polite, Vern, just saying."

"Fuck off, Karl!" Baldy took a second to regain his composure, then hefted his baton. "Here's how it works. You guys give us all your money, and then you go away, and you never come back, or we fuck you up. You get me? No one steps on Havoc turf without paying a fee."

Craig turned to me. "This is America's fault. All those damn gangster movies. Used to just be neo-Nazis here, now we got Aryan guys who think they're black."

Vern stabbed a finger at us. "Oy, we ain't racist, you racist.

We're . . . capitalist."

"You're morons," Craig said, "and pussies. And I'm not racist. But I am confused as to why the fuck we're having a conversation. What the hell do you want?"

"Give us all your money."

"Right," Craig said, and threw a punch so fast I'd have missed it if I blinked. Vern's head snapped back and his arms went down to his sides. Then he fell straight back, hit the cement sidewalk, and lay silent.

I would have gasped, but the other four went into a rage and attacked. Craig became a whirlwind of fists and feet and I thought maybe if I stuck close to him I'd get out of this unharmed until one of those batons caught me in the shin and sent white hot pain up my entire body. I wailed and went after the guy in a blind rage. He swung again and I turned my body into it, caught the blow in the flesh of my upper arm. It hurt like hell, considering I'd been shot there recently, but I embraced the pain as I plowed into the guy and drove him to the ground. He threw punches but I didn't feel them, because all I could see was Christa's head in the middle of the floor upstairs.

These idiots had come out to harass us and now we'd never catch the killer. And that pissed me off so much I couldn't stop myself as I slammed my head into this guy's nose and shattered it. He groaned and kicked but I got my knee into his groin three or four times and felt his balls shove up into his body. He stopped throwing punches and started trying to defend himself and at that point I knew I had the best of him. I used my elbows on his broken nose, trying to turn his face into corn meal.

He finally got a knee into my ribs and stunned me enough to throw me off. But instead of hitting me he got up and ran off.

I turned to see if Craig needed help but sort of went still as I watched his fight play out beside me. He was yelling at the other three like a madman. "Hit me! C'mon, again!"

Karl had snatched up Vern's baton and swung it at Craig's head. Craig didn't move, didn't even blink. He just took the shot to his head. I saw blood arc out from behind his ear. "Again!" he said, and Karl obliged. The baton caught him in the shoulder blade and I could hear the *crack* it made. But Craig didn't move.

Karl and his two buddies punched Craig in the face. Repeatedly. Craig's face opened up like a time-lapse video of a flower blooming. Blood ran everywhere. But he didn't punch back. I didn't understand why. I could see on his face that he was in a different state of mind, like some kind of ninja monk or something. He wasn't re-acting to the blows like a normal person. He was just taking them. And then, a second later, when it was obvious the three Havoc thugs were getting just a bit winded, Craig lashed out. Kicked two in the groin, and grabbed the baton from Karl. With three in-credibly strong swings, he got them all in the mouth and their teeth went everywhere.

"Fuck me," I whispered.

All three of them put their hands over their mouths and stum-bled away in shock, leaving their leader sleeping peacefully at our feet.

"You okay?" I asked.

"No," Craig said, "I probably need some stitches."

"And a neurosurgeon. Why didn't you hit them back?"

"Because that's what Craig does. He waits." It was Katrin. She had come up beside me silent as a cat fart. "Right, Craig?"

"Not the time, Katrin. Where were you, anyway?"

"What, like I was supposed to fight five guys with truncheons?"

"Coulda flashed a knife at least."

"I take it you didn't see the guy who left that girl in bits up there?" she asked.

"No. We didn't have time," I said. "Soon as we got down here the Havoc Tards showed up. The guy is long gone."

"Or he's watching us," Craig said. Which made all of us study the shadows again.

"No," Katrin said, "he's gone."

"What if he's not?"

"Trust me. This area ain't safe. He wouldn't hang around after that. Not here, alone. C'mon, we got work to do."

"Like call the fucking police," I said, holding out my hand for my phone. She pulled it from her pocket and handed it to me.

"Don't call here," she said. "They won't believe you."

"The fuck they won't! That girl up there is nothing but sliced meat. There's a fucking TV up there with a video in it of the guy killing her. They gotta get out here and find this guy!"

"Roger, James has told them about this guy and they don't buy it. You know this. And all they'll find in there is a lot of fingerprints. Yours, mine, Craig's."

"Yeah, because we came to save her!"

"If they feel like it they might see it that way."

"Of course they will."

"Consider also that they've got her phone calling yours at the exact time she died. They've got your phone receiving the call in the exact building she was killed in. They've got a cab driver who will come forward eventually with our description of coming here. They'll get testimony from someone who saw you and her at the bar. Hear what I'm saying?"

"But what about the killer's fingerprints. He must have left them all over."

"The killer? He's been doing this for years. If he was stupid enough to leave fingerprints he'd have been caught ages ago. He probably puts glue on his hands or just cuts his prints off for all we know. But he ain't that stupid."

"I don't care. We need the cops on this."

"All they'll get out of this is that you were the last person to see her alive. You, who's been here for—"

"Only forty-eight fucking hours!" I yelled, amazed at how ridiculous my life had become.

"Yes. Two days. You're a confessed killer, who's been in the city for two days, who picks up a girl who ends up mutilated, who's only communications around that time are with you. You've got her blood on your pillows! Trust me when I say, we head back to the city and call in a tip. There's nothing more we can do here."

"And get rid of your sheets when you get back," Craig suggested.

"Are you insane?" I screamed. "What about the tape? What if there's more on it? What if he left a clue? What if he left something to tell us who he is? You want to just leave?"

She held up her phone. "I took photos. I checked around the room as well. There's nothing. It's covered in blood and stinks like hell but there're no clues. Trust me, I know."

"How do you know? Did you dust for prints?"

Craig put his hand on my chest. "Seriously, Roger, you gotta trust her on this one."

At our feet, Vern moaned, blinked his eyes.

"And then there's this wanker," Craig said. "Who saw you come out covered in blood. Cops ask him if he saw anything, he's giving up our faces. This is why James gave up on the police. And it's why we need to get lost."

I couldn't just leave like this. I had to know for myself that there was nothing worth pursuing in that room. "I'm going back up to check. Don't stop me."

"Fine. Hurry up," Katrin said.

It took me a minute to get back up to the room, where I simply stood in the door wanting to throw up. It smelled like copper and I could already hear cockroaches coming out to sup on the remains. I wanted badly to look for clues but there was just so much gore, and the head of the girl I'd just slept with sitting in the middle of it all staring at me with hollow eye sockets. It was too much. I checked the TV for anything useful but it was just your average piece of crap with a built-in tape player. I hit eject, popped the tape out, saw it was an old school Memorex. Nothing written on it. Maybe there *was* some kind of DNA on it, but I didn't have a police lab at my disposal so taking it would only hinder any legitimate investigation by the cops.

I shined my phone light on it, hoping for a hair or a flake of dandruff. Anything.

But the more I looked the more I knew there probably wasn't anything to lift off the tape. Based on the precision of his cutting and the meticulous way he'd set this all up, I knew he was too smart to leave prints.

Could be he recorded over himself fucking his dog. Tooth's voice in my head, offering unwanted help. *Maybe the tape glitches and you see his face somewhere. Maybe his vagina singing Prince songs. Something.*

"Doubt it," I answered. "He's too smart for that. It's a new tape. Her death is all that's on it."

I left it on the TV and walked out, careful not to look at the body parts all around me lest my brain suffer a mental breakdown of some kind.

Outside, Katrin and Craig were nudging Vern, who was starting to sit up.

"Ready?" Craig said. His neck was covered in blood and his eyes were blacking.

"I can't believe we're just gonna leave," I said.

"C'mon, we can walk to a better area and call for a cab."

Without so much as an apology, Katrin and Craig started making their way down the dark street. I stood in place for a heartbeat, furious and lost, numb from life, and so confused by everything I could barely speak. All I could mutter as I finally started walking was, "I'm not a confessed killer."

Chapter 9

An hour later we called in the anonymous tip from a payphone on the other side of the city. Once that was done we took the U-Bahn home and tore all the sheets off the bed, wadded them up and put them in the trash. Sure, I thought about finding DNA evidence on them from the killer, but I knew that was a lost cause. Besides, forensics can be manipulated. Happens all the time. I once read a book about a rapist who collected soil samples from all over the country, then dropped little bits at his own crime scenes. Cops thought they were looking for a guy from Nevada, Utah, California, Miami, and Tennessee, to name just a few.

Tomorrow morning I would have to figure out a way to burn the sheets.

I grabbed spare sheets from a hall linen closet. Then I collapsed in bed, smelling Christa's perfume on my pillow. I pushed it off the bed and fought back tears. Which wasn't easy. I saw Jamie all over again in that abattoir, saw her severed foot in the EMT's cooler as they took her body out of Skinny Man's basement.

At one point I rolled over and called Fountain's number, got his voicemail again. I was pissed. "If you don't call back and talk to me I'm fucking leaving Berlin first thing in the morning. Whoever this guy is, he came after us tonight and it's your fault. He used me to get to you and I don't even know how the hell he knew who I was. So either you come back here tomorrow or I'm gone. And hey, fuck you."

I hung up and stared at the ceiling.

I couldn't sleep for shit.

It would be three days before the report of Christa's murder showed up on the news. None of our names were mentioned, which I couldn't decide was a blessing or a curse bigger than a moon crater.

But no use getting ahead of myself here. What made me irate before I saw the news report was that when I checked my phone in the morning I saw a message from Fountain. All it said was, "I'm sorry, Roger. I haven't been truthful. I'll fill you in if you meet me here." He then gave an address I could barely pronounce.

I got out of bed and found both Katrin and Craig at the dining room table.

"Anyone sleep?" I asked.

Craig shook his head no. He had four large gashes above his ear held closed with bandage tape. His swollen purple eyes looked like someone stuck plums to his face. Krista grunted, which I took as a no as well. I told them about the message from Fountain, and they shared a look that told me they knew where the place was.

"It's cold there," Krista said. "Wear a jacket."

"And this," Craig added, taking something from around his neck and tossing it to me.

I opened my hand and stared at it. It was a crucifix.

"Just put it on," he said.

"But—"

"Do it," Katrin said.

So I did. Then I pointed at the trash. "We need to burn those."

"We'll take care of it," Craig said. "Don't worry your little head, mate."

"If the cops come here and find even a trace of those—"

"We're on it," Katrin said. She shoved me back toward my bedroom. "Go see Fountain. We'll be here when you get back."

Chapter 10

I grabbed a coffee near the Stasi Museum, read the posters outside about their new exhibit. It was something about apartments from the 70s, listening devices and black market blue jeans. It all boiled down to showcasing how people lived under the iron fist of a murderous government, hoping your neighbor didn't rat you out for having Western ideals. Paranoia city all around. Too bad they didn't run an exhibit of how the public beat and tortured the Stasi when the wall fell, but Berliners are more civil than that; they don't revel in revenge.

Me, all I could think about *was* revenge.

It took me about two hours on the U-Bahn to find where I was going because the name of the street wasn't listed anywhere, and every time I got off at a stop thinking I was right, it turned out I was beyond wrong. I had to stop in a handful of cafés at different locations in the city before a barista caught me staring at my phone, told me it was basically an alley that had been walled off years ago.

"Then how do you know about it?" I asked.

"I explore," he replied, showing me on a phone map where I could find the alley. "The sewers lead there."

"Hell of a hobby."

"The architecture is amazing. You should see the Paris sewers. New York City isn't bad either."

"I'll pass."

"Anyway, Berlin's is an amazing place. Check out the hub under there if you can. There's like twenty tunnels going off in every direction. Very cool stuff."

"I just want to find this place. I don't need to explore tunnels."

"Well, you can either jump the wall if you know how, or come up from the other side."

"Come up how?"

"Through the hub, like I said." Then he wrote something for me on a napkin. It read BERLINER UNTERWELTEN, and when I typed it into my phone's browser back on the train again, it took me to a number of websites devoted to people who traipsed through the Berlin sewer system. Didn't they have theme parks here? Fucking weirdoes.

So I was gonna have to wade through pools of shit to get to Fountain? What the hell was up with this guy? Couldn't he ever just be straight with me?

After skirting flocks of pigeons picking at bagel crumbs in the street, I found the alley in question. It was blocked off by a solid wall stretching between two buildings. It was higher than I was able to jump, so I moved around the street looking for something to stand on but found nothing. Realizing I was licked, I entered the building on my right, which was a rundown office building with bullet holes in the mortar; scars from the war that would never really heal.

Inside, the building was musty, sepulchral. The wooden doors lining the dim, tiled hallway were closed and I would have thought the place was deserted had I not heard a man cough somewhere down at the far end. My footfalls echoed as I made my way under some dusty windows until I found what I was looking for. The elevator.

The doors squealed as they opened, and I said a prayer as I entered that this old contraption still worked properly. As I'd been hoping, there was a basement button, so I pressed it. The elevator descended with a labored groan, like an old man taking a shit, and I got scared the whole thing would just break and drop me to my death.

A minute later I emerged into a basement barely illuminated by a yellow 25-watt bulb. Moldy concrete walls and old metal shelves stacked with cleaning supplies were the extent of this room's charm, so I moved off to the only door I could find and pushed through it. It was pitch black, so I turned on my phone light. I made my way past a large oil drum until I found yet another door, which, sure enough, opened up into a tunnel that stank so bad I thought I'd crapped myself.

I looked at my feet, saw a river of sludge running along the floor. It wasn't much, perhaps two inches wide, but if there'd been paint on the walls here, it would be stripping off in ribbons.

Yay for sewage.

I showed my phone light down to either side and saw that the tunnel stretched on beyond my sight. But I found what I needed just to my left. A ladder. It went up a narrow well that ended at a grate. As I stood on the rungs, I could hear movement above me and hoped it wasn't a rabid rat waiting for me up there. When I moved the grate aside and emerged into the alley, I saw it wasn't a rat but a group of homeless men regarding me with annoyance.

"Berliner Unterwelten," one of them said, waving a metal pipe at me. "If you do not have euros then get out."

I peeled off ten euros and handed it to the guy. "Nice racket you guys run."

"You're in our home, motherfucker, not the other way around, so suck my ass nuggets."

"Fair enough. I'm looking for James Peter Fountain."

"Who?"

"Ah," said another homeless man. He sat on a leather recliner that he'd clearly pilfered from someone's trash. Though how he got it in here was beyond me. He pointed at my neck. "Look. He wears the cross. He's a guest of the church."

I fingered the Crucifix Craig had given me. "Yeah, I guess so."

"The door at the end," the first man said. "Pay my friend."

"Pay me," Recliner Man said.

"Jesus, I'm gonna go broke in this town before I get to actually buy anything." I handed him ten euros as well. "Now where's this door?"

"Right there," he said, pointing down the alley past a small fir tree that had started growing up through cracks in the ground. Behind it there was a heavy wooden door that looked like it might stop a battering ram. I grabbed the handle, found it unlocked, pushed it open and felt a chill wind crawl over me.

I moved down a wood-paneled hallway full of shadows that seemed to go on forever. At the end of this was another door. I opened it, saw stone stairs leading down into a stink that made my nose curl. Mold and something that should have been thrown out long ago. Some kind of fetid cheese stench that made me thank God I hadn't eaten breakfast.

I descended down the spiraling stairs, round and round and round, going farther down than the sewer tunnel I'd passed through. By the time I saw light I figured I was at least four stories below the street. The light was seeping through the hinges of a rusted metal door that looked like it may have once housed a bomb shelter.

When I tried the knob it was locked. "Fucking great."

So I did the only thing I could think of. I knocked. *Bang bang!*

A half a minute later it opened, and James Peter Fountain stood before me. "Roger!" he said. "What are you doing here?"

"What do you mean? You told me to meet you here."

"Yes, but I expected you to ring the doorbell. On the street. I was going to come up and meet you in the church. Not in this building. How did you even get down here?"

"What the hell are you talking about? This is the address you gave me!" I showed him the message he'd sent me on my phone.

"Ah, I see. Sorry. That nine is supposed to be a zero. I was typing too fast. The street wraps around the next block, you see, to the entrance of the church. I told the caretaker to call me when you arrived. Well, no matter, you're here now, albeit smelling of something I dare not ask about."

"And twenty euros poorer."

"Piotr and Oscar got to you, huh? Well, they do serve a purpose I suppose. They like it there in that alley, and they scare the riff raff away. I'll pay you back. C'mon in. Care for a drink?"

Chapter 11

The room was large, made of stone, furnished with old pews and floor-standing candle holders. Many of them were in use, which caused the walls to dance in orange starbursts. At the far end of the room, incense burners had been hung on the candle holders, which explained the awful smell.

"What is this?" I asked. "Eau du Hobo Scrotum?"

"It's a house blend. I'm not sure what, though. I didn't make it. But let me introduce you to the men who did."

We moved over to a large wooden table cluttered with stacks of old books and even more candles. I felt like I was in a scene from a bad Dungeons & Dragons game.

"This is Walter and Uri," Fountain said, sweeping his hand toward two men standing at the head of the table. The first, Walter, was older than Fountain, perhaps late sixties, sported a white beard and wore a black fedora. Uri, on the other hand, was younger, not much older than me, and wore a freshly pressed suit. He was clean shaven, his hair neatly cropped, and I caught a glimpse of a gold Breitling watch as he approached me and extended his hand.

"Roger Huntington, I assume," he said.

I shook his hand. He had the kind of grip you had to admire. Not too hard, not too soft, with skin that had seen plenty of manual labor, albeit not for some time. "That's me. What is this place?"

"This," he said, running his eyes over the room, "is a long forgotten dream of Berlin."

"It was a records office, way back," Fountain said, pouring me a glass of water from the carafe on the small serving tray next to us.

"The smell you ask about," said Walter, "is a combination of myrrh, frankincense, and brimstone."

"Brimstone?" I had heard of it in comics, in horror stories, knew it was a type of sulfur, which explained the stench. But why someone would use it for aromatic purposes made no sense. "You trying to hide a fart?"

He chuckled. "No. It merely exists here, from back when this church was full of Sunday morning adventurers."

"But why burn it? Why even bring it here in the first place?"

"Why do you think?"

I took a guess. "I honestly have no idea."

Walter nodded. "Do you know the story of Sodom and Go-morrah?"

"I saw the porno."

"You jest," Walter said, smiling, "but there are, in fact, many pornographic movies made about its destruction. I've seen my share too. I was once a young man with hormones. It's a good ex-cuse to film an orgy."

"I feel incredibly uncomfortable now."

"Sodom and Gomorrah was so detestable and sinful, bent on pleasures of the flesh instead of pleasures of the soul—"

"One could argue they're the same."

"Indeed. As I was saying. They put their flesh before their soul and so God rained down destruction in the form of fire and brim-stone. It burned up everything it touched. Do you know why He chose brimstone?"

"Because it still smelled better than the gallons of baby batter making all the floors sticky."

"Because it is a miracle element of rebirth. It helps plants grow, kills fungi, and most importantly it kills pests."

"So He burns the cities to ashes, then makes sure no pests can return? That part was never taught to me."

"It's not the pests that are the concern. It's those who would re-turn to a life of debauchery . . . that is the true affront."

"So you burn brimstone to . . . what? Keep the rats and flies away?"

Walter looked up into the ceiling's pipes. I followed his gaze and saw the remnants of old wooden beams up there. "Sometimes it's not meant for things we can see."

"Come again?" I said. "What're you looking at?"

"Things that try to poison us. Ill winds. Voices. Faces."

"I didn't know any better I'd say you're talking about ghosts and shit?"

"Perhaps. Or perhaps there were those who long ago gave up their souls in exchange for something far more sinister."

"More sinister than ghosts?" I remembered the one-eyed wolf statues in Marshall Aldritch's mansion. They were Psoglavs, hellish beasts that ate humans. Marshall and his followers thought they were Psoglavs themselves, and maybe they were. Who knows? I still didn't buy into that kind of crap.

"Walter's ways are not all our ways," Fountain said, smiling. "Sometimes I think he just likes the awful smell. Fact is, it keeps the roaches out, so closely connected to the sewers as we are."

"Which again makes me wonder why you're here in this... cave?"

"I admit it's not a glamorous penthouse suite," Fountain said. "But our work is not about watching the sunset. This place, it was bombed in the war. The locals rebuilt it, then transformed it into a records office, then abandoned when it was commandeered and occupied by the Stasi, and when they left we bought it. Now it is protected as a historical building, and we provide tours on weekends."

"Church services?"

"I'm afraid not."

"Why? Seems like it would be a great place for that sort of thing. Very...overbearing."

Uri spoke up. "It wouldn't be appropriate."

His eyes bored into me, daring me to ask more. But I decided to let my unspoken question hang in the air. I knew if I asked I would either get another fanatical answer or a history lesson that involved the death of millions of Jews. Plus, I hated taking bait from people.

"So the rest of the time you're down here in the stink reading books?" I asked.

"Ledgers," Uri said, picking one up and showing it to me. The pages were full of names and dates and money amounts and addresses and various other bits of personal information that meant nothing to me. Not to mention most of it was in German, and some in Latin, and perhaps Klingon for all I knew. Thing about people who congregate in sub-basements of old churches, they love to hoard shit in other languages.

Fountain put his hand on my shoulder. "Roger, I'm sorry, I—"

I whirled and got in his face. "I don't care what you think you're sorry for or what kind of Illuminati bullshit thing you've got going on here. Where were you last night? Do you know what happened? Speak up." Shit, I sounded like Katrin.

Fountain hung his head, which was good for him because I was feeling real close to punching his teeth out. "I'm sorry, again. I heard from Katrin this morning. I can't believe what happened."

"Do you even know what happened? Do you! He cut her fucking head off! He cut every bit of her body apart and videotaped it for me. She's probably still in pieces up in that building!"

"I know. I'm sorry."

"Did you alert the police?" Walter asked. He stepped back when he saw the anger in my face.

"Of course! And now you need to start spilling it, Fountain. How did this happen? How did this guy know about me? Did he already know about Katrin and Craig? I thought you said you hadn't seen him in months? Why is he really trying to kill you? It's not just because you're chasing him. Because he was in Argentina and he could have just stayed there. But he didn't. He flew to Berlin to find you. That makes this a very personal issue for him. What aren't you telling me?"

He poured himself a glass of water and leaned against a support pillar made of concrete. "This man we seek—"

"Who now seeks us," I corrected him.

"This man…he has been in my life for over a decade."

And there it was. The first bit of truth I'd heard him speak since I'd arrived. I didn't know whether to thank him or punch him. "How so?"

"I had a wife, I was married, we lived in New York City. She was a philanthropist and worked with homeless children, when she wasn't teaching at the youth center. One night the school was having a fundraiser, and normally I would have been there with her, bid on some silent auction items and indulged in crab cakes and free pinot grigio, but that night I was pressed to finish work for my firm. From what I was able to find out, the night went off without a hitch. They raised over twenty thousand dollars. My wife was a delight, and she agreed to stay and help clean up. And that was the last anyone saw of her."

I felt my breathing slow down. My anger was taking a hike, probably because I had an inkling where this was going. Fountain took a sip of his water and continued.

"She never made it home. I was frantic. I called everyone I knew until I finally called the police. Four days later they found her, decapitated, eviscerated, in an abandoned warehouse near the Chelsea piers.

"My world ended, as I'm sure you can guess. To lose the love of your life is one thing, to have to identify her severed head is quite another. I had a nervous breakdown, started drinking, you get the picture. I wanted to kill myself, but was deterred through the kindness of some friends who dragged me to church on an almost daily basis. Despite my being raised in a monastery I had sort of lost my religion for a while. I had become more interested in business. But this, her death, it brought me back to God. Angry though. Angry at Him for taking her. See, when you lose someone like that, God often doesn't numb the pain. You mostly curse at Him."

"Yeah, I've been there," I said. Sometimes, I'm still there, but I kept that to myself.

"You have, yes, which is why you're here. But I digress. The killer was never caught. The police had no leads and no one at the fundraiser had acted suspiciously so no one knew what had happened. Well, I made it my business to find this person, and after hiring numerous private investigators who turned up nothing, I made it my life's work to find this monster myself."

"And you did."

"Sort of. About a year after my wife's murder, I approached a group of college kids in a bar. I heard them talking about Internet programming and what not. It was Greek to me then, as now, for the most part. I told them my story, showed them a picture of my wife, offered them money to help me. I'd exhausted all of my physical leads, I figured—what could it hurt to try the Internet? I honestly had nothing to lose and nowhere else to turn. They thought I was crazy, of course. But one of them, a boy named Jason, took the money and said he'd dig around. He came back to me a week later with nothing but a website link. He told me I would not want to watch it, but that I should get the police to look into it. He'd traced the user to a location in Mexico, though he said the trace was probably rerouted."

"What was on the site," I asked, cutting to the chase.

"It was a website full of people dying. One of them was my wife. Her murder to be exact. Frame by frame I watched as my wife was hacked to pieces. I cried and cried, but I forced myself to watch in the hopes that something, anything, would betray who this killer was. That I might see a tattoo, or a freckle on his wrist, or just some kind of movement that I could single out. But there was nothing. Just my wife screaming, knowing she was dying, pleading and crying as a pair of arms in black gloves took an amputation saw and dug it into her throat. She gurgled, then the air escaped the wound and her pain could only be read in her eyes. The saw cut back through her windpipe, her esophagus, and then hit her vertebrae, which took near a minute to get through. When he was done, her head fell off to the ground. He had to reposition the camera to show it. Then the video went black."

"I'm sorry," I said. And I meant it. I could feel bile rising in my throat.

"The video was labeled as an Al Qaeda assassination. So nobody seeing it would know it was a forty-six-year-old woman from New York. But that's not the worst part. The worst part was the comments section underneath. I still remember them. 'Damn, that bitch screamed.' 'That shit is hardcore. Where can I see more.' And my favorite: 'Is it wrong that I jerked off to this?'"

"People are scum. The whole planet is full of filth."

Walter and Uri did nothing but listen to our exchange. I wanted to say they were uncomfortable, but they almost looked bored. My guess is they'd seen the video, or at least heard about it, a dozen times.

"I assume this is where Interpol comes in," I said.

Fountain nodded. "After a sweep of the warehouse where her remains had been found turned up nothing, the New York City Police had their best cyber crimes people trace the video, but by then it was being hosted on a new site . . . in Russia."

"So your pleas fell on deaf ears."

"Actually no, the site responded, and apologized, and in fact took down the video."

"Score one for the Ruskies."

"But it resurfaced. Nothing on the Internet goes away. Once it's there, it's there forever, and the video can be found on hundreds of morbid sites. These sites hide behind Net Neutrality, or bury themselves in the Deep Web, but I know that my wife's torture and murder only brings them advertisers and money. And the comments get worse and worse. Needless to say, I don't look."

"But knowing they're there must kill you."

"Indeed."

"So then…what? How does all that get you here?"

"Years passed, as they say. I spent time searching for this man, and at some point I returned to the monks that raised me, to seek some guidance and perhaps try to find peace. I found Uri and Walter instead."

I looked at the other two men, feeling like I still had more puzzle pieces in my hand and no clear idea how to join them. "And what do you do exactly?"

"Let's just say we serve a higher power," Uri said.

"Oh yeah? Like who? God? Vin Diesel?"

"We all serve God, boy, but who we serve beyond that is not for you to know."

"So it's Vin Diesel."

Uri didn't smile, but I didn't really care. Sometimes the best victory is just knowing you're bugging the shit outta somebody. I looked back at Fountain. "So this guy who came into my room last night . . . this is your guy? Here in Berlin. The guy who murdered your wife. Who butchered Christa. Who's killed numerous other women. And he wants you not just because you're onto him, but because you're some kind of extension of your wife. If he gets you both he wins some serial killer achievement badge?"

"I believe I got too close to him, scared him somehow."

"Scared him? Not enough to fly here across the globe. No, you didn't scare him. You excited him. He wants to look in your eyes as he kills you and tell you that it *was* him that killed your wife. He'll probably describe every detail of it and it'll be all you know before you die. It's a form of acceleration. He's bored with just killing women. He wants to kill the men who love them too."

"Oh," said Uri, "then what about the girl last night? He wasn't too bored for her."

"Well, he needs to kill. There are phases. The kill is the high. Depression comes after the kill, which is why he needs to kill again. It's cyclic. But it's like any Ivy League drug. You always know you'll come down from the clouds and get depressed, and so you get high again. But in the back of your mind you're wondering if there's a drug that will get you so high you might be able to stay high. That's what he gets from killing you. It's a stronger drug, feeding his needs. Shit, if you don't catch him he'll probably start murdering women, their husbands, their grandmothers, their dogs. Their employees. He's not just destroying one life, he's destroying clans. It makes him a god."

"You've done your research, Roger," Fountain said, smiling like he was proud of me.

"Only we still don't know who he is or where he's hiding. But he knows you, and he knows me, and he's gonna come at us again. Jesus, Fountain, why the fuck did you bring me into this?"

"Because you have a gift. You find these types of people. I just didn't think he'd appear to you so fast."

"Well, he fucking has!"

Behind the stone walls near the bookcases, I heard a low gong, like a pipe falling over in the distance. Uri, Walter, and Fountain exchanged glances and Walter looked at his watch.

"We must go now," Fountain said, "but I will be back tonight."

"Where are you going now?" I demanded.

A false door opened in the stone wall, just a crack, but enough for me to see more candle light inside. What was on the other side?

"Trust in your abilities, Roger." With that, he and his two cohorts disappeared through the door. I caught a glimpse of old men inside wearing suits and one or two in liturgical vestment garb, robes and stoles and funny pointed hats. Then the door shut and I was alone.

Alone and confused and pissed off.

"Where are you going?" I yelled through the wall. "Who are those men? Fountain!"

Nobody answered. I stood alone in a room that smelled like shit.

So I left.

Chapter 12

I used the front door this time, which was a lot faster and more convenient than the sewer, and made my way back to the apartment where I found Craig and Katrin at the kitchen table sucking down coffee.

"How'd it go?" Craig asked.

I tossed him the crucifix. "How'd you know I'd need that?"

"Fountain and his boys keep some subtle security nearby. I assume they clocked you?"

"Actually, I think I surprised them. Then they took me for twenty euros."

Katrin snickered. I ignored it and kept my gaze on Craig. "Bigger question is, are we working for that church?" I asked.

He guffawed. "You think the church hires people like us?"

"Well, truth be told I don't even know what you do, besides get in fights."

"I also quilt."

"Really? Paper piecing or appliqué? Or are you straight stitch in the ditch?"

"Say what now?"

"I thought so."

"Whatever. You know you smell like shit?"

"It's brimstone."

"I mean, seriously like shit. Like a dog's arsehole exploded on you, mate."

"You know what, dude—"

"How are you holding up?" Katrin asked, changing the subject.

"Well, the first girl I met in Berlin is dead, and the cops are probably going to arrest me for it in a few hours, and the guy is still out there and knows who we are. Oh, and I just walked through the sewer for no reason. So I'm doing okay."

"But you're meeting interesting people," Craig assured me. "That's worth something, right?"

"You mean Walter and Uri?" I asked.

"You met Walter and Uri? Bloody lucky, you."

"Why so?"

"Them blokes are like ghosts. And usually when you see them, you don't live to talk about it."

"Very dangerous," added Katrin. "They must like you."

"Well I don't like them. And you can tell them when you next see them. I don't appreciate being run around like this."

"So you're going to leave?"

"Maybe. Why not, right?"

She ran her hand through her pink hair. "Don't go yet."

"Why not?"

"Well for one, what if this guy follows you to America?"

The odds of that happening seemed slim, but I had seen so many fucked up things in my life I wouldn't put it past some killer to track me all over the globe if that's what he wanted. I knew Fountain was his real quarry, but I was now connected to Fountain. And this guy had possibly drugged me and been in my room. I couldn't risk him following me to my family.

"And two," she continued, "you've only been here for a couple of days. We need to retrace your steps and find out how this guy knew about you."

"He knew about me because he knows about Fountain. For all I know he reads his emails."

"Or he just saw you two in public," Craig said. "Where'd you go the first night you went out together?"

"We went to a restaurant," I replied. "You already know that. The pigeon, remember?"

"Is that it?"

I shook my head. "No. Actually, Fountain thought we were being followed so we went to a bar. The same bar where I got Christa's number."

"Okay then," Katrin said. "We have two places where he might have seen you. Which means someone might have seen *him*. Or seen *someone*, anyway, who didn't belong."

I sighed, knowing full well I was in the thick of things again. And despite not even knowing Christa's last name, I owed it to her to figure this out. "Okay, let's go look. But first I need to wash up. I stink like shit."

● ● ●

It turns out that when I mentioned the layout of the bar to Craig and Katrin they had no idea what I was talking about. Apparently Fountain had never taken them there. I didn't know if I should feel special or creeped out. I texted him to get the name but he didn't answer. No doubt he was too busy playing grabass with his clergy assassins.

"Wonder why we've never been there," Katrin said.

"Fountain's a smart bloke," Craig said. "He probably took Roger somewhere new to feel him out. No sense bringing him to the local haunts he brings us to if he was gonna end up being useless."

"Or maybe he just thinks the two of you aren't worthy of nice establishments," I said.

Craig laughed, but then I saw him retreat into his own head and I think he was really wondering if I'd gotten some kind of special treatment. Which of course had to be the truth.

Once we hit the restaurant a lot of my man-date came back to me. "That's where Interpol was watching us from a van," I said, pointing out the curb across the street from the restaurant's entrance.

We skirted the eatery altogether and made our way down the back road, to the back door, so that I could get my bearings on which way we'd walked to the hotel bar. It wasn't far, and we strode into the hotel like we belonged there, glided past the front desk, and got in the elevator. On the basement floor, we exited and I pointed to the door at the far end.

"That's the bar."

Problem was, when we tried the door knob it was locked.

"Too hip to be open this early," Katrin said. "Probably won't open until sundown."

We headed back to the elevator, and when its doors opened two men in suits stepped out and looked us over. The man on the left had a goatee and dark sunglasses and the man on the right had such bad dandruff he looked like he'd just returned from Aspen.

"Where are you all going?" asked Goatee.

"Just checking out the bar," Katrin said. "It's closed."

"What do you want with it?"

"A drink," she replied. "Usually what one does at bars. Now excuse us we're trying to go on up."

Dandruff Man stepped in front of her and blocked the elevator door. "Hold up," he said, finally brandished his police badge. "What's your name?"

"Graham Cracker Fart Mouth," Katrin said.

"And you?" He pointed at Craig, paused at the sight of his black eyes. "Who are you?"

"Your daddy . . . according to your mum." Craig smiled.

"Do you work for the bar?" Goatee asked.

"No. We just wanted a fucking drink, mate, like my friend explained. Early birds and worms and all that jazz. Why is that of concern to you?"

"Because we think someone came here the other night and picked up a lady who worked here and then . . . murdered her. So indulge us…mate. Were any of you here two nights ago?"

"Shit no," Craig said. "Your mum made me meatloaf and were retired early."

"Mention my mother again and I'll arrest you on the spot. Got me?"

Oh shit, I thought. Here we go. Trapped in a desolate basement hallway with two detectives and a bigmouth who likes to fight.

"We're just asking questions, Craig," Dandruff said. And at that point all our eyes went wide because we knew Craig hadn't said his name.

Craig squinted through his bruises. "How do you know me?"

"It's my city," the cop replied. "I know you."

"He's lying," Katrin said, walking right up to the detective. She looked in his eyes, and he took a tiny step back. His partner's hand slowly went to his gun holster. "He's seen you on a computer screen before, seen your name, probably an old mug shot, but he doesn't know you."

"Are you the assholes that came to our apartment?" Craig asked.

"No," the cop replied.

"He's telling the truth," Katrin said. And I gotta admit, the way she was acting, I was getting turned on and freaked out all at once. Fountain had said he'd hired "people like me" and I was starting to see that there was definitely more to Katrin than met the eye.

"Bravo, girl," the cop said. "Do you want to guess my weight next? No? Well, understand this: I will go back to my office and look you up again, Craig, and I will find out why you're in the system. And as for you two, I'll find out who you are as well. And if you're wanted for anything, even littering, you'll be in jail by tonight. Or, you could just answer our questions and save us time having to find you later."

I debated telling them that I had been here, that I had grabbed a drink with Christa, that she'd come home with me. But something told me they were looking for an easy collar and there was no way I could explain my way out of this mess yet. For fuck's sake, our fingerprints were on every door knob in that abandoned building Christa had been killed in. I needed to get on the phone with Teddy and figure out what my legal options were here, not first of which was how to get off the hook from withholding information regarding a murder.

"We just came to get a drink," Craig said, finally stepping past our interrogators. "We weren't here the other night and we don't know about your murder. And if you want to know about me, just friend me online."

We got in the elevator and rode up. I stared at Katrin the entire time. What was her deal?

• • •

We hit the restaurant on the way back and grabbed a coffee inside at the bar. This gave us an excuse to check out the staff and spy on potential tails; it was possible Mr. Video Death was watching us even now.

Every table was occupied with people in work suits discussing business deals, or movies, or whether chocolate was good or bad for you this week, or whatever the hell people in suits talk about, so it was hard to tell if any of them had ulterior motives. It seemed unlikely any of them were our killer.

On the wall next to the bar hung some photos of the management and I ran my eyes over them but nothing stuck out. The waiter who'd served us that night was in the staff picture, and it looked to be a couple years old, so I gave him the benefit of the doubt he wasn't a globetrotting serial butcher. I didn't recognize any of the others.

"Anything?" Katrin asked.

"No," I replied.

"Me either. We're wasting time," she said.

I gave the place one last look over and we left.

Outside, I suggested visiting the flea market, but we all agreed it was too big an area to cover, with too many people. The place could be filled with men dressed as Abraham Lincoln and we'd never find them.

That meant the comic shop.

When we got there, Craig's fling was behind the counter and she squeaked like a mouse. She rushed out and hugged him." Why'd you run off on me? What happened to your face? Are you okay? Answer me."

"Emergency, love," he said, "but I'm back now. Right as rain, as they say."

"Well thank God," she replied. "I thought you hated me." She gingerly touched his bruises from our fight with the Havoc Crew. "Answer my other questions."

"You don't remember the rough sex we were having?"

"Course I do. Why do you think I want you back. But I wasn't hitting that hard. Who'd you fight? Does it hurt?"

"Only when we're apart."

"Barf," Katrin said, before walking off to give the evil eye to other people in the store.

"She's kind of rude," Comic Book Girl observed. I realized then I'd forgotten her name.

Please don't ask about me, I thought. But sure enough she finally turned my way.

"Roger, right?" she asked.

"Yep," I said. "And how are you...buckaroo?"

Please kill me.

She tilted her head like a dog hearing a distant whistle.

"Roger's a wanker, Brit," Craig said, accentuating her name for my benefit. "Ignore him."

"Oh, I like Roger," she said. "Speaking of which . . . what happened to that girl you met, Roger? The one who liked your comic book. Ooh, that reminds me, I want to order some. Who's your publisher?"

"Wankers R Us," Craig said.

I didn't know why Craig was back to treating me like shit again, but I was starting to see a bit of a routine with him. In front of the ladies, he felt the need to be the tough guy. Couldn't say I blamed him; Brit was rubbing his arms even as he put me down. Subconsciously she liked his alpha male asshole attitude. Problem was I hated it, and I had visions of me swinging an axe into his head.

"Just friendly ribbing, Roger Roger," he said. "Snap out of it."

I did, and for some reason *I* felt like a prick.

"And call your girl," Brit said. "Let's all get drinks again. And you…" she poked Craig in the chest, "you come over tonight so I can take care of those wounds. I'll give them some extra love and attention. Plus I've got a new set of handcuffs I wanna use." She looked at me as she hugged her new manly man. "You ever use handcuffs, Roger?"

"Once. In a nightmare."

"Well I like 'em. Hope you do to, Craig. See you tonight."

She sauntered back to the counter to help a small boy buy some Spider-Man books, which were apparently popular enough to be sold in English. The older ones behind the counter were called *Die Spinne*. They had a *Die Spinne 129* and I seriously considered blowing the rest of Fountain's money on it for myself.

"That bird is mental," Craig said. "I might be in love. Like for real."

"Thought you said all comic readers are nerds?"

"Yeah. But didn't say I wouldn't fuck them."

Katrin returned, staring at Craig like she didn't know whether to high five him or kick him in the crotch. "She's an idiot, but it's your life."

I spun in a circle for a second, remembering we'd come here for a reason. Oh yeah, looking for clues of who'd tailed me last night. "See anything?" I asked.

"No," she said. "Just nerds and comics."

"You too, huh?" I said.

She squinted, scanning the room. "I'm trying to remember who was here, but I can't get a clear picture in my head. I don't have an eidetic memory."

"Me either. I just remember a bunch of twenty-somethings.

Maybe some older folks. Also some teenagers. Shit, that doesn't help at all."

"There's a stock room over there." Craig pointed to a door covered in comic posters. "Could be someone was inside it, watching us. Maybe someone who followed us home."

Katrin went over and knocked on it. A second later it opened and an overweight man in a button-down shirt and black-rimmed glasses leaned out. He was holding a coffee cup, looking mildly annoyed. Behind him a TV set was playing an anime cartoon. I could just barely see a computer on a small desk next to that.

"Yeah?" he asked.

"Let me see your hands," Craig said.

"Excuse me?"

"Raise your fucking hands or I'll raise 'em for you, mate."

Confused and suddenly afraid, the poor guy eased his arms up.

"They're too fat," I said, shoving decorum aside. "They're not the hands on the tape. Who else goes in that room?"

"Just me. I own the place. What the hell do you guys want? I've got the police on retainer."

"No one else goes in there?" I asked.

He dropped his arms, realizing now we weren't a threat. Now he was pissed. He walked at us like he might bowl us over. "No one. Now if you're not buying books I'm gonna need you to leave."

"You got video surveillance in there?"

"Do we look like a museum?"

"I dunno," I said," you've got some nice landmark issues on the wall there. Hulk 181, House of Secrets 92, both in mint condition."

"You gonna buy them?"

"Wish I could. So you're telling me you don't keep cameras on them?"

"I reiterate . . . no, we have no surveillance. But if you're thinking of robbing me—"

"Relax, mate," said Craig. "We're just looking for someone who was giving us a hard time. We thought maybe he followed us here the other day. But even if he did we wouldn't be able to confirm it so all's well in nerd land. Take a breath and go back to playing with your toys. We'll be jogging on."

So we left. And the day got more interesting.

● ● ●

We made our way to the bar where we'd drunken ourselves stupid the previous night. It was chock full of 'punters', as Craig called them. I still didn't know if it was a nice term or not. I asked the bartender if he remembered anyone weird from last night but he said he hadn't worked last night and that if I wasn't drinking I needed to leave the bar seats open for people who were.

I thought we might be setting a record for getting asked to leave places.

"I don't suppose you have video cameras in here?"

"No. Why?" He almost looked like he was going to reach for a baseball bat under the bar, or whatever German sporting equipment was the equivalent. The way he stared at Craig's puffy face told me he was on edge.

"Someone stole my purse," Katrin said, lying, diffusing the situation. "We just want to see if it was caught on camera. It has a lot of my stuff in it."

"We're not responsible for lost belongings. And I can't let you see the tapes, but I'll tell the manager when he comes in if you want to leave your number. If he sees anything, he'll call you."

Katrin humored him and wrote down her number, or a fake one. I didn't know.

"Well we're at a dead end again," I said. "Shit, he could have been at any of those places."

"Even if he was, it doesn't matter," Katrin said. "It just dawned on me that all we need to do is go back to the hotel bar. Think about it."

"I don't follow."

"He *must* have seen you before we got to this pub otherwise how would he know you were working for James. He had to have been at the bar in the hotel."

"Currently under watch by *das bullen*," Craig added. "So we're kind of out of luck for now."

"So the day was a waste," I said. "Meanwhile, this is all about Fountain but he's out playing games in a church basement for God knows what reason."

"I'll have a pint," Craig said to the bartender. He looked at me with a grin. "What? When in Rome."

• • •

Ten minutes later we were all downing lagers and trying our best to
be Sherlock Holmes but failing miserably. We'd gone through every
scenario in our heads a dozen times and couldn't figure out how
this guy was able to watch us, possibly slip me a sleep aid, and follow us home without us hearing or seeing him. Then to get Christa
out of the apartment and across the city in time to butcher her,
record it, and fuck with us.

"Can we even go back to the apartment?" I asked. "How do
we know he's not there waiting?"

"I'll go," said Craig. "Soon as I'm drunk. If I don't call, don't
come back."

"How long will that take?"

He downed his beer in one long gulp, tapped the empty glass
on the bar to get the bartender's attention. "Not long," he said.

"Can I ask you something?" I looked at Katrin.

"As long as I can answer how I want." She almost seemed in-
trigued.

"That thing you did in the basement of the hotel. When you
stared at the cop and knew he was lying or telling the truth…is that
like, a trick or do you have some mind-reading powers I should
know about? Because if so, I'm embarrassed at what you may have
found in my head since I arrived."

"Some people are just easy to read, Roger. If you know how to
play them."

"So that's it? Educated guesses? No Madam Xanadu stuff?"

"I have no idea who that is and I'll thank you not to refer to me
as Madam."

I took a sip of my beer, eyed a couple of college-aged girls sitting at a table not far away. They'd ordered a bottle—nay, a contraption—of absinthe. I'd never seen real absinthe before. In the
States it doesn't contain wormwood, but I assumed it was the real
deal here. The bartender showed them how to pour the hot liquid
over the sugar cubes and dissolve it in their glasses. It looked like
fun, and I wished Tooth was with me. He'd love it here. Getting

hallucinogenic drinks, meeting girls from Italy and Prague.

Craig slammed his beer down and burped. "Alright, you cunts, I'm headed back to the comic store for a little midday snacking, if you know what I mean. I'll check the flat after that, and give you a call. I suggest we get Jimmyboy on the phone and tell him we need new accommodations as soon as possible. If he ever crawls up from his cave."

I thought Craig was going to leave, but he eyed a pestle the bartender had left in a shaker for muddling. He grabbed it up slyly.

"Not here," Katrin said.

"Fuck off," he responded. "I'm pissed, and you don't get to tell me what to do." He took the pestle and smashed it down on the back of his hand. The sound it made just about echoed off the walls. I said, "Jesus," and let my jaw hang open. The guy was crazy, breaking his own hand.

"Hey, you!" The bartender rushed back over and took the pestle away from him. "Get out. Now."

"I was just leaving," Craig said. He flipped us all the bird as he backed out the door, the other patrons watching him like he was a lit stick of dynamite.

"Your friend is not welcome here anymore," the bartender said to us.

"He won't be back," Katrin replied. "Not that you'd stop him," she added, after he moved off to the end of the bar.

"The fuck was that about?" I asked.

"Craig has his kinks."

"He just broke his hand!"

"Probably not. Well, maybe he did, I dunno. He'll be fine though, don't worry."

"I'm not worried, I'm lost."

"Boys will be boys, right?"

"I don't do that shit. Had a friend that was like that once, though. My best friend growing up. He was kind of crazy and I never knew what he was gonna do to get us in trouble. Craig reminds me of him a bit. 'Cept Craig might be even more unpredictable."

"If he was always getting you in trouble why'd you stay friends with him?"

I thought about that. In fact, I'd thought about it a lot in the last ten years. "I think because my life was boring otherwise. I mean, I didn't know it then, and it used to piss me off a lot, but the fact is I think I knew, somewhere in my mind, that I'd never feel truly alive if I wasn't always on edge like I was around Tooth. Plus he always had my back. So even if he got us in trouble, I knew he'd get us out somehow."

"James told us your best friend was murdered before your eyes. That him?"

I hung my head, but only for a second. No use getting sad around her. "Yeah, that was him."

"Sorry." She sounded like she meant it, which was something.

"What about you? Friends? Family? Fountain told you about me, but he didn't really tell me about you. Why are you wrapped up in this?"

"No big secret. I ran away from home when I was seventeen. Mom and Dad couldn't handle me. James found me sleeping on the street, took me to his home, fed me, let me stay for a bit."

"Wait, hold on. He told me he met you in a coffee shop. Said you punched your boss in the face and he gave you a job. Was that a lie?"

"Don't act like you were taken advantage of, Roger. You may not hate your past but I hate mine. So I asked him to come up with a story if anyone ever asked about me. Truth is I was on the streets, and I was desperate."

"So…what? You just got in a car with a strange man? Fountain is seriously freaking me out the more I learn about him."

"Wasn't like that. I kind of approached him."

I was afraid to ask why she'd done that, but she saved me the trouble and told me. "I was sleeping with old men for money. Don't fucking judge me either. I was young and homeless."

"But you had a home. The one you ran away from."

"Mom and Dad wanted to commit me, and I didn't feel like seeing shrinks. Seventeen-year-olds have issues, but sometimes they don't require padded rooms. So I left. And I needed money. And old guys like blowjobs so—"

"Okay. Whoa. Please stop. I'm not asking for details. Get back to Fountain and how you met him."

"Yeah, well, he turned me down, because he's good like that, offered to take me to a shelter, even gave me twenty euros for some food when I said no thanks."

"But then why did he take you home with him?"

"I sort of... I told him something he needed to hear."

"Which was what?"

She looked at her phone, showed me a text message. It was from Fountain and it said he was coming by. "Time to go."

"What? No. Finish the story."

"Another time. We gotta get back."

She got up and left and I sat there fuming, yelling after her. "Fuck this! You can't just leave in mid-story like that. This ain't some movie where you tell me I have to follow you but when I ask why you say there's no time. Fuck that! There's always time. How hard is it to say, 'because terrorists are gonna blow up the building,' or 'because a meteor is headed our way.' Three fucking seconds! Watch! Time me! 'Because a meteor is coming.' See! Two fucking seconds even! In the time it takes you to say, 'I can't tell you,' you could've told me! Not to mention we still have to take a cab back to the apartment. That's gonna take like a whole ten minutes! Fucking bull-shit!"

The bartender leaned over and took my glass, which was still half full. "Get out."

• • •

The streets were starting to fill up with people leaving work early. Or just people waking up late in the day. I saw a few tourists snapping pictures, and the occasional Hare Krishna, believe it or not, but mostly it was the happy hour crowd ducking into bars and cafés.

"Wait up," I called as I chased after Katrin.

"Heard you yelling," she said as I drew up next to her.

"Seriously, that's how you leave me hanging?"

"For now, yes. And if you must know, I don't feel like getting into it yet. I barely know you. All I know is that since you've ar-rived, someone came into my home, killed a girl, and now we're being hunted."

"Don't put that on me. That's Fountain's deal, and you agreed

to be his mercenary, or whatever it is you do for him. Are we getting a cab?"

"No, there's a U-Bahn station up here."

She skirted a woman pushing a stroller and turned left down a
narrow tree-lined street. I stayed beside her lest I get lost in the
maze of apartment blocks. We passed two more women walking
dogs, and I moved over to avoid a teenager in a purple hoodie riding a skateboard toward us at an alarming speed.

Katrin wouldn't look at me. I guess I pissed her off. I felt bad.
"Hey, Katrin, listen—"

I didn't get to finish my thought before Katrin was dropping to
the ground, barely registering that the purple-hoodied skateboarder,
zooming by us, was swinging a scalpel. It whizzed over her body,
just missing her head. The board's momentum carried him to me,
and he kicked me square in the stomach as he jumped off. I flew
backwards into a lime tree the city had planted on the sidewalk and
felt my body wail in protest. Old wounds, and some not so old,
flared up like fire. I saw the tiny blade coming at me again, and
threw my arm up to block, but the swing was caught in mid arc by
Katrin, who was on his back now, her legs wrapping around him
like a spider attacking prey. I just had time to notice he was wearing rubber gloves before she flung herself backwards, taking the
guy with her. They both fell hard on the sidewalk. Katrin lost her
breath as the guy landed on top of her.

I was up in an instant but so was the guy. Coming at me with
the scalpel. I prepared for it to slice open my face. But he flew right
past me, suddenly flailing. All that was left in his wake was Katrin's
outstretched leg, left hanging from where she'd kicked him.

I spun to grab the guy, to pull his hood off, knowing full well
who he must be, but he was rebounding off the building and swinging his blade in a wide arc.

I jumped back, noticing now how his face was hidden behind
a thin black biker bandana.

He came at me again but Katrin was there, her own knife in
hand, and she got him in the ribs with its blade.

The guy yelped and kicked her in the stomach and down she
went.

"Fucker!" I yelled, running at him. But I'm no martial artist, and when he swung his blade at me again I instinctively stopped, giving him enough time to race off down the sidewalk at a ridiculous pace. The guy was like an Olympic sprinter, lithe and spry and all legs. I blinked and he was gone, around the block.

I took off after him, found him already at the end of the next intersection. He ran through people and dogs and baby carriages, never touching them, like he was made of mist.

He took another turn. My heart raced and I got a stitch in my side. When I took the same turn, I didn't see him anywhere.

He was gone.

"Shit." I bent over to catch my breath, waiting to see him emerge in the distance, but he never showed. Minutes ticked by. It felt like an eternity. But still he didn't show.

I made my walk of shame back to Katrin.

She was on the ground moaning, trying to catch her breath, so I helped her sit up. "Are you hurt?"

She finally sucked in air. "Yeah. Everywhere. You're cut, by the way."

I looked down and saw the gash in my thigh, right through my jeans. Damn, I thought I'd accounted for every swing the guy had taken. Now that I saw it, the stinging sensation began. "I'll live."

"That's deep. You're gonna need stitches. Fuck, I can't believe he got away."

"He was so fast. He just . . . disappeared."

"Did you at least see his face?"

I shook my head, cursing myself for not grabbing him when Katrin had taken him down.

"Where'd you learn to fight like that?" I asked.

"I wouldn't call it fighting so much as flailing."

"It was better than what most people would do."

"You think that was the guy?" she asked

"Had to be, right?"

"Who knows. Either it was him or it was a random guy trying to mug us in broad daylight with a surgical knife. Germany's weird but I don't know it's *that* weird."

I looked up and saw a few people staring at us, but most people seemed to keep on moving. If they were like most people they probably didn't want to get involved.

"If it was him, why attack us like this? In the street, on a damn skateboard of all things. He's got to be at least in his 40s. What forty-year-old rides a skateboard?"

She finally stood up. "He was swinging for my neck. If he'd connected it would have taken a second before either of us even noticed and he'd have been away in a heartbeat." She walked over and picked up the skateboard, looked it over, hoping for a clue.

"You got forensics people in Berlin?"

"No," she said, handing me the board, "we only have white-haired alchemists and Nazi wizards."

"I didn't mean—"

"Of course we have forensics, but I don't see a footprint. And he was wearing gloves."

"Yeah, but, could be a strand of hair, even a bit of his sweat."

"It rode all over the streets of Berlin. If it's got DNA on it it could be anyone's. Not to mention the police don't allow walk-ins to swab random skateboards. Which is beyond the fact that we should be laying low from the police for a bit."

"Alight, point taken. You okay?" I asked again, like an idiot. Of course she wasn't. The guy had targeted her for death. Why would she be okay?

"I've dealt with street thugs before. I'll be fine. You really do need to clean that cut though. And let's bring the board. Maybe you're right after all. Maybe it'll help us."

"If that was him," I said, "he's probably been watching us all day. He knew where we were headed and gave himself enough time to get a head start."

"Yeah, that's what scares me."

Chapter 13

Back at the apartment, we found Fountain and Craig hunched over a laptop, waiting for us. I hobbled in holding my leg, blood still rushing out like its time was money. The riders on the train had eyed me like I was a crazy person, but Katrin had positioned her knife in her pocket, hilt sticking out, to keep anyone from approaching.

Fountain rushed over. "What happened?"

"That time of the month?" Craig asked.

"He attacked us on the sidewalk," I said. And then before he could ask *who*, I said, "Pretty sure it was the guy who killed your wife. I take it he didn't come here?"

Fountain went stoic, which was anything but a stretch for him. "Not that we've seen."

Katrin stepped in behind me and shut the door. She dropped the skateboard on the floor. Craig took one look at her face, growing purple with a bruise, and jumped up. "Let me get you ice." He bounded to the kitchen, wrapped some ice in a paper towel and pressed it to her cheek.

"Thanks," I said. "I'll just stand here and bleed out. It's fine. The wooziness is pretty relaxing."

He swatted me on the back. "You'll be fine, ya twat. Just need to sew it up. There's a needle and thread in the bathroom. Wash yer hands first."

"Nonsense," Fountain said. "Sit down, Roger. I'll patch you up. And you tell me about this guy who attacked you. Did you see his face?"

"No. He was wearing a hoodie, came at us quick on that skateboard, swinging a knife. It was all just a blur, but his face was hidden. Katrin jumped him but he tossed her off and ran away. I tried to catch him but..." I trailed off, annoyed that I'd failed to catch the guy.

Fountain retrieved the first aid kit from the bathroom, took out the needle and thread and wiped the needle with rubbing alcohol.

"We can take you to the hospital," he suggested, "if you don't want to do it this way."

"And attract *das bullen*," Craig added.

"Just do it," I said.

And so he did, driving the needle into me and suturing the wound with six stitches. It was unpleasant to say the least, but Craig was nice enough to pour me some vodka they had in a high cupboard. I hate vodka, but any port in a storm.

When he was done, and my insides were finely martinied, Fountain taped a bandage to the stitches, sat back in the chair before me and tried to read my thoughts. At least that's what he looked like he was doing. That or trying to hold in a fart. He picked up the skateboard, studied it. "Question is, why attack in broad daylight?"

"He was going for my throat," Katrin said. "Trying to kill me. But I have to admit, I almost think he's fucking with Roger."

"Roger? How so?"

"Well, he could have killed Roger when he came here and abducted Christa. I mean, she was in bed next to him. But he didn't. And then he made Roger chase him to a remote area of the city, made him think he could save her, only to reveal he'd already killed her. And now today he swings a scalpel at *my* jugular."

"On a skateboard," Craig added. "That takes skill, let's give the boy credit."

"Shut up, idiot. My point is, if this was about getting to *you* through Roger . . . why not kill *Roger*? Right? But he didn't. Both times he went after people Roger was with."

Her logic made sense; the guy had had the element of surprise and chosen to ignore me both times. He'd taken one girl from me, it was possible he'd wanted to take another. "Why's he after me and not you?" I posed the question to Fountain, who was now fingering his earlobe.

"I've been searching for this man for over a decade. You're right. Why would he target you and not me? Why now, after all this time, after chasing him around the globe when I've had the chance, does he come out of hiding but then keep focusing on you?"

"He knows plenty about us and we know nothing about him," Katrin said. "It pisses me off."

"We know some things." Craig brought the computer over and showed us what they'd been looking at. It was one of the disgusting websites that hosted execution videos. "Here's a new video we think is him. Young girl, in her twenties. He posted it as an Al Qaeda video. It's disgusting."

"Please don't make me watch it."

"I'm not going to. It's not worth it. You've seen one you've seen 'em all."

"Did you tip off the cops?" I asked.

"No need to. Someone in the comments section said they were sending it to the F.B.I."

"Fucking Americans," Katrin said. "Trying to save the world through the Internet. Don't suppose you saw Christa on there?"

"No. Not yet. But it doesn't mean he didn't get a video out somehow."

"But he left the tape," I said, realizing it was a moot point.

"He could've recorded the TV, or used his own phone. It's possible."

I shuddered at the thought that I might see Christa pop up on one of these sites.

"So what does this video tell you?" I asked.

"It tells us he was in France recently, likely right before he made his way here," Fountain said. "The victim yells *au secours* more times than I can count."

"Well thank God we know his travel itinerary," I said. "What, are we supposed to track everyone in Berlin who was recently in France? We'll be dead before we get all that information. I meant, does it reveal anything about who he is and how we find him?"

"Fuck no," Craig said.

Fountain stood up, checked his watch. "I must be going."

We all stared at him like he'd punched us. "What?" I said. "Where?"

"And do we pack up and leave or what?" Katrin asked. "Does this guy know where we live?"

Fountain nodded. "You will all stay at the church until further notice. Please pack up your bags and head over. I've alerted Uri and Walter you will be coming by."

"And where are you going?" I asked.

"I have a prior engagement."

"Screw you, Fountain. Ever since I got here you've been elusive."

"You saw me this morning. And we had dinner two nights ago."

"And what do you want, a blowjob? You keep disappearing, and when you do, people die."

"You think I'm responsible for what has happened? I'm trying to end it. And you're here to help me. I'm sorry I have other engagements in the meantime, but I do. It's not to annoy you."

"All I know is I don't know shit about what's going on. About who you really are. About what you and your friends really do."

He sighed. "Would you like to come with me?"

"You keep leaving and...what?"

"I agree with you. I was keeping you at bay to ease you in, but if you are to be a part of our organization, you are entitled to see it in its entirety. I was merely concerned about letting you get comfortable here, but the timetable has obviously changed."

I looked at Katrin for advice. She just nodded her head as if to say, go with him, we've all done it. Fuck it, I told myself, and went to change into pants that didn't have blood on them.

Chapter 14

And so it was ten minutes later we were in a black sedan heading down Schwarzewaldstrasse

into a sullied area of East Berlin that looked like it had been gentrified and then abandoned during a rent hike. Despite the modern architecture and newly paved sidewalks, graffiti now covered the doorways and loose trash blew down the street. To be honest, it was probably no worse than any street in South Boston, but here in Berlin, where so much of the city was clean and reconstructed, it felt dirtier than it should.

The sun was setting and shadows were peeking out from the edges of the world. We parked outside a brown apartment complex in front of which stood an old woman in knee-high stockings smoking a pipe.

That's your girlfriend, Tooth whispered.

If she was, I thought, she'd be dead soon.

Fountain got out and waited for me to meet him on the curb. "When we get inside, stay close."

I felt my muscles go tight. I wasn't sure what I was preparing for, or if I was even right to be so tense, but when someone tells you to stay close, it's usually not just because they enjoy your body heat.

We strode into a shaded foyer that smelled of dust and mold. The interior of the place was pale blue. Drab as shit. The sun clawed through some dusty windows and made pink swirls on the opposite wall. It reminded me of sunsets I used to paint in California, back before I met Marshall Aldrich and his wannabe Psoglavs.

"This way." Fountain passed the elevator and opted for the stairs, hauling us up five floors to the top.

"I mentioned my leg was just gashed open, yeah?" I said. "Perhaps I need to explain it in a series of one-act plays?"

As usual, he found no humor in my words, and waved me forward to the end of the hall. I heard booming bass coming from the nearest unit. From another came the smell of something that could only be dirty socks soaking in cow shit. I tipped an ear toward the latter door and tried to hear animals mooing but got no result.

Ahead of me, Fountain was knocking assertively on a door like he'd come to deliver a package. Short, loud raps. "Who are we meeting?" I asked.

He didn't answer. Nor did he even bother to look at me. His demeanor had changed and I could see his mouth tightening, his jaw clenching. The man who usually gave off an air of patriarchal leadership now looked like someone I'd be afraid to meet in a dark alley.

The door opened. A man said," Who are you?"

And Fountain punched him in the face, pulled a small stun gun from his pocket and jabbed it at the guy. The air crackled and I saw blue sparks dance in the dim light. The guy was launched backwards into the apartment and Fountain rushed in after him.

"Shit," I said, and ran in too, closing the door behind me, making myself small lest any fists or guns or weapons came out of nowhere at me.

On the floor, Fountain sat on top of the guy and punched him again. The guy's head rebounded against the floor and Fountain punched it again on its way up. This time, the guy's nose erupted in blood and he started wailing, kicking and punching and flopping about. Somehow he managed to knock the stun gun out of Fountain's hand and bucked his way out from underneath. Fountain went sprawling into a refrigerator.

The guy was all rage now. He ran right at me, bear hugging me, lifting me up and slamming me into the wall. My back wailed in protest. I didn't even know who this guy was! Why was he doing this?

He screamed in my face and I saw all the way down his throat. His blood speckled my face and all I could think was, please God, don't have AIDS or Ebola or some European shit I've never even heard of.

I got my elbows up over his head and brought them down on the back of his neck. Once. Twice. Three times. My own shoulder threatened to dislocate from the socket, but that last blow was enough to make him drop me. As I fell, he leaned over to his kitchen counter and drew the bread knife from the knife holder. He came back at me and I rushed him, getting under his swing and lifting him up like he'd done to me. I was all adrenaline, scared shitless, confused and pissed that some guy I didn't even know wanted me dead.

Atta boy, killer! Give it to him. Get that knife and ram it up under his ribcage. Go for the heart!

Skinny Man's voice was lost in the haze that was my fear and rage as I rammed this guy into his fridge, knocking glass bowls off the top. They smashed on the floor, shards flying everywhere.

Fountain's fists came from behind me and caught the guy in the jaw. Two shots and the guy's eyes rolled back in his head. His knees buckled and his arms went slack.

"Let him go, Roger." Fountain was shoving past me and grabbing the guy by his collar. As the man sagged, Fountain got him in a headlock, and dropped him to the ground, tightening his arms around his carotid, utilizing the type of sleeper hold maneuver they only teach to military and MMA fighters.

Finally, the guy stopped moving altogether.

I leaned back against the wall, bent over to catch my breath. When I could breathe again I stood up. "What the fucking fuck! Twice in one day, man!"

"Are you hurt?"

"Twice in one day."

"What's twice in one day?"

"Knives! Two guys coming at me with knives! What the fuck!"

"Did he cut you?"

"No! Jesus. Not this time. But shit, you just stitched up a knife wound an hour ago. If those stitches are even still in place . . . Why did you bring me here? Who the hell is this guy? Wait, is he . . . ?"

"He's not our killer, if that's what you're wondering?"

"Only thing I'm wondering is whether or not to call the cops on you. You're fucking certifiable, you know that?"

He moved to the other side of the kitchen, picked up my Red Sox hat and gave it to me. I hadn't even realized it had fallen off. It had fresh blood on the rim, but that was nothing new for the hat, which said a lot about my life.

Fountain opened the fridge, took out a gallon of orange juice that was nearly full. "Come here," he said, moving into the living room.

I pointed at the unconscious mystery man on the floor. "What about this yahoo?"

"Leave him. He'll be out for a few more minutes."

I made my way into the living room and saw Fountain texting

to someone. He hit send, put his phone away, and motioned for me to follow him down a small hallway. He stopped outside the door at the end, tried the knob. It was locked. He bent down and peered under the crack at the bottom. Next, he stepped back and kicked with all his might. The door flew open and banged off the wall and I heard voices squeaking, like rabbits or squirrels.

But when I looked in the room it wasn't wildlife I saw, it was women. Lithe, malnourished, sunken-eyed women. They cowered as we entered the room, retreated onto the dozen mattresses that were strewn about. They shook, pulling blankets up over their mouths and noses, peering at us from beneath.

"It's okay," Fountain said, offering the gallon of juice to the closest one. She was young, maybe seventeen or eighteen, and she hesitated. I could see in her eyes she didn't trust this situation.

"It's safe." Fountain unscrewed the cap and took a swig of the juice, making sure she could see he'd really swallowed it. He offered it to me. "Have some, Roger."

I could barely take my eyes off the girls, but I grabbed the plastic jug and drank from it, then handed it back.

"See? Safe," he said, offering it to the girl again.

This time she took it, sniffed it, and downed several big gulps. Slowly, like frightened cats, the other women came out from under their blankets and reached for the jug. They all passed it around, starting to smile, to laugh even, making sure they saved enough for everyone.

"You're safe," Fountain said.

A skinny woman in her mid-twenties came forth and hugged Fountain, then hugged me, and I didn't know what to do. I just stood there, numb, lost, and angry. Because it was all starting to make sense now. The track marks in their arms, the bruises on their legs and faces. The finger marks on their necks and biceps.

It was a sex slave operation, and this was some kind of storage house.

"*Danke,*" she whispered in my ear. "*Du bist ein engel.*"

I could feel the scabs on her arms against my neck. She'd been pumped full of heroin, and was probably dependent on it now. I felt like punching something, and then remembered the man in the kitchen. When she let go of me I turned and tried to storm out of the room but Fountain grabbed me. He knew what my intentions were.

"Leave him," he said. "That man will be dealt with. Help these women gather what little belongings they have and meet me in the foyer."

He turned and left and I stared at the collection of sad and hopeful eyes before me. "Anyone speak English?" I asked.

They kind of tilted their heads.

"English?" This time I felt like a dick. Like I was insulting them. Why would they know English. The guy in the kitchen, and his buddies, probably went to great lengths to make sure these women didn't know English.

"*Ya ne govoryu po-angliyski,*" said the woman before me. She was dressed in a pink wife beater and had on shorts that were stained with dirt. "No English. *Izvinite.*"

I smiled, enjoying her smile. "I'm sorry. I don't speak…whatever that is you speak." Instead of trying to communicate I moved to the only closet and opened it. A collection of lingerie hung on hangers. Disgusted, I ripped it all down and tossed it aside. The girls laughed as I did this, and a few ran over and started pulling the bras and panties apart at their seams. I did find what I was looking for though, a beat-up old suitcase, and I picked up some jeans and T-shirts that were on the ground and tossed them inside. Seeing what I was doing, they followed suit, gathering whatever meant something to them. Mostly some shoes and some jewelry that may or may not have been what they'd been wearing when they were abducted.

Shit, I thought. How long had they been here? What had they suffered? I could only imagine, and truth be told I didn't want to know.

I saw the youngest in the room, a girl of maybe ten or eleven. My heart sank as she kept behind one of the older women. The child didn't feel safe yet and I didn't blame her. For all she knew she was just being moved to a new slave house.

When we had everything packed we all swept out of the apartment, but not before I raided the fridge again and let them take whatever they wanted. They grabbed granola bars and apples and cold cuts and a bottle of cheap wine and went to town right there, savoring every bite. After they'd stuffed their pockets with the remainders, we crushed into the elevator, all nine of us—as I was finally able to count—and rode down.

In the foyer, I found Fountain waiting with our friendly neighborhood enslaver, who was groggy at best. Fountain took the guy's wallet out, stuck it in his inside pocket.

The women stayed to the other side, still afraid of this guy, even though he was in vegetable mode.

"They're addicts," I said to Fountain. "What do we do?"

"It's being taken care of."

Before I could ask what that meant, two large, black SUVs pulled up out front, and Uri and Walter got out of them respectively. They came inside and looked at me, at the women, then at Fountain.

No words were spoken as Uri put handcuffs on the creep and hauled him outside, threw him in the back of the SUV.

Walter spoke something in German, or Russian, or Ukrainian, or all three for all I knew, and the girls followed him out to the second SUV and got in like it was a clown car. As the door was shutting, the youngest girl came back in, and for the first time looked at me in the eye. Then she hugged Fountain. He pet her head and said, "We're going to get you home."

She let go of him and came over to me, smiled up at me, and wrapped her arms around my waist. I saw the track marks on her arms and felt tears well up in my eyes. I knew pain, knew physical abuse. But this was something different. This was a life ruined before it even began, and it gave me heartache throughout my entire body.

She ran back outside and climbed into the SUV.

Fountain and I stood there silent until both vehicles left. Then he looked at me. "You did well."

"Why didn't you tell me before we arrived? You told me about the guy who killed your wife the first night I was here. Why not tell me about this?"

"Because I want you to know that behind every closed door you see, the potential for depravity and sickness abounds. Just because you can't see it, doesn't mean it isn't real. And that's what we do. We find them. The *way* we find out what's behind these doors, and how we kick them down, is why we operate the way we do."

"But . . . why not just tip off police? Why the subterfuge?"

He held up the guy's wallet, opened it up, tapped the photo in the plastic casing. A picture of our man in a police uniform.

"He's a cop? Fuck me."

"We don't believe we're above the law. We just know we're better than them. And at the end of the day, Roger, we only trust ourselves. This is the family I'm letting you into."

I thought of Teddy back home in New Hampshire. One of the good ones, as they say. He was the kind of cop that could restore your faith in law enforcement. "They can't all be bad," I said.

"Of course not. But they're not all good. And the ones that are bad . . . are very bad. Our way is better. It's effective."

"Yeah, so I'm learning. Vigilantism. It's the new black."

"So now do you understand why I can't always tell you where I'm going? We have secrets that must remain secrets. Sometimes, anyway. Because there are ears listening to us all the time. We can't risk alerting the enemy."

"Gotcha."

He put a hand on my shoulder and squeezed. It felt almost fatherly. "C'mon," he said, "let's go discuss our next move. Someone is out to get us, and we're too exposed."

• • •

The ride back to the church was quiet and somber. I tried to listen to the radio, even found stations in English, but didn't know the politics they were discussing. I settled on a rock station playing some INXS, which brought back memories of my childhood, but then made me remember how the singer had supposedly killed himself trying to jerk off while dangling from a noose. Whether it was true or not, I didn't know, but it spoke a lot to the mindset of people in positions of power. Not that Michael Hutchins was a prominent political figure or a corporate CEO or a war general or what have you, but the guy did have access to plenty of money and girls. You'd think he could have fucked anyone he wanted to. But no, the guy decides the only real way to achieve enlightenment is to shoot his jizz on the walls while playing hangman.

What is it about sex that makes some people equate it with death?

When I was in college, I took a course on Shakespeare. It was a Gen Ed requirement, and I like some of his plays, so I figured I could skate by. I think I got a B. Point is, there's a scene in *Romeo and Juliet*, wherein Juliet is daydreaming about Romeo, and she says:

> *Give me my Romeo, and when I shall die*
> *Take him and cut him out in little stars,*
> *And he will make the face of heaven so fine*

Turns out that back in Shakespeare's time the word "die" was slang for having an orgasm. Once you know that, you can see what Juliet's really getting at.

Imagine yelling that during sex: Oh right there, baby, I'm gonna die!

I remembered Skinny Man and the way he would strip naked before he'd torture us. He made Mystery Woman's severed head give him a blowjob. It was vile.

And yet, here it was all over again. A man torturing a naked woman on video. Just because we couldn't see if he was naked or not didn't mean his videos weren't about sex. I mean, they were about voyeurism, and voyeurism is all about sex. The people who watched these disgusting videos on the Internet, they were watching because it was a vicarious thrill for them. It was power without the guilt.

Is it wrong that I jerked off to this? That was a comment under the video of Fountain's wife's murder. And I believed the commenter probably did crank one out to those fucked up images. After what I'd seen tonight, I believed that the world was just one cataclysmic event away from digressing into a big orgy of bloodshed.

Just people fucking and dying.

At that point my mind had come back full circle to the INXS guy, and the notion of power.

What made people desire power over others? Was it as simple as saying they'd been raised under an abusive fist that left them feeling helpless, that this was how they expunged those memories of being powerless?

It only made sense if when you left out the part about the sex.

No, people like the man in that apartment, like Skinny Man, like

Marshall Aldritch and his followers, they desired the pleasure that came with power.

And those types of people, as Fountain had said, hid behind closed doors. Even if they were public figures, they still had doors they closed when they got home. And what was behind those doors was anyone's guess.

Only now it was ours. Our guess.

I never wanted to be sitting at Fountain's side as badly as I did on that ride home.

"What are you thinking about," he asked.

"Things," I said, because I couldn't even begin to put all those thoughts into a sentence.

He didn't press further.

I watched the crucifix dangling from the rearview mirror sway back and forth as we drove. I had forgotten I still had on the one Craig had given me. I saw it in the light from the streetlamps, and for the first time noticed its markings. Little swirls and runes and what looked like an upside down eye in the middle.

No, not an eye, something else. A star. And there was something in Latin scrawled down the center. It was tiny, almost looked like general wear and tear, like little scratches, but I'd read my fair share of comics on my phone and had developed a keen eye for tiny text. *Peccare Comendenti.*

"What's it mean?" I turned down the radio and pointed to the cross.

Fountain looked at it, looked at me, then back to the road. "You can read that?"

"What I can see of it. Pretty much need a magnifying glass."

"It's Latin. Do you speak it?"

"Oh yeah. Along with Klingon, Kryptonian, and Wookie. Of course not, that's why I asked. I suppose I could look it up on my phone if you don't want to tell me."

"It's the motto of my people," he said. "It means 'Sin-eater.'"

I didn't know what to say. I'd heard the term before, bandied about in books and movies, but I didn't know it was a real thing. Of course, just because it was on his crucifix didn't make it real. It just made it real to him.

"You take on people's sins? Is that was this is all about? Is that why Uri and Walter took that asshole away, to make him say five Hail Marys?"

"Hardly. It would take more than that to save his soul. If he even has one."

"Then what? You go home, eat some Eucharist wafers and ask God to forgive that scumbag?"

He paused. "Do you see the falling star in the middle?"

"Yes. I was wondering what it was. Why is it falling?"

"Why does anything fall?"

"Because of gravity."

He took a left, and I saw a man on a skateboard zipping down the sidewalk. But he didn't have on a hoodie and he was too fat to be our killer. Still, I felt my knuckles clenching. For all we knew Mr. Scalpel was trailing us in the shadows.

"Falling," Fountain continued, "is to lay down. In other words, to sacrifice. We sacrifice ourselves for a greater good."

"But what are you really sacrificing? Besides your sanity...and mine?"

"Sanity is a worthy price. What we do, it comes with a price. That price must be paid."

"Tell me about it," I said, thinking of the years I'd spent on anti-depressants, seeing shrinks, giving vague answers to people's questions. "But you don't seem too fucked up to me."

"My mind is fine. Well, with the exception of old age. If I had a euro for every time I can't find my keys and realize they're in my hands I'd be richer than the Queen of England. My sanity, to get back to your question, is not what I sacrifice. But that's for another time. Look, we are here."

I could see the church looming ahead of us. Its sixteenth-century architecture was a splendid juxtaposition to the apartment houses and business offices that surrounded it. We passed by the wall blocking off the alley, went past the front door, and parked off the street on the west side.

I noticed one of the SUVs was already back, and it was empty.

I got out of Fountain's car, walked by the front of the SUV, and glanced inside. There was blood on the passenger seat, and a footprint on the windshield.

Someone had put up a struggle.

Chapter 15

Inside, the church was silent and cold. The vestibule lights were off and any and all tours that might have come through were long gone. Fountain closed and locked the giant wooden doors behind us and we made our way down the stairs to the basement, then to a second set of stairs that dumped us out into the sepulchral room I'd been in earlier. Only a few candles illuminated the walls, but there was an electric light glowing blue on the big table laden with books and ledgers.

I saw Katrin's face swim out of it as she got up from her seat and came to us. Lord, did she looked pissed.

"Why didn't you tell me?" she asked Fountain.

He nodded, like he knew he was in trouble. "I made the call to go alone."

"You knew I'd been working on that case too. I'm the one who tracked the last girl to her buyer. I almost got caught that night. Shit, I thought you were just taking Roger to see your apartment or something. You should have let me go!"

"I'm sorry, Katrin. But I needed Roger to get a look at things. And I couldn't risk you being jumped again after your attack."

"I can handle myself."

"I know that more than anyone. But better you come here and rest, keep Craig company, and wait for things to settle."

"It was *my* case." She hung her head. I could tell she was furious but there was also a hint of acceptance in her attitude. I assumed Fountain had done this type of thing to her before. "Craig's not here," she said. "He went to see his stupid booty call, said he's coming by later."

"The doors will be locked," Fountain replied.

"It's okay, he knows the back way in."

"Ah," Fountain said. "And where is Uri?"

She pointed to the room from earlier, the one I'd not been let into. "They're in there."

They had to be Uri and the sex slaver.

"Uri didn't take him to the cops?" I asked.

Fountain said nothing to this. He took off his jacket and laid it across the back of the chair closest to him. Then he opened the door to the strange room, entered, and closed it behind him.

"Why does he do that?" I asked the air. I started for the door myself, intended to barge in, but Katrin grabbed me, stopped me.

"Don't," she said. I saw something in her eyes. Something like a warning. Or maybe it was a suggestion. Either way, it stopped me cold.

"Alright," I said, "but if he's going to take me out into the hood to kick the shit out of scum, he'd better start telling me everything. And I mean everything. Like, where are the girls we rescued? How long have you guys been chasing that guy? And what the fuck is in that room?"

"In that room...you don't want to know."

"Um . . . yes I do. That's why I asked."

"Maybe later. And the girls are headed to Poland...is my guess anyway."

"You're sure of that?"

"Yeah. I know because I set up the contact with the halfway house there myself. They'll call when the girls are settled. And then they'll get them home."

"Again...are you sure?"

"Yes, you twat. You think we'd send them to another hell? This isn't the first slave ring we've broken up. I've gotten letters and calls from previous ones. Trust me, they're fine. And in a few days they'll be brought back to their homes and reunited with families. Or taken to places where they can get help. Or taken to people who will take them in, give them jobs. Only you won't see it in papers because we're not politicians and we're not after votes. And to answer your other question, I've been helping James track these shitheads for four months now."

"Okay, fair enough." I noticed now that she had brought my bags with her. They were plopped on the floor near a couple of cots. "Thanks for that," I said, pointing at them. "I take it we sleep down here now?"

"Yes. For now."

"Seems cold. Colder, anyway. And what about rats?"

"It's not bad under blankets. And rats steer clear of this place for some reason."

Brimstone, I thought.

I took in the room again, the massive stone walls, wrought iron sconces, religious artifacts engraved with Latin words, tapestries of angry monks. In case you're wondering what an angry monk looks like, imagine an aging bald man in a dark bathrobe who just had to take a freezing shower because his teenage son used all the hot water. "Christ, my first two days here and I'm sleeping in a basement and nursing a knife wound. And, lest I forget, hiding from the police, who think I killed a girl. A girl, by the way, who died alone and afraid because of scum like the man in the next room."

"We're working on it. We'll find him."

"I'm just saying, it's been a deplorable few days."

"You've had worse."

"Sadly, it's true. Although I don't think you know the half of it."

"I do. We all do."

In the Other Room, I heard noises that made my teeth itch. Chains jangling and iron bars scraping against stone. "The hell is going on in there?" I asked.

She studied the door for a moment, then turned her back on it and began to undo her sleeping bag. "Penances. Justice. Things like that."

"You know you could just talk straight with me. I do understand English?"

"Yes, but you don't understand everything, and I'm not the one who's supposed to be teaching you. Shit, I didn't even ask for you to be here. I thought it was just gonna be me, Craig, James and Paulo. But then you showed up, so don't expect me to fill you in on everything. This is James's gig, and when he's ready to tell you he will."

"Fuck that! Tell me now. What's going on in that room?"

"I told you. Penance."

A man can only take so much double talk, even from a cute girl with the knife skills of a ninja. I'd hit my breaking point with all the vagueness around me. "Screw it," I said, and marched over to the door.

"Don't!" Katrin yelled, but her words were meaningless to me.

I grabbed the big wooden handle on the door and gave a yank. It didn't budge, so I put my back into it. It moved an inch, but stopped. So I put my foot next to the jamb and pulled with all my might and it gave another inch. It was barely enough to see past but I put my eye to the crack and peeked in.

The room seemed to slither with flames, and in the middle of it all a man was on his knees. Circled around him were other men in hooded robes, just like in the artwork on the walls. They each held a flagrum and whipped at the kneeling man's exposed back. Blood drew up in thick red vines before running down his back to his naked bottom. I could not see who the man was because the flames seemed to grow higher and higher now in front of me, but he looked to have Fountain's figure. Past him, up near the front of the room—as much as I could see through the flames—a second man hung from the ceiling by chains. Large metal hooks pierced his back and legs like he was meat in an abattoir, and he swayed with his mouth wide open, screaming in agony. Only there was no sound, as if his voice box had been removed. The flames grew hotter and hotter, and then just when I thought they would burn my eyebrows off, one of the hooded figures looked my way and pointed at me and for the first time in a long time, a genuine chill of fear ran down my spine.

I'd had enough. I slammed the door, which closed so easily it might as well have been on greased-up ball bearings. I backpedaled into the center of the room, and only stopped because I felt Katrin put her hands up on my back.

"Do you see why I don't bother explaining things now?"

I turned and looked into her eyes. "What the hell was that? They were whipping him. Hard."

"If you say so."

"Was that Fountain?" I was pretty sure it was, but I hadn't seen the man's face so it could just as easily have been Uri.

"I don't know."

"Who are the other guys, the crazy monks?"

"I don't know that either. I just know that they pay my rent, and so I don't ask questions."

"But…why the hell are they making him pay that kind of a penance?"

"Why else? So we don't have to."

Two hours later we were lying in our cots, staring up at the ceiling. Fountain had never come out of the room, nor had anyone else gone into it. At least the noises had stopped. It had been quiet ever since I'd shut the door.

I rolled over and looked at Katrin, who was in the cot next to mine. She was turned away from me reading something on her phone, and I couldn't help but notice her sleeping bag had curled up over her hip, exposing her ass to me. She was in pink boy short underwear, and it looked damn good. She was toned, smooth, and part of me very much wished she'd throw me to the ground again.

And then I remembered Christa and how she was nothing more than pieces in the morgue now and that killed my desire. I cleared my throat and stared up at the ceiling, waiting for her to roll over and realize she was mooning me. She did, and covered herself before asking, "You okay?"

"Yeah. Hey?"

"What?"

"When we were talking earlier, you said you told Fountain something he needed to hear. When you first met him. That that's why he took you on to his crazy team of religious vigilantes. What was it? What did you tell him? And don't tell me, 'Another time.' We're not going anywhere so spill it."

She sighed. "I told him I knew his wife."

"No shit. Did you? For real?"

"Sort of. I knew of her. Point is she'd sort of said something to me."

"What did she say?"

"It wasn't so much words as a look."

I sat up in my cot. "For the love of Pete, just be clear."

She sat up too, annoyed. "Look, nerdboy, it's not that fun for me to tell this shit to people because they think I'm crazy."

I remembered her saying her parents had wanted to commit her, so I eased up and put out my hands in a gesture of submission. "Okay. Sorry. But look, I've seen crazy first hand. I killed crazy with my bare hands. Trust me, you're not crazy."

"Well, I saw her ghost standing next to him as he was offering to take me to a shelter."

Okay, she was crazy.

"His wife waved at me, then looked at him, and the look in her eyes…it was unmistakable. She just wanted him to move on. To stop blaming himself for her death. And anyway I said this to him and he looked at me like I was crazy. And I said, 'No really, mister, she's right behind you.' He didn't believe me, just like my parents never did. Until I described her, right down to the rings on her fingers."

I was going to play devil's advocate here and tell her she could have just seen the video of Fountain's wife's death and remembered the details somehow, but I let it go. Still, it could have explained a lot. Some people have eidetic memories and don't even know it.

"Before you ask, I hadn't seen the video at that point. In fact, I've only seen it once, after James told me who he was. I ran to the bathroom and threw up after I watched it. Those images . . . they don't go away."

Okay, toss that theory out the window. Unless she was a pathological liar, which was a vibe I'd never gotten from her. If anything, she was honest to a fault, at least when it came to telling people what she thought of them.

"So he believed you," I said.

"Yeah."

"And so what now? You're like his psychic viewer? Emma Frost to his Magneto?"

"Don't try to get me to nerd out. I don't read that shit. I barely tolerate the movies. But yes, more or less, it's pretty much why I'm here."

A silence passed between us as I thought about this new revelation. Was she really psychic? Did such a trait even exist in real life? I'd seen my fair share of the unexplained but mediums just seemed like carnival folk who were good at reading a person's gestures and physical appearance. And right then I remembered how she'd read the cop in the basement of the hotel, outside the bar. Was I to believe there'd been a ghost there? No, that interaction had had nothing to do with ghosts; that was her getting control of the situation. She'd read him like any cheap fortune teller. I had to admit she was good, though. She almost had me going.

"You think I'm nuts?" she finally asked.

"Uh…no?"

"I'm not lying," she said. "I don't care if you believe me or not. It's a pain in my ass, to be honest."

I had a sudden urge to see just how good she was. "You get any weird vibes from me?"

"I'll tell you this much…it's not the guy in the baseball hat who leers at me that bothers me. It's not even the creep with the long hair and tattoos all over his body yelling at me like a psycho that is the biggest problem with talking to you . . . "

The hairs on my arm started to stand up. I wanted to rationalize how she knew this stuff, wondering if she'd read the news reports about me and Tooth. Perhaps she'd even seen pictures of Skinny Man on one of the sites that had interviewed me. But the way she described their mannerisms was definitely concerning.

"What's the biggest problem then?" I asked.

"It's the other chick."

I felt a chill move through my chest. "What other chick?"

"There's a girl following you."

It had to be Jamie, I thought. "She young? Like fifteen years old?"

"No, she's older, maybe in her twenties. She's lost, and she thinks she knows you but I don't think she does."

What the fuck? Who the hell was she talking about? "Describe her," I said.

"She's pretty, skinny, long brown hair, big eyes and she's wearing a skirt and a designer T-shirt. She's crying, and she keeps reaching for you. And I can't stand looking at her face because it's starting to make me sad. She's terrified."

"Who the hell…?"

"She's making a motion to me now. She's rubbing her stomach. Now she's rubbing her face. Now her eyes. I don't know what she's trying to say but something horrible happened to her. Only she doesn't speak. She's trying to but she can't. Whoever she was she thinks you're going to save her."

"I don't . . . "

"She wants very badly for you to save her. But I'm guessing you didn't."

And then I had it. Oh my God, it was the woman from Marshall Aldritch's house. The one they'd eaten alive. I turned and looked behind me, seeing nothing but a concrete wall. I think I started to really get weirded out because I stammered over my next words. "I couldn't . . . I couldn't save her. Oh Christ, there was nothing I could do."

I wondered if that was true. I didn't really know. Maybe I could have run into that dining room and done something, but I'd probably have ended up dead as a result.

Then I mentally kicked myself for even believing in Katrin's carnival trick. She's playing you, I thought. But still, the specifics of her visions were so spot on I wondered if maybe she wasn't telling the truth.

"That girl . . . " I said, and let my voice trail off. I could feel tears welling up, could feel anger building and guilt drifting in on top of everything.

Katrin got out of her cot and came over to mine, pink underwear and all, and I barely noticed until she was against me.

"They're people I watched die," I said. The words didn't make this any less creepy.

"They were important in your life."

"Well, one of them. I think the other two latched on for some unknown reason. Can they see me?"

Jesus, why was I believing her?

"I think so. It's like a shimmer, you know. Not always there. Sometimes I look at you and you're alone, and you kind of have a glow about you—"

"Now I know you're lying."

"And other times I look at you and they're all there, all fighting for your attention. Do you hear voices sometimes?"

"Yeah. I mean, I did. My shrink put me on meds that helped some. She was an idiot."

"But they never really made the voices stop, right?"

She got that right. All they really did was make me borderline narcoleptic. "No, I still hear them from time to time. So you're saying they watch me?"

"Like I said, sometimes."

"That's embarrassing. Do you have any idea how much I jerk off?"

Her eyes widened. "Um, I wasn't thinking of that, but I assume a lot. Hey, maybe that's why that girl is always crying."

"You're a laugh riot."

Now that she had told me what she'd seen, I couldn't stop thinking about it. Were there really ghosts behind me right now? Had the voices I'd heard not been in my head? It all seemed like so much bullshit, and yet, I was starting to believe her. Those voices, whenever I heard them, they seemed so real, to converse of their own free will.

"What are they doing now?" I asked.

Katrin looked over my shoulder, cocked her head a few times like a dog listening to a distant whistle. "Nothing. I can't really see them anymore. Like I said, they come and go."

"Thank you," I said to the room. "Next time please let me know you're here so I know not to walk around in my underwear. Like maybe flick a light on or knock a book off a shelf or something." I smiled at Katrin. "You think they heard me?"

"No, but good try."

It was then that I realized she hadn't gone back to her own bed yet, and I started to have typical guy thoughts, wondering if maybe she wanted me to make some kind of move. But part of me felt like that would be inappropriate for more reasons than just being creepy. Namely, that Christa was still fresh in my mind, and I was mad at the whole series of events that had led us here.

Dude, she's half naked in your bed. What're you waiting for? Touch her tits.

It was Tooth's voice in my head. Instinctively, I met Katrin's eyes, waited for her to say something, to tell me she could see Tooth standing behind me again. That she could hear his voice, too.

"What?" she asked.

"Nothing. I just thought I heard something."

Stop being a pantywaist. Walk your eyes up her body, let her know you're interested. That's why she's sitting here.

"So…um…" I glanced down at her underwear, wondering at what ecstasy was hidden beneath it, hoping Tooth was right, ghost or not. As far as percentages went, he'd generally scored with these types of moves, so I figured he had to know.

Katrin reached out and wrapped her hand around my neck and squeezed.

"Ow," I whimpered, fighting for air.

"If you're gonna be a pervert, do it to someone else. I'm not in-terested in you, and for fuck's sake a girl just died. Have some fuck-ing respect. I only jumped in bed with you because I thought you needed a hug is all."

With that, she got and up and went back to her bed, slipped under the covers and rolled away from me. "We're teammates, that's it. Figure there'll be times we see each other in our underwear. Thought you could handle it. Guess not."

I sat there rubbing my neck, feeling ashamed. "Sorry. Really, I'm sorry."

"Accepted. Now get some sleep."

Oh man, I could hear Tooth laughing somewhere over my head. It sounded so much like him, but who knew. I was probably just in-sane and needed my meds again.

I was going to apologize once more when the secret door opened and Fountain emerged from the shadows. He appeared hunched and broken but I knew it was him. He took the stairs up to the rooms above us, saying nothing. The secret door began to close on its own but stopped short, remained slightly ajar. I snuck outta bed and crept over to it.

"Don't," Katrin said.

I ignored her.

Inside it was dark. Empty. Where had everyone gone? How had they exited without me seeing? There were no fires. Just a metal contraption at the far end. I moved in deeper, felt the cold, marble floor beneath my toes. When I got to the metal contraption, I pulled my phone out and used its flashlight feature to get a better look at it. It was a gibbet. The kind of thing you'd put a criminal in and leave to die a slow horrible death.

Inside the gibbet was a man, long dead, mummified and leath-ery, wrapped in black cloth. I almost wanted to say it was fake, be-cause there was no smell, but then who am I to pretend to know the attributes of proper mummification.

I poked it with my finger, felt how its arm was both hard and papery.

I almost wanted to say the eyes looked like the guy I'd beat up earlier, but that wouldn't make sense. Would it? No, couldn't be.

Had to just be a really good fake, or something from a museum that the church was storing.

I scanned the room with my light, saw a series of doors at the corners, and figured that was where the robed guys had gone. I was almost going to go explore when Katrin appeared beside me, still in her underwear, though I was trying hard not to notice.

"We're not allowed in here."

"What is it?"

"Penance. I told you. Now get out before they hear us."

The tone of her voice made it clear she'd hit me again if I didn't, so I shut down the phone light and left, went out and crawled into my cot.

I tried hard to make sense of it all but it wasn't working. Instead, I thought of Katrin's underwear and eventually fell asleep.

● ● ●

In the morning I heard footsteps above my head, realized a tour was coming through the church. I could hear children laughing and the occasional cell phone going off. I laid still till they left, praying they had no cause to tour the basement.

After I heard them leave, I got up and washed in the cold, tiled bathroom that someone had been nice enough to hang some potpourri in. It mixed as well with the stench of brimstone as toothpaste mixes with orange juice.

With the sleep washed out of my eyes, I tried the door to the strange room again but found it locked. It figured.

The images from last night still played in my head. The gibbet. The mummy inside. Fountain's head hung in pain as he exited. What the hell had they really been doing in there?

I found Fountain upstairs near the altar. He was hunched over praying, and when he heard me approach he quickly said, "Amen," and stood up. I could see the curve of his swollen back through his button-down shirt.

"You hurt?" I asked.

"A little sore. It goes away. How much did you see?"

"Oh, I dunno, just you getting whipped, some crazy guys in robes walking through fire, a mummy that looks very much like our slaver hanging in a metal cage. Not a whole lot, really."

He smiled, winced; even this caused him pain. "You must put it out of your mind. It's not something that concerns you. Were it not for the sudden change in our plans, you wouldn't have even seen it."

"Do they force you to take that beating, your friends in the robes?"

"No."

"It's voluntary?"

"It depends, I guess."

"Depends on what? Whether *you* chose to hurt someone or *they* ordered you to?"

He refrained from answering but I could see the truth in his eyes.

"Did you and your friends kill him?" I asked. "The slaver?"

"Of course not."

"Then who was in the cage? Looked like a corpse that had been burned."

"No one was burned. Covered in ash, perhaps."

"More brimstone."

"It has its uses."

"Is he alive then? Where is he?"

"He is alive, and he's been taken elsewhere."

I looked at his back again. It looked like he'd added two inches of skin to his torso. "This is all the sin eating shit, huh? I still don't get it. Why take a beating for his sins?"

"I'm not taking on his sins, I'm taking on ours. See, Roger, he was but a player in a larger game, an international game. We were hoping he'd have information that could lead us to others."

"Did he?"

"Yes, he did."

"So you're telling me you tortured him."

"We got what we needed. And now he's being dealt with in another location. Would you really care if he was dead now?"

He had me there. Did I care about a guy who kidnapped and sold women, shot up children with heroin? "No, fuck 'im."

"Then let's move on. You did good work last night." He pulled out a wad of cash and handed it to me. "Your share, for last night's job. I'll give Katrin and Craig their shares later. Catching that man was a major coup. You should be proud."

"I didn't really do much. Just hit him a few times."

"I'd say you did more than that. I was lucky to have you. Now, where's my jacket?" He found it draped over a pew and put it on as slowly as he could without hurting himself.

"Why don't you go to the hospital?" I asked.

"Like I said, it'll pass. Tomorrow I'll be right as rain." He made his way through the vestibule to the front door and opened it. Outside the sun was bright and the sky clear. I had already forgotten what day it was in all the commotion, but judging by the amount of people on the street I figured it must be a weekend. The scent of fresh croissants and crepes hung heavy in the air and my stomach rumbled.

"The bakery is open," he said, moving down the front steps. A city bus passed in front of us and I scanned the windows for any suspicious looking individuals. There weren't any, unless you counted the young boy flipping me the bird and laughing. I made a mental note to find out who he was and kick him in his nuts when they dropped, nip his breeding possibilities in the bud.

"Should we just be out in the open like this? What if our skateboarding friend knows where we are?"

"We have people watching the area."

"Big deal. You have no idea what he looks like."

"No we don't, but we can't live in fear either. I'm serious about that bakery, it's the best in the city. Go get yourself some breakfast."

I was starving and had a new wad of money in my pocket and needed to get away from the craziness for a while, do a little investigating on my own. My Spidey senses were starting to go haywire. All the secrecy, all the glossed-over information . . . it was piling up too much to just get shoved under the rug.

"Later," I said. "I need a new pair of jeans. My favorite ones have a giant slash in them."

"There are clothing stores a couple blocks over. Maybe go with Craig. Watch each other's backs."

That pissed me off for some reason. Granted Craig was bigger than me, and had a definite screw loose, but I was the guy who'd killed lunatics before, the guy with the supposed luck powers. You'd think he'd trust me to go a couple blocks on my own. Not that shopping was really my intention.

"Can't. Craig never came home." It was Katrin, standing behind us. Neither of us had heard her approach. Fountain suddenly went rigid, forgetting all the pain in his back.

"Why not? Why didn't he come here with you?" he asked.

"He went to meet a girl. Don't look at me like that. I'm not his keeper. "She held up her phone for us to see. "Don't worry, he just texted, said he's heading over in a few."

Now Fountain went back to looking hurt, but did his best to fake not feeling it. He turned from us and headed toward his car.

"Where are you going?" Katrin asked him.

"My home. To gather up things. I didn't have a chance to do so last night before we came here."

"Thought you lived here," I said, indicating the church.

"Hardly. I would have shown you my apartment eventually but now there's no use. If it hasn't been compromised yet it soon will be."

"And yet you're going to it? Doesn't that seem counterintuitive?"

"Perhaps, but there are items I cannot risking falling into the wrong hands."

"What if you fall into the wrong hands? We couldn't save Christa, remember?"

He tried to respond, came up with nothing. Instead he settled on, "Get your jeans, Roger, then hurry back."

He moved off down the sidewalk leaving us surrounded by pedestrians walking so fast you'd think there was a race going on. If our killer was one of them he'd be on us before we knew it. I didn't know what made Fountain think this street was so safe, and I felt myself go on high alert.

"Jeans?" Katrin asked.

"No. Not really, but I needed to tell him something." I headed in the opposite direction, noticed Katrin hadn't come with me, then turned back and yelled to her. "You coming?"

She flipped me off, but then hung her head and came after me.

Chapter 16

The flea market in Mitte was as crowded as ever, or at least as crowded as I knew it to be. Katrin told me it was a bad idea to be there. She said we should go back to the church and lay low. But I didn't care. I needed to talk to someone who could provide me with information, and even if Michael didn't like me, I knew he liked money and would offer up something if the price was right.

He looked me up and down as we approached, a half smile smeared across his smug face. When we got close enough, he reached out and hugged Katrin, who squinted her eyes as if to say this display of affection was new to her. I could tell Michael was just doing it to get a rise out of me. I didn't really care.

"To what do I owe the pleasure?" he said, his arm still around her.

Katrin pulled away. "Not for me. For Roger."

"Don't much like, Roger, so the answer's no, whatever it is."

I held up twenty euros, waved them a little and watched his eyes follow them like a dog's might follow a biscuit. "Just a couple questions. We'll be fast."

"Depends on the question."

I waited till a patron scooted by us and was out of earshot. I'm sure he was nobody, and I was just being paranoid, but there was a fifty-fifty chance we'd been followed—*caution* was the word of the day. "I want to know everything you know about James Peter Fountain. And I mean *everything*."

Katrin blanched, whirled on me. "Are you fucking serious? What're you getting at?"

"Not sure. But I want to know," I said. "So, what about it, Mike? What can you tell me?"

"Why would I tell you about his private life?"

"I get it, you're friends. But I'm not trying to hurt him, I'm trying to help him."

"By spying on him?"

"Sort of. Are you going to humor me or not?"

He snatched the money out of my hand. "First answer is on the cheap, but others will cost more than this."

"Just spit it out."

He started to walk away from us, then waved for us to follow. We collected at his till, where he kept a laptop computer showing a video feed of his make-shift store. I could tell from the angle that the hidden camera was above us to our right. He closed the feed down and brought up his files, which were all encrypted like something out of *The Matrix* films. He chose one at random, or so it seemed, and opened it up. Fountain's picture popped up, along with a bunch of documentation.

"Alright then," he said. "Born in Poland. Raised by monks. Check and check. Both true. Inherited a large sum of money from the monastery but pays no taxes. Ever. Religion and State and all that garbage."

"I can't believe you have files on him!" Katrin said. "Do you have files on me? On Craig? Tell me!"

"I have files on all of you. It's what I do."

"I want to see mine," she demanded. "Now."

"Thousand euros," Michael answered. My guess was he knew it would be dangerous to show her her own file. His answer only seemed to piss her off more. I almost expected her to go for the knife in her belt.

"Fountain," I said, getting us back on track. "I want to know about his marriage. His wife." To save time, I peeled off another twenty and tossed it at him. "Just tell me."

Michael pulled up another file, this one showing Fountain's wife. She was walking down a city street in a long black dress, classy formalwear, off to some event. The pearls around her neck looked real and the diamond watch on her dainty wrist all but screamed *I have money.*

"Wasn't his wife," Michael said.

"Wait, what?" This from Katrin, who moved a little closer to the screen. "Yes, it is, that's his wife. I've seen a million pictures of them together."

"Wrong, my love," Michael said. "Not his wife. Co-worker as far as we could ever tell. Not even real sure of her name. It says Angeline Mathias on her passport, but fuck me if we can find her in the system anywhere before 1980 by that name. Found a few Angeline Mathiases, of course, but none that are her."

"But . . . I don't get it," she said. "A co-worker for who?"

"Her past is murkier than beef stew, but as far as we tracked it, she was working for a non-profit owned by the monastery. She's listed as the chairman. Chairwoman, I guess, if you're gonna be a twit about gender roles."

"The monastery that raised Fountain?" I asked.

"The one and same."

"Non-profit that does what?" I asked.

"A sort of one-for-all type deal. Called it the Soaring Skies Network. You know, feed the homeless, save the dogs, educate the kids, all of that shit rolled into one organization. This picture was taken at a fundraiser for that charity."

"Is that New York?" I asked.

"No, this is Japan. See the Japanese writing on everything, idiot. That's a clue that it's Japan."

"I see a lot of English too, asshole. Sue me. What else do you have on her?"

"Got another picture of her here, attending another fundraiser. Seems like that's what she did for the most part."

He brought up the new image. She was bent down hugging two little boys and a little girl.

"Until she disappears," Michael continued, "and ends up in the videos you no doubt have seen."

"One more question."

"Gonna cost you double, just because I don't like you and because I told you I wasn't gonna stay cheap. But mostly because I don't like you."

"How's this?" I gave him one hundred more and stuffed the remaining few bills back in my pocket with a grunt to punctuate the fact I was done doling it out. I was going broke fast and I didn't exactly have a job. And getting more money would mean asking the guy I was snooping on right now. Bosses tend to frown on that sort of thing. I looked him in the eye for effect. "At what age were you orphaned and living at Fountain's church, and why are they having you keep files on everyone?"

His eyes went wide and he slowly closed the top to his laptop as if it might bite him were he to make any sudden movements. "What?"

"I'm speaking English, not Japanese, idiot. When did you go to live at the church? You do know the people from the monastery, right?"

"What makes you say that?"

Katrin was now looking back and forth from Michael to me like there was a tiny tennis match going on between our noses.

I pointed at the necklace around his neck. "I noticed that when I first met you and it tells me your assholish attitude is a front. Well, part of it anyway. I bet you *would* hit a guy with glasses, but you'd pull your punch, if for no other reason than you might get in trouble. But you're not here to start fights, are you?"

He was mute, fingering his gold chain like he'd forgotten it was even there. But I hadn't forgotten.

"*Peccare comendenti*," I said, continuing to point at it. This drew a look of genuine shock from him but I ignored it and continued. "Yeah, I know what it says. You know Fountain through the church. And you know this stuff—" I pointed at the laptop— "because you're looking for leads at the same time we are. Right? The church also has you keeping tabs on everyone, right?"

He gave a slight nod, not exactly the kind that said he'd been bested, but the kind that said he may as well reveal some truth to save us all time. "Yeah, I was raised at the monastery. I was seven when they found me in the streets. My parents were taken to prison for drug trafficking."

"Fountain found you? Or Angeline?"

"Neither. Father Adelburts. He's dead now, before you ask. I only met Fountain recently. Never knew Angeline. And that's as much as you get to know."

"I don't believe this," Katrin said, her mouth hanging open. "You piece of shit. You're spying on us? James doesn't trust us?"

Michael waved her off, back in tough guy mode. "It ain't him, as your friend Dick Lacey here just figured out. It's the others. Fountain's got nothing against you. Him letting you play Mystery Men, that's on the up and up. But I'm sure he's told you you're on a need to know basis, so lighten up."

"Dick Lacey?" I asked.

"I couldn't think of anything funny. I was rushed."

"Like, I wear lace?"

"Whatever, dude."

"Wanna try again?"

He stabbed a finger at me. "No. Now fuck off. Get out. I have customers."

"Why does the church need to keep tabs on us?"

"Same reason they keep tabs on anyone. They're historians. They collect information. Beyond that, I don't know and don't care. Now . . . we're done."

"C'mon." I moved past Katrin, left the stand, and she followed me with heavy footfalls, like she was trying to kick the earth.

"I'm gonna ream James when we get back," she said.

As I strolled past the next stand, which was selling screen-printed T-shirts, I swore I heard Michael yell: "Dick Gaysey!"

Chapter 17

On the U-Bahn I asked Katrin where the nearest Internet café was. She said they were all over East Berlin and we might as well just take the next stop and ask someone or check Google. So we disembarked in a quaint neighborhood that had obviously been gentrified in the last ten years to resemble something like the West Village in New York, complete with art murals on the sides of buildings and little eateries on the corners. The building facades had been remodeled to ensure the historic pre-war architecture mixed seamlessly with the contemporary cubist blandness. Part of me liked it, part of me wept for it.

The Internet Café our search engines directed us to was a neat little art deco affair (the 60s are always in vogue somewhere) that served beer and wine, which suited me well enough.

"Two Shirazes," I said to the woman behind the counter. I handed one to Katrin who gulped it down in one sip.

"I needed that," she said. "Why are we here?"

"I need to talk to a friend, but first I want to look something up."

"You can't look shit up on your phone?"

"Well, I may want to print something out. We'll see."

I pulled up a seat and got to work on my search, quickly finding information on the Soaring Skies Network. I didn't find the exact picture of Angeline Mathias that Michael had shown us, the one with her posing next to three children, but I found a similar one. This one was taken in Dublin with a group of four young boys who'd been found abandoned in a farmhouse a year after their parents had been killed in a random IRA-related bombing inside a bank, (correction, *alleged* bombing). According to the article they were all brothers and Angeline, along with the Soaring Skies organization, had gotten them into foster care, and even brokered the sale of their parents' house so they'd be somewhat financially secure later in life.

Nice lady. I kind of liked her. I could see why Fountain missed her.

"Can't believe it's not his wife," Katrin said. She was still upset.

"Question is why lie about it?"

"Why lie to *me*? I never gave him a reason to distrust me."

"Men are pigs. It's just nature."

A few more searches and I found what I was looking for, an article from the *New York Times* about the event Michael had shown us. Angeline wasn't in the picture, but one of the little girls was. She was too young to have her name printed, but I grabbed a screen shot of it and emailed it to a friend. That done, I pulled out my phone and dialed said friend up.

"Roger?" Teddy answered, sounding sleepy.

"Shit, I forget about the time difference. Sorry."

"You always do. What's Germany like? The beer as good as they say?"

"It's not bad. Though right now I'm drinking a Chilean Shiraz. Or is it Shiras? Is there a difference?"

"I think one is Australian and one is…who gives a shit. If it's good, drink it."

"Way ahead of you."

"You're making me jealous."

"That's my goal. Why else do I call?"

"Most times you call me it's because somebody is in serious trouble and you're near death. Do I need to call…shit, who would I even call? Interpol?"

"No! Don't call them. I'm fine."

"Well, thank Christ. For once nobody died."

"I didn't say that. Girl I met two nights ago, she's in pieces, literally, and the scumbag who did it knifed me in the leg yesterday."

"I'm calling Interpol."

"Seriously, don't. Listen, I need a favor."

"Roger, come home now. Come home and bury yourself in a bunker and don't ever go out again. Please? I'm begging you."

"Teddy, this is serious."

"No shit! You go halfway across the globe and in three days someone's murdered and you're being attacked. It's beyond serious. It's like an HBO series, only they'd never make it because it's too outlandish. Shit. I can't help you, Roger. I'm in fucking New Hampshire, not Dusseldorf! Call the fucking police and then come home."

"Do you have connections in New York City?"

"No, why would I?"

"Nobody? It's important."

"Maybe. I dunno. Yeah, one guy I spoke to on the phone a year ago. A cop. But I don't really know him. Like I said, I spoke to him for a bit is all."

"Spoke to him enough to have him owe you a favor?"

"Not really. Some perp that came down from Canada. Stole a car here, robbed a liquor store in Providence, then tried to rob another in Brooklyn. We coordinated on the case and they got the collar. I got shit. Fine by me."

"So he does owe you."

"He doesn't owe me shit. This isn't *Law & Order* and I'm not Ice-T. I helped him because I didn't want the guy coming back this way and taking more cars. We're a peaceful town with one major blight on our record. Which, by the way, is the topic of some Netflix documentary now. Did you authorize your image for it?"

"I don't even know what you're talking about."

"Then forget it. Point is, I can call this guy but whether he helps me or not is up to him, and I can't guarantee anything."

Teddy had told me a while back that there wasn't much in the way of professional courtesy between cops when you worked in different zip codes. So I knew this might go nowhere. But I also knew once Teddy got on the case he wouldn't let it go. He had that nagging itch that good cops had; had to make sure things were wrapped up one way or another.

"I emailed you a picture," I said. "Can you look at it now?"

"Not while I'm on the phone. Unless I get out of bed."

I waited, counted to ten in my head, finally heard him groan.

"Shit," he said, getting up. "Why should my sleep be sacred when you're out drinking wine and getting knifed halfway across the globe."

It took another minute of groaning, and then he said he was looking at the picture on his laptop. "So what am I supposed to do with this?" he asked.

"See the kid?"

"Yeah. Who is she?"

"She's was rescued by a woman named Angeline Mathias. She chaired a non-profit called Soaring Skies."

"What did they do?"

"A little of this, a little of that. In this case, Angeline Mathias rescued children—the child in that photo—from poverty."

"You want me to look into Angeline Mathias?"

"No. I know where she is. Dead. Butchered. In fact you can watch her death on a hundred websites full of people dying. It's labeled as some bullshit fanatic Islamic propaganda, but it's a straight-up murder."

"Fuck me. You report it?"

"To who? You can't see the killer. The walls of the room are blank. Just her getting stabbed a whole lot. It's fucking reprehensible. But the little girl in this picture…I want to know where she is now."

A moment of silence passed while Teddy thought on everything I'd just told him. Or maybe he was writing it down. Or maybe he was picking his nose. How the hell did I know? Finally, he spoke up. "There's no name printed here because she's too young. Maybe the photographer knows, but the press generally isn't very helpful. Best I can do beyond that is try to find a rep for this Soaring Skies company in New York."

"And see if your contact can ask around. Check local orphanages, schools for homeless kids, foster parent agencies. Maybe someone knows her."

"That's a lot to ask of a guy I hardly know."

"So you'll help?"

"I'd like to say no, but I have nothing going on today besides paperwork for some DUIs and looking for a contractor to redo the deck on my house."

"So it's a 'yes.'"

"It's a 'screw you.'"

"That means 'yes.'" Of course I knew the real reason, but I kept it to myself. I preferred letting old softy think he was too tough-as-nails to care about victims outside his jurisdiction.

"Roger, I'm serious," he said, "get protection. Go to the cops. Then come home. Don't be stupid."

"The cops are dirty."

"Dirty cops steal weed from the evidence rooms. They don't harbor murderers."

"Here they steal women."

"Jesus Christ. What are you involved in?"

"That's what I'm trying to figure out. Call me as soon as you know something."

We said goodbye and hung up, at which point Katrin handed me yet another glass of wine and pointed toward the front door. I glanced over and saw Craig walking in, a trickle of blood dripping down his face from behind his ear.

"Drink up, pussies, we're going out."

"What the hell happened to you," I asked. "Your eye is turning black as I watch. And how'd you find us?"

"I got into a bit of a squabble with a mailman. And Katrin called me."

I didn't know which one of those revelations to focus on, so I looked at Katrin and hoped for an answer. She ignored me, just glared at Craig before telling him, "Fountain lied to us, Craig. He fucking lied to us."

I noticed two things right then. One: Katrin had stopped using Fountain's first name. Two: She never seemed to care that Craig was always covered in fresh blood and bruises.

"Always figured he was lying to us," Craig said. "Lots that didn't add up."

"Like what?"

"Like why he offered me a job after he saw me take on a pub full of West Hammers. That's football to you, Roger. Real football."

"Yeah, so I've heard."

"I broke four fingers in that fight," he continued, "but I walked out the winner. I think, anyway. Don't remember much beyond the blood. Any man offering me a job after that had to be keeping some secrets. But fuck if I've ever figured out what exactly. Figured it wasn't my place to ask."

"Do you like working for him?" I asked.

"Put it to you this way . . . I heard you got the cunt that was trafficking them women."

"We did," Katrin said. "Well, Roger did."

"Good for you, Rog. Me and Katrin here only spent months tracking him down. I got punched in the head for asking questions in some dingy places. Glad you got to take the credit."

"Sorry. I wasn't trying to steal anyone's thunder. But I had no idea where I was going."

"Yeah, well, I did. Figured as much when I saw Fountain leave with you. That's why I went off and got my dick wet."

"Speaking of which, you need to be more careful. We're being followed."

"If the bastard jumps me he'll get the fight of his life. But let's not talk about me. What's all this about Fountain? What did you find out?"

"His wife wasn't really his wife," Katrin said. "She was some woman who rescued orphans or some such shit."

"What a bitch," Craig said.

"Can't you be serious for one second?" Katrin spat.

"Maybe. Maybe not."

"Why would he lie to us, Craig?"

He scratched his chin. "Maybe they were married in secret and nobody knew."

"No. It's something else. But what?"

"A red herring," I said. "If we thought she was his wife we'd be gung ho to help him find the killer."

"None of the women you rescued last night were his wife and we were still gung ho to help," she replied. "He doesn't need to lie to us to convince us torture and murder needs to be stopped. The person we're looking for needs to be put down like a rabid dog . . . would we have said no to helping if we knew the woman wasn't his wife? Not me. I'm all in either way."

"True," I said. "Then what're we missing?"

"Pints," said Craig. "I'm missing a glass of alcohol. Let's go get some."

"There's beer here," I said.

"And there's dingleberries in my ass. Doesn't mean I want to play with 'em."

I shook my head. "I don't even know what that means."

"Means we're going to get a beer elsewhere. Here, gimme that." He grabbed the wine out of my hand and downed it in one gulp, put the empty glass on the counter. With a fist pump he burped, said, "Follow me," and walked out the front door with his head held high.

I heard Tooth's voice: *That guy's an asshole.*

• • •

Through the streets we went until we found ourselves back at the Lux Moderne. As it turned out, Craig had actually been working while he'd been away. He'd asked the concierge for some names of regulars, made some threats and paid out some euros, gotten the name of a regular who knew the bartender, who in turn had the keys to the place. I had a feeling there'd been more threats involved than he was mentioning but I wasn't going to argue with his results.

The bartender had agreed to meet Craig, after Craig had told him we had information on Christa's death.

We made our way down to the basement and through the corridor to the bar entrance. The door was open and the lights on inside—the fluorescents, none of that late night atmospheric shit. The bartender was waiting for us behind the bar, flanked on either side by two bouncers. I assumed they were bouncers anyway, since they each looked like they could body slam a moose.

"Over here," the bartender said, waving us in. "Which one of you is Craig?"

Craig raised his hand, almost too happy to be called on. "Right here, mate."

As we approached, the two muscleheads got behind us and locked the door. I saw Katrin's hand go to her belt, ready to pull her knife at a moment's notice.

"You Leon?" Craig asked.

"Yes," the bartender said. He held up his phone. "Got the cops on speed dial. Uwe and Tom there are gonna stop you if you run. No offense, right. Just don't know you."

"Fair enough, mate."

"Now, from what you said on the phone, I want to help. But first I want more details. Is the piece of shit that went home with Christa here?"

I gulped. Perhaps too loudly because Leon looked at me, his eyes narrowing.

"You?" he asked.

"Thanks. Craig," I said. Then to Leon, "Yeah, it was me. But I didn't..."

"Didn't kill her? How do I know that? What's your fucking

name?"

"It's Roger. And because I wouldn't be here. We're all trying to piece this together. I swear."

"Cops were here last night," he said. "They want to talk to you, Roger."

"Call him Roger Roger," Craig said, "he likes that."

"Yeah, we saw a couple detectives in the hallway yesterday," I added. "Wait, how do they even know about me?"

"The video tapes. We keep all footage on a hard drive for up to a month. And since I'm the bar manager, I know the passwords. See the cameras in the corners of the ceiling?"

I turned and looked up behind me. Sure enough there was one over the door, watching people enter and leave. I also spotted one near the hallway to the bathrooms, and one above the bar.

"They want to talk to everyone in the video," Leon said. "But they seemed particularly interested in you and your older friend. Then of course there's the part where you and Christa exchange numbers. That's about what, twenty-four hours before she's murdered?"

"It wasn't me," I said. Then I told him what had happened, how we'd chased the killer, how we'd been too late. How we'd called the cops and how the killer had later attacked us. I even showed him my leg. I think he believed us, if for no other reason than the real killer probably wouldn't come back like this.

"We want to see the tape," Craig said. "You said on the phone we could see the tape, too. Do we get to do that?"

"Sure," Leon said. "But why didn't you go to the police, Roger? After you were knifed? It seems very guilty to me. Why shouldn't I call them right now? Have Uwe and Tom knock you lot out, and sit here till they put you in cuffs?"

"You don't want to do that," I said. "I will not ever be put in cuffs again, come hell or high water. And if you try—"

"Then answer the question."

"The cops are dirty. Some of them, anyway. I've seen it. Trust me."

"Yeah well, that's a given. But you think they had something to do with Christa's murder?"

"Maybe. Who knows? But if they arrest us, the killer will still be out there and he'll find more women. Do you want that on your conscience?"

"I want Christa back. I want her to have never met you. I want her walking through that door for her shift. I want to see her face again. I want . . ."

He trailed off, at a loss for words. We could all sense him battling new emotions in front of us.

Krista spoke up. "You liked her?"

Leon hung his head. "We dated for about two weeks. Yeah, I really liked her. She said I was not her style and that she didn't want to date a co-worker anyway. I can see the way she looks at you on the video, Roger. She was...excited."

"She read something I wrote. It's nothing. Bigger issue is, who else might be on the tape that saw her come to our table."

"I've got it cued up. Come and look."

We all followed Leon into a small office off the bar and crushed around the computer while he hit play. From there we watched the video, occasionally letting Leon fast forward it. It was pretty boring stuff. People came and went. People drank. A few people ate some appetizers. Two or three guys sat at the bar all night ordering martinis.

"They're Italian," Leon said, as if that explained everything.

He fast forwarded again to the part where Fountain and I arrived and I watched Christa come over and serve us. As she left to get our first order, she glanced back at me. Leon didn't like that, but I gotta admit it made me feel good. Even Craig smirked. "She was a looker," he said. And only now that I knew Craig well enough to know his vibe did I realize he was feeling a bit down. In fact, I think we all were as we watched her work.

Myself, well, I felt pretty insensitive because as she swerved between the tables I remembered the way her ass did that when she rode me in bed. I felt like I should have found another memory to think about, but most of what I did remember involved sex.

You should have slit her throat and fucked the gash.

Oh shit, Skinny Man's voice was back. I willed it away, wondering again about what Katrin had said. Was he really here with me? I told myself no. I still refused to believe in such madness. It was my PTSD acting up again.

We watched it all the way through again but still didn't see anything suspicious. Granted it was hard to know what to look for. No one was leering at Christa. No one was looking at me or Fountain. No one really seemed out of place. And with so many people coming and going, there were plenty of moments when some people blocked out others.

"Who're the bartenders," Craig asked, tapping the monitor.

"One's the owner, Thomas, and the other is his nephew, Otto. They were both questioned by the cops and given a clean report. They were actually working the next night too, when it all happened."

"They travel much," I asked.

"You're asking if the owner of a bar travels? You don't know much about the bar industry, do you?"

"So they're not globetrotting," I said. "Which leaves us with fuckall."

"What now?" Katrin asked, putting her head in her hands. She still looked upset about the whole Fountain lying thing.

"Well, may as well get some drinks," Leon said. "I'm here, you're here, Uwe and Tom are here. I'm certainly not going home to nap. What do ya say? On the house."

● ● ●

Two pints later (on top of my wine) I was feeling tipsy and angry. Angry because I was really hoping someone on that video would have stood out. We were all squeezed into a corner wraparound booth and Leon was telling us about the funny things Christa would say at work, about how she named the mice in her walls at home, or how she wanted to visit Florida and see alligators.

"Florida would be brilliant," Craig said.

"It's not," I told him. "It's so humid you want to die and you have to drive for hours to get anywhere."

"But there's girls in bikinis, right? They sunbathe topless! I've seen pictures."

"I guess. In Miami. But it's a dirty place. And they won't talk to you anyway unless you've got one hundred pounds of muscles on your chest."

"Correction: They won't talk to *you*. They'll talk to me because I'm British."

"So?"

"So I've got an accent. American birds like that, right?"

"Actually . . . yeah."

"American girls are super dumb, huh?" Katrin asked. "Like on the TV?"

"No," I replied. "The ones I know are smart, driven, successful. Just the ones you see in tabloids are dumb. Which is a lot, I admit."

"I've got muscles," Craig said, and took off his shirt.

I thought Leon would get mad but he just laughed and told Craig he smelled bad. Wacky Europeans.

But that's when I noticed all the scars on Craig's chest. Too many to ignore, crisscrossing in a latticework that made him look like he'd slept on a hot chain-link fence.

Katrin shifted her eyes away. Leon kind of stared but said nothing. But it was getting harder and harder to ignore the fact that Craig walked around looking like he worked as a crash test dummy.

"What happened to you?" I asked.

"Gave your mother the rough stuff," Craig said. "And she rode hard." He thought that was funny and downed his beer as a reward.

Katrin punched him in the shoulder. "Don't be a cock."

"I'm serious," I said.

"And I'm pissed. So if you'll excuse me, I have to go open a valve." He hopped over us and strode to the bathroom.

I turned to Katrin, hoping to find answers. "He's always hurt. What's the deal?"

She took a long sip of her drink then fingered her glass for a moment. "You know how I told you I can see things?"

"Yeah," I said. At this, Leon's interest was piqued.

"Craig has a little issue himself," she continued.

"You see things?" Leon asked her. "Like what?"

"Like the creepy tattooed guy standing behind Roger. He's been here ever since we came in. And the six ladies in the corner over there, dressed in black. Their faces are bruised and their heads are lumpy, kinda funny."

Leon looked over his shoulder, his eyes wide. When he looked at us again he seemed a little paler. "Seriously? There're women in here? Like ghosts?"

"Might be more than six. Hard to tell sometimes."

"Creepy. Yes, some women were murdered here by the Stasi, before my time. This was all an apartment block before it was converted. They were shot for being traitors. I don't know the whole story, unfortunately, but it's not an uncommon one. Probably every building in East Berlin has a similar story. The owner told me about it."

She's playing psychic, I thought, just like the guys on TV who claim to speak to dead relatives. I'm sensing someone in your family whose name begins with R. Shit like that. Like Leon said, every building here could make the claim to be hosting the ghosts of people murdered during the Stasi regime. But the other half of me, the half that gave her the benefit of the doubt, thought that if it was true, well…now it really sank in why Katrin was so moody. Even if she just *thought* she saw things, she probably felt ghosts everywhere. Such an affliction could be debilitating, even if it was psychosomatic.

Either she was a twinge crazy, or she was making herself crazy. Couldn't be good.

"What're Craig's issues?" I asked, trying to keep us on track. "Besides being an asshole."

She glanced back toward the bathrooms once, making sure the topic of our discussion was still relieving himself. She looked guilty. Perhaps she'd sworn not to reveal his closeted skeletons, but she did it anyway. "He doesn't feel pain."

"Yeah, because assholes don't care about anyone but themselves," I offered.

"No, not emotional pain. Real pain. Physical pain."

"Come again?"

"Like, if he stubs his toe, he doesn't even notice. If he closes his finger in a door, it just annoys him more that he has to open the door again. He doesn't feel shit. Nothing."

"Sounds like bullshit to me," Leon said. "I know his type. I think he just wants to be macho."

"It's not bullshit," she said.

"But I saw him get punched by those street thugs," I said. "I heard him, you know, make a noise, like it hurt."

"Doesn't hurt him. Just pisses him off. And partly because he doesn't feel it."

If what she was saying was true, and trust me when I say I took everything she said with a grain of salt, then it might explain the wounds on Craig's body. "So he goes out and picks fights?" I asked.

"No." Katrin shook her head, double-checked the hall outside the bathroom. "He does it to himself. It scares me. I've watched him do it. He'll ram his head into the wall till it bleeds and show no emotion. He cuts himself too. Anything to try to feel. But not like, you know, a teenager who's depressed . . . He really wants to feel the pain to be normal. It's become an obsession with him."

"*Ach, quatch,*" Leon said, "I'm pouring more drinks," and made his way to the bar just as Craig came back. No doubt that's why Leon left in the first place.

Craig slid in and saw the suspicious look in my eyes, and the evasive one in Katrin's. "What're you cunts chattin' about?"

"You," I said. "Why're you always covered in bruises and cuts? Some of those are fresh."

"Some twat started shit with me today. He got what he deserved."

"That one looks like a razor blade slice."

He ran his fingers over the gash on his forearm, then glared at Katrin. "You fucking told him?"

"Well it's kind of hard not to notice, you idiot," she spat back.

"So, like, you feel nothing?" I asked.

Took him a moment to answer, but he leaned back and said, "Nothing at all."

"What's it like?"

"What the fuck do you think it's like? It's like being dead. It's like not existing. It sucks, and it's all I've ever known."

"You've never felt pain?"

"I've felt pain. When my Dad died, that hurt." He tapped his heart. "Hurt in here. Tons. But that's a different pain, you know. But this pain . . . " He picked up his glass and smashed it over his head.

I sat up straight, my jaw dropping open, as a trickle of blood ran down his forehead and dripped off his nose.

Tom and Uwe went wide-eyed, didn't really know how to react. Katrin brushed the glass shards to the edge of the table, away from us.

"That," he said, "didn't feel like anything. Wouldn't even know I'm bleeding except I can see it dripping off my nose."

Not only did that gross me out, but it raised a bunch of other questions. If he couldn't feel pain, how did he feel his body? How did he even know he was sitting? How did he know he was done taking a shit?

"How does it work?" I asked.

"It's called congenital analgesia. A mutation in my nerves. Far as I can tell, if I apply extreme pressure to my body, I just get an absence of sensation. But, since I can see you're about to ask, yes, I can feel certain things. If I run my hand through my hair, or the wind blows on my face, I can feel that stuff. It's the pain part I can't feel."

"So then, you've got a condition everyone in the world would kill to have."

"Yeah, I used to think that, but it doesn't work that way. Pain is an indicator you're in trouble, that you need to move, to change. Like, if you feel extreme heat, your house might be on fire. If you step on a nail you should pull it out before you get tetanus. Shit like that. When I was a kid I'd put my hand on the burner on the stove, watch my blood sizzle on it before my mum would snatch me up, screaming like a banshee. Broke my wrist when I was ten, jumping a fence, and didn't even realize till it swelled up so much I couldn't move my arm. If my dad hadn't noticed it the bone would've set so funny my fingers would be upside down."

"So it's extremes," I said.

"It's a burden. A fucking annoyance." Craig got up and went to the bar to get a towel for his head.

I looked at Katrin. "He's crabby."

"Wouldn't you be?"

"Hardly. If what he's saying is true, he should be thrilled. Who wants to feel pain?"

"Like you said, it's the extreme things he doesn't feel. There's extreme pleasure in the world too."

"What, like, he can't . . . you know . . . get off?"

"I never asked. But I heard him in the shower a few times. I'm not sure what happens but it isn't normal."

"Must work, though. His new female friend is into it."

"Depends on which version of the story he tells you."

"You think he's lying?"

"I think he doesn't feel any pain, or extreme sensation of any kind. What the truth of it is, I dunno. There's something wrong with him, that's all I know for sure."

"How long have you two been working together?"

"Little over a year. He can be annoying but he's also a good guy to have in your corner."

"He is pretty tough to take," I said.

"Yeah, well, he's had a shit life. But then, fuck, haven't we all."

"Shit life how?"

"His father was killed by a drunk driver. His mother lives in a nursing home. She's got dementia and doesn't remember him most times he calls. He doesn't have any friends. Grew up ostracized. He was the weird kid in school, you know."

And right then I heard a commotion at the bar, saw Craig reach over the counter and grab a knife and draw it across his arm. "Believe me now!" he yelled at Leon.

Dammit, Leon must have been questioning the whole thing, and Craig was a bit buzzed. I jumped up and ran over to grab him but Uwe and Tom beat me to it. They lifted Craig up in a bear hug and started carrying him to the door, but Craig threw his head back and broke Uwe's nose. Or maybe it was Tom. I couldn't remember who was who anymore. I just knew my adrenaline was coursing and this was getting out of control fast.

"Goddammit, Craig! Stop!" Katrin was beside me, grabbing Craig's arm, getting him down from his captors and getting between them. She whipped out her knife and held it in front of her face. "Nobody is fighting! It's over."

Leon came around the bar, wiping off the knife Craig had used on himself. He tossed it in a sink. "Tom, back off. Uwe, are you okay?"

On the floor, Uwe held his nose and nodded his head. "Been hit worse. This guy just got in a cheap shot."

"Cheap shot, my ass," Craig said. "I'll kick your ass. Any day.

You name it."

"Get out," Leon said. "Get out of this bar and never come back."

"Your bouncers are pussies!"

"We'll get him out," Katrin said. "C'mon, Craig."

"No," Craig yelled. "Nobody believes my hell. Nobody knows what it's like."

Katrin inched her face closer to his, their noses almost touching. "I believe you. I do. But this is a business. They were nice to us when they didn't have to be. Let's just go."

"You don't believe me."

She held his arm up and showed him the cut. It was deep and might need stitches. "I believe you. I do, Craig. But this is not the way to prove it to everyone else."

He took a few deep breaths and collected himself, ultimately turning to Leon and apologizing. "I'm sorry. Really. It was wrong of me. Too much bubbly this early makes Jack a crazy boy."

I apologized myself and threw twenty euros from my stack on the counter. "If we hear anything, we'll let you know," I said. "Just don't tell the police anything. Not yet. Not if you want the truth to all this."

We were halfway down the hallway when Leon stuck his head out the door and said, "I'll give you your money back if he can prove it."

"Prove what?" I asked.

"Prove he doesn't feel pain."

"Are you serious?"

"Yes. I wanna know if he's for real. Not just a tough guy looking for an excuse to fight."

"Why?"

"Because I want to hope maybe you guys find this fucker that killed Christa. And this gives me hope, a man who doesn't feel pain. Indulge me, okay?"

And so Craig walked himself back toward Leon and stuck his chin out. "Go ahead, hit me."

"Not me," Leon said, "Tom here."

Tom lumbered out into the hallway like a grizzly bear trying to squeeze through a straw. I was pretty sure if he sat on coal it would turn to diamond.

"Alright then. Hit me," Craig said to him. "Ya fat fuck."

Tom landed a punch that resounded off the walls and Craig went flying like a wad of shit thrown by a monkey. I raced after him, moving to pick him up as he dripped slowly down the baseboards. To my surprise, he got up on his own and made his way back to Tom, stumbling like his legs had been replaced with putty.

"Dizziness I can feel," he said, giving his head a shake. "That counts for something, so thank you. But the rest of it…felt like a fly landed on my lips."

"Yeah, well your lips don't look like a fly landed on them," Katrin said, "unless that fly was swinging a lead pipe."

Craig spit blood on the floor. "Right then. Let's get outta here and get back to work."

To anyone else it certainly appeared that Craig didn't feel pain from the punch, even if his chin was pouring blood down his neck. But I'd grown up with Tooth, and I knew it didn't prove anything if you liked getting hit. It just proved you were nuts. Still, Leon gave me back my twenty euros.

"Find this guy," he said.

"We will," I replied, hoping it was the truth.

• • •

As we were walking back to the church my cell phone rang. It was Teddy. Damn, I thought, that was fast.

"Hello?"

"You're paying me back for these charges, you know," he said.

"I got a guy will send you money. I think. Depending on what you found. Did you find anything?"

"Yeah. My pal in New York got some kind of commendation as a result of nabbing our liquor store perp. Turns out he was wanted for murder in Canada. Can you believe it?"

"I thought all Canadians did was watch hockey and ride moose."

"And kill their wives, it turns out. Over groceries. So my friend was all too happy to run things through their computers for us. Turns out the girl in your photo is Courtney Tibbets. She was abandoned when she was five. Spent the next several years on the streets until social services found her sleeping in a garbage bin. Your other person of interest, this Angeline Mathias, got her Soaring Skies foundation to place Courtney in one of their halfway houses. Even hired one of those Make-a-Wish groups to help her get her life on track. She wanted to be—get this—a gangsta rapper."

"Don't they all."

"No. They don't. Anyway, she gets back into the school system, Ds and Cs, but what else do you expect from foster care, and then she disappears when she's sixteen. No real family or friends so everyone assumed she just ran away again. Want to know where she surfaces?"

"At Dr. Dre's house?"

"Who's that?"

"You need to get out more."

"Oh, he's that headphone guy?"

"Sure, let's go with that."

"Moving on. Her body is found in a cabin in Tacoma, Washington a year later. She's completely mutilated. I mean real sick shit."

I stopped in mid-walk, my stomach lurching. "Was it on video?"

"Jesus, I hope not. That's some disgusting and heart-wrenching stuff. Poor girl gets saved only to end up a murder victim."

"Think hard. I'm serious. Did your friend in New York say anything at all about it being videotaped? Was it on the Internet? Are they sure it's the same girl?"

"No, he didn't say anything about a video. Then again, I didn't ask. But you're getting ahead of me. After they find her body, they start running her prints. They're in the federal database because she's a person of interest in a number of human trafficking collars."

"Wait, now I'm confused. Why is she involved in that?"

"I don't know. Neither did my source. Only thing we can guess is she was at the home of a white slaver. At some point, anyway."

Now alarms were going off in my head. Was it merely a coincidence that Fountain and I had just raided a slaver's apartment the other night? That Fountain, Katrin and Craig had been chasing down leads on kidnapped women? Of course fucking not."

"Did they catch the slaver?"

"In fact they did, but he wouldn't give up his sources, and he was later shivved in prison so that's a dead end now."

My gears were really starting to turn now. "Teddy, I need a favor. Can you check on a couple more things?"

"Roger, I've been a cop for almost twenty years. You think I don't know what you're going to ask?"

"Do you?"

"Well, let's see. The woman who saved this little girl is dead. Murdered, or so you inferred. The little girl ends up in white slavery stock houses, and is later murdered. And some guy is after you, who just killed your new girlfriend. The whole fucking scenario reeks. You think it's all connected."

"I do."

"I know," he said. "And so I am now spending my brunch doing some research. And guess what?"

"You have every Dr. Dre album, you just didn't know it?"

"I've found at least eleven other girls who are associated with the Soaring Skies Network listed in reports for prostitution or just listed as missing."

"That's significant, right?"

"Maybe. Maybe not. Statistics will tell you most runaways end up on drugs and working the streets, even if they *do* spend time in foster care. What concerns me are the two others who end up dead. Mutilated. One in Tijuana, and one in Cuba."

"Cuba? Why the hell are they going to Cuba?"

"My guess is it was against their will. Slavers will ship where they need to ship. But this is New Hampshire, so we don't get too many of those cases, or, you know, any of them."

"So how does it all fit together? Girls getting saved by Soaring Skies ending up dead all over the place. The Chairwoman of the organization murdered on video."

"There's one last thing. I came across an article in *Variety* called 'Slave for Year.' A girl named Jenny Seaboldt was kidnapped when she was nineteen. She was working in a coffee shop in Boston, and as she was walking home one night someone jumped her, threw a bag over her head, and forced her into a van. For the next year she's pumped full of heroin and sold to creeps as far away as Dublin. Six times she's moved, until she ends up in Dubai, and she escapes by biting her new owner's dick off. An American businessman spots her running naked through a parking garage. She begs him to take her home to America, so the guy—turns out he's an ex-marine—does the right thing and gets her home."

"Where are you going with this?"

"Well, back before she starts selling coffee, she's in and out of orphanages. But at sixteen she gets a lease for an apartment to live on her own. Guess which organization helps her make that change?"

"Soaring Skies?"

"On the nose. Again, it could be total coincidence, stranger things have happened . . . "

"But you don't think so?"

"Do you?"

"I don't know what to think right now. This is a lot to take in and I need a moment to process it."

"Me too. I'm calling my New York friend back in a few. This smells hinky to him as well. And it's making me very worried about you. Are you sure you're okay?"

"I never am. Listen, I gotta run, I'm about to get on the train back to the church—"

"You're going to church now? Didn't even know you were religious."

"I'm not. Well, I kinda am. I don't really know. That's a discussion for another time. Thanks, Teddy, you may have just saved a ton of lives. I don't really know how yet, but I think you did."

"Roger?"

"Yeah?"

"This isn't a game. Come home. Now."

"I can't."

"Why?"

"Because I didn't save her."

"Jamie?"

I would always feel the sting of regret associated with her name. "Yeah. But I can save others."

"You're not Batman. These guys . . . they'll kill you. We'll never find your body. Come home. Please."

"I gotta go. Thanks, Teddy."

Chapter 18

We made it back to the church a half-hour later, the wine and beer starting to wear off a little. Fountain was still out and the rest of the place was empty. I was pissed. I wanted to talk to him. I could tell the other two did as well. We wanted to get some real answers from him, about why we'd been kept in the dark about Angeline Mathias.

We didn't bother going to the basement, and instead sat up in the rectory for a few minutes, mulling over the info Teddy had given us.

"Here's what I think," Katrin said. "Our killer was watching the Soaring Skies organization. Maybe he was out to ruin the organization's reputation. So he killed some of the girls that got saved."

"Sounds thin," Craig said. The cut on his arm was swelling up. "Easier ways to ruin someone's rep than multiple murders. That's a fact. Maybe he was just a guy who asked for their help and was denied."

"That really doesn't hurt?" I asked. "Your arm?"

"Not a bit," he said, but I still didn't know if I believed him either.

"So he kills Angeline as payback for not getting him off the streets," Katrin added, running with his theory. "Could be. You spend enough time on the streets you get abused for sure. You get your money the hard way, and people don't play fair. Trying to get food and a hot shower . . . who knows what he had to exchange for it."

"And in the end he kills Angeline as payback." I said. "Except . . . why keep killing once she's dead? He got what he wanted. It doesn't fit."

"Because . . . maybe Katrin is right. It was about the organization. And the organization continued without her," Craig said. "At least for a while. I think."

"I haven't heard James mention it since I met him, other than as a thing of his past," Katrin said. "And do we even know if the other girls murdered on film were part of it?"

I held up my phone, opened the Google app. "Only way to find out is to get screenshots, send 'em to the feds and see if they can match them up, right?"

"Oh goody," Katrin said, "get me the popcorn and let's get

cozy. Seriously, I don't want to watch that stuff."

"We don't need to watch them at all. Just the faces of a few. We can put two and two together after that."

"Can't wait."

Finding the videos was a bit trickier than we had anticipated. I knew how to find Angeline's and one other, but despite our search parameters—Al Qaeda, torture, execution, you name it—we only found one other video we could say was most likely our killer at work. Problem was the woman's face was in shadow for most of it. It looked like it was an older video, judging by the woman's hairstyle, which was inspired by Jennifer Anniston's character on *Friends*. Perhaps it was one of his first attempts. Mostly likely from the mid-90s. The room in the video was bare, the walls made of concrete blocks, like a college dorm room or a stock room. His usual MO.

We gathered in a semicircle around my phone and did our best not to look away, lest we miss her features. My phone app had a scrub function, but it wasn't working so great just off the cell data network in the city, so watching in real time was best.

And also the worst.

It started with her crying, pleading and begging. And then two gloved hands appeared and wrapped duct tape around her head a half-dozen times. Her cries became muffled, though no less desperate. Then out came a scalpel and a pair of pliers. His body moved in front of the camera, just his waist to his shoulders, and the screaming became shrill.

"Just fucking turn it down, mate," Craig said, somber as all hell now.

When the man's torso moved away the woman was writhing. Blood spattered on her beige skirt as she flung her head about. Unfortunately, the shadows were still too thick to see her face. The man turned to the camera and opened his hand to reveal two little bits of bloody flesh.

"It's her eyelids," Katrin says. "He's making her watch him."

The man went back again, and this time his cutting motions were wider, less precise. The woman flailed and her body spasmed and the next time the killer stepped back I caught a glimpse of the woman's head, a glistening blotch on her right side where her ear should've been. The killer showed the ear to the camera and dropped it on the floor.

We all watched the woman shaking in agony.

"Freeze it and take a screenshot," Craig said, but I was already ahead of him, taking a couple and labeling them for future reference.

"Is it enough," Katrin asked?

"Not for a facial recognition match," I said. "You can't really match a missing ear and half a chin."

"You can kinda see her eyes."

"We need more. Her nose or her mouth or something."

The killer wiped blood on his dark shirt and went back for more, using pliers this time, stepping to the side, enough to give the viewer a better idea of his methods, though his arms blocked her face. He forced open her mouth, yanked out a tooth and tossed it away. Yanked out another and when she convulsed he punched her in the face. She went completely still. Even in the room's darkness I saw blood running down her neck. He must have broken her nose.

"Jesus," Katrin said. "I want to kill this fucker. I want to kill him so slowly."

As he backed up I got a quick shot of her eyes, which were wide on account of her not having any lids, and a flash of her nose. I took a screenshot and saved it. It was better, but I still needed something clearer.

Next, the killer yanked her lips out and started slicing through them, taking them each off one at a time. She woke up screaming again, trying as hard as she could to break the ropes binding her to the chair. The killer left the frame for a minute, just letting her loll her head and suffer, her mouth nothing but red goop. Her hair fell over her face and her features were all but lost.

"Dammit, just move your head back, lady," Craig said. "All we need is to see your face."

I felt my stomach getting a little weak, probably on account of the alcohol; it doesn't mix well with live human mutilation. "I don't even know that she has a face anymore."

The killer returned yet again, and this time he had a spoon, and he sat on her lap and took that spoon and jammed it into her eye socket.

"Fuck!" Katrin screamed, finally getting up and moving to the other side of the room.

"I don't know how much more I can take," Craig said. "I don't even feel pain and I can tell that's beyond anything people can withstand."

I kept watching, studying it for anything we could use. The killer worked the spoon in under her ocular bones and started scooping out the eyeball. It took several tries and then it fell out, dangling on some gristle. He left it hanging there and went after the other one, just jammed that spoon in and rotated it viciously, scooping and boring, like a kid trying to shovel frozen ice cream out of a carton. There was so much blood. The woman's body shook and undulated, but he held it firm with his weight. I could finally see the back of his head, which contained a shock of dark hair, but it wasn't much to go on.

After a few more seconds he got up and the woman sat there with her two eyeballs dangling on her chest. She was alive, but just barely, and I could only pray her suffering didn't last much longer.

"I'm gonna be sick," I said.

"We all are," Katrin responded. Her face was turning pale and I could tell it was a struggle for her to keep watching.

"What's that?" I said, pointing at the phone's screen. "Is that—"

"An eyebrow ring," Katrin said, leaning over my shoulder. "It's got two beads on it."

"That's something," I said. I took a picture of it and then bookmarked the page. Before I closed the browser I couldn't help but notice the top couple comments, which were from a few days ago: "I'd feel bad for dis bitch if she wasn't born in da land o camel jockeys." And another: "He shoulda fucked that ho before he cut her head off." There were more, older ones, but I was too disgusted to care.

We found one other video and repeated the process, but thankfully this time the killer had improved his filming techniques and gave us a clear shot of the woman about two minutes in, which meant we only had to sit through some warm-up mutilation, if you could call it that. The scene was the same. Same drab walls, same duct-taping, same methodical way he carved her as she cried, only this time it was the tip of her nose that came off first. Then he opened her cheek like he was gutting a fish. That was when she screamed so loud the duct tape slipped below her chin and we got a good shot of her face.

"I think two is enough to confirm our theory," I said.

Katrin nodded, her eyes studying her feet. She was angry and trying to stay calm. Craig was playing with the puffy bruise under his eye. "I agree," he said. "I don't need any more of them images in my head. Need to sleep again at some point."

I emailed them off to Teddy with instructions, then we went to our cots.

Chapter 19

Sleep did not come, but I didn't mind. I was doing my best to think things through, put two and two together. I was pretty sure our theories were correct, though it brought me no closer to our killer. It still scared the shit out of me that he knew who I was and I didn't know him at all. I prayed he didn't know where we were right now, but chances were good he was watching. I knew Piotr and Oscar were standing guard, and Uwe and Walter were onsite somewhere, so he was going to have a hard time getting to us without being seen, but it wasn't an impossible task either. He'd evaded capture for years now, and he was good at hiding in the shadows.

The three of us had fastened some of our own burglar alarm systems around the room—leaned empty bottles against the windows, stood metal candle holders in front of the door, and positioned a circle of chairs around our cots. Even if he had night vision goggles he'd be hard pressed to get to us without making noise.

At some point Craig got a text, sat up and said, "See ya, tossers, pussy beckons."

"You're leaving?" Katrin asked. She was not happy.

"Yeah. That's what I said."

"It's not safe. Don't be an idiot."

"I'm not afraid of him. What's he gonna do, cut me? Ouchie. Oh no."

"He could do worse."

"Fuck 'im. The quicker he shows himself the quicker we put an end to this. But for now . . . " He made a V with his fingers and flicked his tongue between them. Classy stuff.

After he left Katrin and I watched the walls and tried to find reasons for conversation. I thought she might ask to sleep in my bed with me again, but she didn't. She turned away from me and I couldn't tell if she was in dreamland or not.

I did what I always do to force sleep, to bore myself. Think of things in alphabetical order, repeat it all until I see ZZZs. I chose female comic book characters this time. Abigail Arcane. Barbara Gordon. Carol Danvers. Dazzler. Echo. Firestorm . . . I cycled through the alphabet three times before I was out.

Then I woke to screaming.

• • •

My head shot up off my pillow. I heard metal candle holders rolling across the cement floor. A body landed on top of me and nearly knocked me out of bed. Instinctively I threw it off, jumped up with my fists raised, ready to swing at anything.

Katrin was up next to me, her eyes in shock, pulled from deep REM sleep with no idea what the hell was going on. "What!" she screamed. "Who!"

"Help me!" came the voice again, and this time I saw a girl on the ground near my bed. I grabbed her elbow and yanked her up. It was Brittany, and she was hysterical, covered in blood. "Please! Help me!"

I sat her on the bed, brushed her hair out of her eyes. Her face was swollen, her nose broken, blood running out of her ear. She'd been beaten.

"What the fuck happened?" I asked, trying to stop her shaking.

"He said if I went to the cops he'd kill him." She looked back and forth between me and Katrin with an utter sense of helplessness.

"What are you talking about? Slow down. Take a breath. Who said what about who?"

"He took my fingers!" She held up a bloodied hand that was rounded into a nub. All five fingers were gone. Black char was crusted on the severed knuckles.

He'd burned the wounds shut.

We've seen this shit before, Rog. Holy fuck, it's like all psychos know about cauterizing wounds. I bet the fucker has a dog too.

"I'll call the *schupo*," Katrin said.

"No!" Brittany screamed. "He said he'd kill him. He said he'd come back for me. I'm so scared. I don't want to die. Please don't."

"Who?" I asked.

"Really?" Katrin said sarcastically. "Isn't it obvious?"

I nodded, feeling so drained, wondering if I'd even gotten an hour of sleep. "Yeah. I know who."

"He was in my apartment," Brittany continued. "He was just there, when I opened my eyes. Just standing in the middle of the room in shadows. I screamed and he raced at me, kicked me into the wall. Craig woke up and rushed him but…he had as stun gun. Craig fell down and the man . . . he choked him, knocked him out. I tried to hit him but he was too strong. He punched me in the face and when I was down he . . . he had garden shears. He cut my fingers off. Oh God it hurts. It hurts so much. Please help me!"

Katrin was hugging her now, rocking her. She had her phone out. "Okay, okay. I'm calling an ambulance. Just hang on."

Brittany was whimpering, tears running into her mouth "God, it hurts so bad."

"Tell us where Craig is," I said. I was afraid if she went into shock or passed out we'd never get the information we needed. "He was alive when you last saw him?"

"He was still alive. That . . . guy started dragging him to the door and he said if I told anyone . . . he'd kill Craig and come back for me. It hurts so bad. I can't feel my arm."

"Why didn't you call for medical help?"

"He said doctors would call the police."

"Yeah, well you're going to hospital," Katrin said, "and that's that. How'd you find us?"

"Craig told me if anything happened I should come here. He said I could find Katrin here."

Well that didn't make me feel very wanted but I pushed aside my pride.

"Where'd he take him?" I asked.

She shook her head, licking tears off her lips. "I don't know. I didn't see. He had a butane torch, and he burned my hand, and it hurt so bad I passed out. I woke up and they were gone, just a trail of blood going down the stairs to the street and then nothing."

Katrin yanked me up and pulled me toward the wall. "He knew she'd tell us," she said. "It's why he let her live."

"Which means he knew Craig told her to come here."

She nodded. "Which means he's been close to us for days. Close enough to hear our conversations."

"Or he just took a guess she'd know where we were. Either way, first things first, take her upstairs to meet the ambulance. She needs medical attention. Find Uri and Walter. They were supposed to be in the building. Where the fuck did they go?"

"They're always in and out."

"They're idiots. Whatever. I'm going to get Fountain."

"How? You don't even know where he is."

"Somebody must know. And he needs to be here for all this. This guy wants Fountain above all. Fountain is his goal. So I'm gonna bring this hunter his quarry. Enough is enough."

Chapter 20

I didn't know exactly where Fountain was, but I had my guess. I took the long way through the church to the back alley, found Piotr and Oscar still there, beers in their hands. They smelled like shit even from ten feet away.

"Way to stand guard, guys."

"Whatcha mean?" Oscar asked.

"Nobody heard the crying girl enter?"

"We don't watch the front, friend."

Fair enough, I thought. "I need to find Fountain."

"He ain't here, boy," said Piotr, relaxed in his recliner.

"I know that. He keeps disappearing. And there's only two places I can think of where he'd be. One is in his apartment, wherever that is, though my gut tells me he's been spending time here at the church because he knows his place has been compromised. The other place is farther away. Perhaps a few hours on a train. A church. You know the name, yes?"

Oscar pulled on his beverage, sized me up with his eyes. "You're smarter than you look."

"You're smellier than you look. And you look like dog shit."

"Aw, that's not nice."

"You gonna help me or what?"

"It's true, he went back to the monastery."

"You know this for sure?"

"Well . . . no. But then again, yes. He's there."

"Where is it exactly?"

"You don't know how to Google something?"

"I do. But I don't know that he's been the most truthful with me so I don't even know if I'll be googling the right place. I can pay you for what you know."

Piotr shook his head. "Some things we don't do. Not for money, not for our conscience."

"Your conscience? You're gonna pull the allegiance card over this?"

"It's our job, no? Keep the trespassers out, keep watch on them passersby. Something like that." He took another long sip.

"As I already pointed out, you failed. There's a girl in there who's been mutilated by the guy Fountain is trying to catch. Craig—you know him—has been taken by this sicko and is probably dead or near dying. This is no fucking joke. Cut the Honor Guard crap and give me the location."

They were both sitting up straight now. "Why didn't you say so? It is just outside of Gorzów, hidden from street view but you can find it if you know where to look."

He rambled off the address and I committed it to memory. A minute later I was back inside, helping Katrin bandage up Brittany's hand. She was shaking and I wished I knew if there was any wine in the undercroft, anything to steady her shaking.

"Ambulance is on the way," Katrin said. She taped off the bandage and then dabbed Brittany's head with a cold towel.

"I'm going to Poland," I replied. "It's a just a two-hour trip. I'm confident it's where Fountain is and we're going to need him for this."

"I still think we should go to the police."

"No!" Brittany said.

"I hate to say it, but I'm with her. If we do, they'll arrest us instead for Christa's murder and Craig will die. Trust me, that's how these things work. He's got Craig an inch from death, and if he smells cops he'll make Craig an example. I know these types. But we have an advantage."

"Which is?"

"This guy wants Fountain, that's why he came out of hiding and attacked us. He's gone full predator. He's done being prey."

"When the hell was he ever the prey? The guy has been murdering women on film for years."

"I mean he realized Fountain was tracking him. And now he wants Fountain out of his way. So he came here and came out of hiding to lure us all to where he wants us."

"What do you mean 'out of hiding'? We don't know where he is or where he has Craig."

"No, not yet. But if I can get Fountain back here, I guarantee he'll give us a clue. He knows Fountain has been chasing him for years and he's going to use that to our advantage."

She stopped wiping Brittany's head. "If he wants Fountain, why didn't he just fucking go after Fountain! Why take Christa? Why take Craig? Why attack us in the street?"

"Because Fountain keeps eluding him. That's why we moved around at dinner that night. He knows not to stay put in one place. So the guy gave up and came after us as a way to lure him out."

"Then you're just playing into his hand."

"Yeah, but we know we are, so we maintain a semblance of control."

"Says you. I say we have no idea how far ahead this guy is thinking. I'm no chess player."

"Fair enough."

She rubbed Brittany's blood off her chin. "Tell me you're not doing this because of the little girl I see behind you. Tell me this isn't about you feeling some hidden bloodlust and I might feel better."

"How little?"

"Maybe early teens."

Probably Jamie, I thought, if I wanted to believe her carnival tricks. I definitely still wanted vengeance for Jamie, but this was also about more than my sister. It was about bad people doing bad things and how I was beginning to get real tired of it. So I wanted to tell her my bloodlust was true but I couldn't be sure what I was feeling. All I knew was I was so angry inside I wanted to hurt this guy. And to do that I wanted to meet him face to face.

"How long will you be?" she asked. "What about Craig?"

"Craig has his own advantage. One I bet our killer doesn't know about."

Katrin's eyes were burning with anger. "Craig can last a while but a slit throat is still a slit throat. If we don't find him soon we'll be watching his death on the Internet."

"Four hours. Maybe five. I'll be back."

"It's too long! We need help now."

Sirens wailed outside and tires screeched near the door. The ambulance had arrived, so we cut our off conversation and hoisted Brittany into our arms. We carried her up into the church proper and laid her in one of the pews closest to the vestibule. Her breathing was shallow and her eyes were closed and fluttering.

"She's going into shock," Katrin said, just as the paramedics burst through the door.

In the confusion I slipped out, ran several blocks away in case someone was trying to tail me, and then hailed a cab. I didn't see anyone giving chase, so I figured I was safe from the killer. Besides, if he had Craig tied up somewhere, then his attention was no doubt on his captive.

Craig was on borrowed time. If I didn't figure this right, he was as good as dead.

Chapter 21

The taxi driver almost balked when I told him how far we were going, but I gave him most of the money Fountain had given me, and he finally agreed. It was probably more than he would have made all night if he'd stuck around the city. Or maybe not; I still couldn't do the euro conversion real well in my head. For as big a city as Berlin is, we were out of it within minutes, then speeding by fields under a starry sky. I looked up and found familiar constellations, proof that no matter where people lived on the planet we were all still on the same ground, living lives that were hard, that were sad, that blindsided us with unexpected pain.

There wasn't much to see on the road to Poland, at least not in the dark, so I got on the Internet on my phone and used Google Maps to get the Earth view of the location around the monastery. I didn't see anything but trees and some parks. Piotr and Oscar had said the monastery was kind of hidden, but I was hoping "hidden" just meant nestled among some trees. Last thing I needed right now was to traipse around the forest in the middle of the night.

Last thing I ever needed again was to traipse around a forest . . . period.

I texted with Katrin to see what was going on with Brittany but she just said the doctors were monitoring her and that Brittany was on a lot of painkillers now and not making much sense. She said she'd call if anything changed. I prayed she didn't do anything stupid like go looking for Craig by herself. Again she mentioned police and I talked her out of it.

Time seemed to pass slower than a Lars Von Trier film.

I emailed my parents, told them I was okay. I told them I missed them but not in some obvious way that I was in trouble. Part of me felt wracked with guilt, that I might die and put them through the death of their only other child, but the other part of me knew what I was doing was the right thing. I just hoped that if I did die our killer made a big enough announcement online that someone found my body. I wouldn't want my parents never knowing what happened, always hoping one day I'd walk through their front door. That's the worse torture.

In time, we were in Poland. It wasn't much to look at, but it was dark out so what did I know. I saw some statues, some old houses, what was possibly a school and park.

Eventually, we were skirting a large city full of lights and my mood brightened. Gorzów Wielkopolski was beautiful to observe by night, the type of place where you could fall in love. Spired buildings set alongside the Warta river, red-tiled roofs and baroque architecture that seemed to spill out of paintings seen in history books. It reeked of culture and I wished I could get out and take a walk, but I didn't have that luxury anymore.

"You sure this address is correct?" the cabbie asked me.

"Far as you know," I replied, trying to make a joke. I felt like it had been ages since I'd laughed at anything truly funny. Same rang true for the cabbie; he huffed in annoyance.

We travelled past the northern tip of the city, took a thin road around a hotel with thick bronzed window frames, then left all that culture and mystery behind us. I checked the time on my phone. We'd been gone from Berlin for almost two hours. Was Craig still alive? I hoped so. I hoped my assessment of the situation was correct, that this killer was waiting for Fountain before he performed his coup de grâce.

The car slowed to a stop. "This is where my GPS is telling me to stop," the cabbie said.

I opened the door and got out, leaned back in the window with my remaining cash and said, "Don't leave. I'll be back."

"Ten minutes. Then I'm leaving. I didn't agree to stay here all night."

"I'll be back."

I looked around me and saw that we were on a thin, paved road. Some buildings lined one side, but the lights in the windows were off. Couldn't tell what they were supposed to be, maybe some offices, maybe some low-income houses. There was a sense of abandonment shrouding it all.

On the opposite side of the street were trees.

"Figures."

I took a few steps toward the darkened buildings, then noticed the staircase leading off the street, down into the trees. The kind of staircase that leads to a hiking trail. That had to be it. If it wasn't, then Piotr and Oscar had screwed me. So I took the steps down into the darkness, heard a small stream bubbling off to my right, the shuffle of a small rodent darting away to safety. The darkness was total, thick, and the wet moss around me smelled like sweat. The steps descended onto wooden planks, some kind of walkway that wound around the tree trunks. It squelched in wet mud as I clomped my way down an incline until I emerged into a clearing, at which point I could plainly see the building I was looking for.

Candles lit up stained glass windows with flickering reds and oranges. Two small towers with arched corbels and brass spires flanked the sides. A small wooden fence ringed the property, beyond which I could make out dark silhouettes I took to be fruit trees. The wooden walkway turned to a cobblestoned path that skirted a small parking lot—no doubt accessed through the woods on the other side—and came to an end at a set of square wooden church doors set under an inlaid carving of a crucifix.

Though quaint by many standards, it was still an impressive bit of architecture.

I slowly pushed the doors open and found myself in a two-story-high vestibule. Two more doors were beyond this, and I pushed through them into a large stone room lit with candles. A man in an abbot's chasuble greeted me like a ghost materializing out of the fog.

"Can I help you?" he asked.

"If you have some clean underwear I can borrow. Maybe give me a heads up before you pull a Dracula entrance next time."

"I'm sorry. We don't get guests this late. I was making rounds and heard the door. Are you in some sort of . . . trouble?"

"You have no idea. I need to find James Peter Fountain. Is he here? Please say he's here."

The abbot looked at the floor, then back at me. "He is here, but he is indisposed."

"I don't care. I need him. Now."

His eyes studied mine, searching for some sense of trust or truth or danger. I'm sure he found all three. "Of course. This way."

• • •

European clergy love their basements. Like the church in Berlin, this undercroft was dank and dark and smelled of dead flowers and dust. Candles jutted from insets in the walls, though one half of the room was lit by old floor lamps so I assumed they'd at least heard of the twenty-first century.

Fountain was on his knees before a large crucifix, his shirt off, his back streaked in blood. Standing above him were members of the monastery, one soaking a rag in water. He took the rag and dabbed at Fountain's back, washed off the gore. I saw a handful of lacerations cutting across his back.

Not this shit again, I thought. What the hell kind of penance was he paying now? I don't know why but it angered me, so I stormed over and grabbed him by his shoulders, spun him around.

His watering eyes seemed genuinely surprised. "Roger?"

"He got Craig."

"What do you mean?"

"Craig. British wanker, doesn't feel pain, lives in your apartment and does what you tell him to. Ring a bell? He's been captured."

Fountain stood up, reached for his shirt. "My God." He groaned as he put it on.

I whirled on the abbot, who had followed me over. "Why are you doing this to him? And don't tell me he does it on his own because someone had to teach it to him. What crime fits this punishment? This is why I don't trust churches. You're still living in the Crusades. It's fucking disgusting. This is cruel and unusual punishment."

"Roger, please . . . ." Fountain began, but I cut him off.

"Shut it. This is sick. They expect you to chase killers and suffer for it too? It's goddamned ridiculous."

Fountain touched my shoulder. I nearly threw a punch at whoever was closest. I could feel myself unraveling.

The abbot held up his hands in acquiescence. "I agree. It is barbaric. I have urged James not to do this, but he insists."

My brain took a second to dwell on that. "Wait, you don't have anything to do with this? But I thought . . . " I pointed at Fountain, who was buttoning his jacket. "What the fuck?"

"Someone has to bear the burden of the lives I cannot save, and it can only be me. It is but a small show of sympathy, and an attempt at empathy, for the horrors they suffer."

"It's fucking Fruit Loops, is what it is. Who are you even talking about? You already caught that asshole with the girls in his closet."

"And we discovered, while interviewing those girls, that two of them overdosed the prior day. Their bodies were removed by accomplices and we have no idea where they are. Had we been a day earlier . . . "

I thought about the little girl with track marks on her arm, wondered what could have happened to her had we been a day late. But I pushed the thought aside. You can dwell on what-ifs till the end of your days, it won't change anything. It was better to focus on the fact we had saved lives, right?

Still, I understood the madness it put him through. How many slavers and rapists and killers had he captured only a day late? It could break a man.

"So . . . what, you can't do this back in Berlin?" I asked.

"I had further business here. I'm supposed to—"

"You have to report in. I get it. No phones. No computers. Just face-to-face clandestine shit, like the old days. Like the Crusades."

"James generously brings us provisions a couple of times a month," the abbot explained.

I was about to make another snide comment when my phone buzzed. It was Katrin, asking for an update. I told her I had James and was heading back as soon as I could get him out the door. I then noticed I had about two minutes before the cabbie left.

"Please tell me you drove here?" I asked.

Fountain fished in his pockets and held up his keys. "Of course. And we must hurry back if what you say is true."

The abbot stepped out of our way, but whispered to Fountain as we passed. "Is this the American you spoke of?"

Fountain nodded.

"He's angry."

Fountain nodded again.

"Very angry."

"I can hear you, Yoda," I said.

"I don't care," the abbot said. "Mr. Huntington, my friend James here speaks very highly of you. I can see you don't trust him, or us, or why you are here. But we are not the enemy. We are trying to stop the enemy."

"You don't say. Okay, maybe that's part of it. But I also think you're cleaning up a mess you made. A mess that started when you decided to fund an organization for runaways. I just haven't put it all together yet."

"I assure you we did nothing to—"

"And I feel like I'm being used. So no, you're not the enemy, but I don't know I trust you yet."

"It will come in time."

"Says you. But all this can wait. I don't have many friends these days, and I'm not sure that Craig is even one of them, but he's one of the few people who's bought me a beer recently that didn't want to know what it was like to kill a man with an axe. All he wants to do is talk about girls and feel something besides boredom. I get that. I like that. And now he's being held by a man with a scalpel and saw and God knows what else. And that cannot wait one second more."

"Absolutely not," Fountain said, taking off for the stairs. "Follow me!"

I chased after him. We exited the monastery, jumped in Fountain's car in the parking lot and took a winding wooded road back to the main street. I never did see if the cabbie had waited for me or not. My guess was he took off the second I disappeared into the trees.

We drove about fifteen miles before my phone alerted me I had a video message. It was from Craig's phone.

"What the hell?" My palms started to sweat and I felt heat race down my chest. I played it and gasped. It was Craig, covered in blood, laughing. A gloved hand came into view, holding a surgeon's knife, then the screen went black.

A text popped up next: *No Police. Just you. I see police, you'll never find his body.*

His now-familiar mantra. I was shaking in both anger and fear. I texted back: *Had to run an errand, sweetie, be there soon enough.*

"Drive faster," I said.

Chapter 22

We made it back to Berlin without saying much to each other; it was a long fucking ride.

Katrin met us at the church, filled us in once more on Brittany's condition, which was stable, and we gathered around a small table. I took out my phone and replied to the video message. *We're all here. We're alone. Where are you?*

A couple seconds later we got a reply: *You'll find the key to my door out back. Looking forward to getting you all off my back once and for all. Just be sure to smile for the camera when you arrive.*

"Out back?" Katrin asked, bewildered.

"There's no backyard," Fountain said. "There's no exterior property at all."

Then I had it. "Oh shit," I said, and leapt up, running out the front door. I hit the street, stopped beside the wall to the small alley and scrambled up and over it. Laying in pools of blood were Piotr and Oscar's bodies. Their heads were missing, and nocturnal bugs were supping at the gore. The whole alley smelled like copper and feces.

"Roger, what the hell is happening?"

I heard Fountain's voice coming over the wall at the same time Katrin's hands appeared. She hoisted herself over and landed next to me. "Holy fuck," she whispered.

"He was here."

"Ya think."

A second later Fountain was coming out of the back door of the church into the alley. He was huffing from running to catch up, and had grabbed a brass candle douter along the way, obviously as a weapon. "Dear Lord," he said. He came over and bent down besides the corpses, ran his hands over their torsos, searching for something. He stopped at the stumps of their severed necks. "Where are they?" he whispered.

"Where's what?" I asked, noticing the way he now fingered his own pendant necklace. Before I could say anything Katrin was shouting.

"Here! Here! Look, the grate's moved and there's a trail of blood."

It was obvious now that the killer had used the same ingress point I had just days ago. Meaning he'd disappeared back into the sewer tunnel. He could have then exited from the same basement room in the next building, or just kept running through the sewers. There was only one way to find out.

"I'll go first," Fountain said. He was still moving stiffly from his wounded back, and I saw Katrin eyeing him with concern, but I figured it wasn't my place to open up that conversation right now. For all I knew she was already privy to his little back-attack fetish.

I went next, and Katrin followed. The trail of blood leading into the darkness of the tunnel made his direction obvious.

I heard Katrin's switchblade open with a *snik*.

Then we were walking in the muck, wondering what was going to jump out at us.

● ● ●

The blood trail led us down a couple tunnels off the main sewer. He'd smeared it on the walls to make sure we could follow. I could only imagine the scene of him walking through the sewer with two decapitated heads, rubbing them on the brick and concrete and laughing as he went.

For a short while we were able to use light from outside street-lamps spilling down through grates, but the trail took us to a tunnel that sloped down and we soon had to use our phone lights to see where we were going.

And it smelled. Bad. Like a dead cat's rotting, maggot-filled vagina.

So we held our shirts over our noses as we went. It didn't take long for me to lose a signal on my cell phone, and when I asked if anyone else had service the answer was a resounding no.

"I hear rats," Katrin said. "And I saw one in the water a minute ago so be careful."

"Rats are the least of our worries," Fountain replied.

We turned left down another tunnel, and at this point the faint streak of blood on the wall got thicker, and formed an arrow showing us the way.

"That's nice of him," I said.

"He's probably watching us right now," Katrin said. "He could be in these tunnels with night vision goggles on, making sure we go the right way."

That thought made the hairs on my neck stand up.

We followed the arrows, taking a couple more turns. The water dissipated here and I suspected we were in a part of the sewer no longer used.

And then we saw the door. It was red and rusted and stood looming at the end of the tunnel we were in. And affixed to it somehow were Oscar and Piotr's heads. We pulled up to them slowly and just stood there for a minute, knowing that on the other side of the door this game was about to enter the lightning round.

"*Requiescat in pace*," Fountain whispered.

Katrin held her knife up in my phone light. "What he said."

"Listen," Fountain began, "beyond this door is a man who is more clever than any you've ever encountered. He's a master survivor. It would be nice to try him for his crimes but there is no way to do that unless he confesses and he wouldn't have lured us here if that was his intent. So if you get the chance, kill him. Don't talk to him. Don't trust him. Just end him."

"Professor X you are not," I said. "And the monastery . . . they're okay with that decision, I assume?"

"Roger, you more than anyone know I pay a penance for my choices."

It was making more sense now, why he flagellated himself. It wasn't just bearing the burden of the victims' deaths, it was also carrying the weight of bleak choices. I didn't know how I felt about that. Didn't know if a religious man killing for the greater good would sit well with the man upstairs, if the man upstairs even existed. But then it was hard to argue with his logic. Because if we let this killer go, who knew how many more innocent women and men would die in front of his lens.

It also confirmed that, yes, Fountain wanted me on his team because he knew I subscribed to the belief that killing for the greater good was, in a fucked up way, virtuous. The whole thing made me hate myself all over again.

Oh suck a sympathy dick, Roger, you like this part of the game. Skinny Man's voice was back, his nasally, gruff voice swimming through my head. *You know that suited-up motherfucker is telling it like it is. Can't have pervs and psychos running around cutting off heads and jerking off on squirrels—not that I ever did the last one. Okay maybe I did once. Fucker kept coming in my yard and staring at me. So I came in his face then barbecued him. Don't you judge me, killerboy. Don't think what you do is any better. It's all about cleansing the world, right? Slice, hack, punch. Wee wee wee, all the way home. Shit, get in there and do your job, pussyboy.*

"Roger, snap out of it."

Katrin was shaking my shoulder.

"Sorry. I just— "

"I know. And I hate to say it, but in this instance, he might be right?"

Fountain was testing the door handle, heard our conversation. He looked at us. "*Who's* right?"

"No one," I said.

"Roger's friend," Katrin added. "He's been with us since we got down here. He's the creepiest thing I've ever seen."

The hairs stood up on my neck again, but for an all new reason. I still couldn't believe what she said about seeing Skinny Man was true, but Jesus it felt real.

I turned to Fountain. "I take medication. When I remember." As if that explained anything. Besides, I think he already knew.

But Fountain was too preoccupied to care. He was opening the door.

"The plan?" Katrin asked,

Fountain whispered. "I don't have one. All these years and I don't have one."

"I guess we're your plan," I said.

Katrin shook her head. "Nice line, cornball."

Fountain opened the door. I stepped back so Oscar's head wouldn't brush up against me. Piotr's either for that matter. They kind of bobbed a bit as the door swung wide,

Then we stepped through into the horror show.

• • •

The stone room was cold and stank of something rotten. A combination of sewage and rodent shit and decomposing trash.

I've gone down on bloody pussies that didn't smell this bad.

"Shut up, Tooth," I whispered. If either Fountain or Katrin heard me they didn't say anything.

Went down on this hairy bush once that had a dead fly in it. Thought I was gonna puke.

"Enough."

Like the tunnels outside this room, there was blood on the walls, lit by a few candles that had been placed randomly on the ground. The other light, the one illuminating Craig, came from the top of a video camera that the 80s had long forgotten. No doubt a VHS recorder, the same one he'd used while killing Christa.

Craig was bound by some kind of metallic wire to an old office chair, the kind made of metal and vinyl with four small wheels on the legs. Duct tape was wound many times around his mouth. His face was awash in blood, and he may have been missing an ear; it was hard to tell. Fountain was moving to him, but Katrin and I knew better, and we both hung back and watched him go. She slowly moved to her right and I went to my left, kept our backs to the walls of the room, inching into the shadows across from us. I saw her switchblade flicker in the candlelight, even when her body disappeared in the darkness for a second.

Besides Craig, the room was empty as far as I could tell. It was circular and wide, and at one time must have been a junction for branching tunnels. I could see two more tunnels coming into view on the curve of the wall ahead. There were likely more farther in, like spokes on a wheel. The European sewer contractors of yesteryear had to have been crazy people to design things like this.

And yet . . . so much of it looked familiar. The concrete. The stains. Then it hit me, the killer had used sewer systems before in his videos. It explained the concrete walls in his filmography. He always shot underground. And likely other subterranean realms—the subway tunnels of NYC, sublevels of other major city public works' departments. He'd known this room was here, had been here before, had known it was a place with too many exits to cover, giving him the advantage.

A voice came back to me: *You should see the Paris sewers. New York City isn't bad either. Berlin's is an amazing place. Check out the hub under there if you can. There's like twenty tunnels going off in every direction. Very cool stuff.*

"Shit," I whispered. "I know who he is."

"What?" Katrin asked, confused.

"I think I know who he is. I think I spoke to him. Maybe. I think . . . I think he tried to send me here before."

"Why?"

"I don't know. Part of his game. He wanted me to see where he planned to kill me. Or he was going to follow me and kill me right then."

"Who is he?"

I stared around the room, taking in the blood stains on the walls. "A barista. Works at a café down the block. Sonofabitch. He's been close by the whole time."

"A barista? Why would a barista—"

"It makes sense. There are coffee shops all over the world. You don't need a big résumé to get a job making coffee. You can find a coffee shop within blocks of any place you want to stake out. It's practically a bohemian lifestyle. It doesn't raise alarms if you do it for a bit then quit and move on. You can do it all over the world. You can learn people's names, their habits, use it to follow them in the open. The fucker was playing with me."

"You're sure?"

"Not entirely. But something he said. 'Check out the hub under there.' This is the hub."

"Where is he now?" Fountain said, checking the bindings on Craig.

"He's in the walls," Craig replied. "Somewhere."

I took it to mean the guy was using the tunnels to get around. Katrin was getting close to me now, having come around the other side to meet me in the middle of the wall opposite where we'd entered. We both kept an eye on the tunnels we passed.

"Can you walk?" Fountain asked.

Craig chuckled. "I can run a marathon if you want. Probably won't win, though. Not feeling myself today, and shit like that."

"I can't undo the wires. They're too big for a knife and he's got them tied too tight. I need wire cutters or something."

He was trying to beat the chair with the douter but it wasn't doing anything to loosen the binds or the legs and arms. Katrin ran back over and tried to use her blade but the wire wasn't having it. Switchblades will slip through flesh like a hot knife through butter but they're shit against anything hard.

"Where did he go?" Fountain was still asking questions. "He's watching. I know it."

Craig shook his head. "I don't know. The goddamn camera light is blinding me. Can't see shit beyond it. Hope it's at least getting my good side."

"What side is that?" asked Katrin. "The side where I can see he tried to flay your cheek or the side where the bone of your chin is shining through your skin?"

"The side where I'm under a pile of naked chicks wearing crotchless knickers. Does that side exist? Just say yes either way."

"It's recording," I said, noting the red light on near the camera's viewfinder. "Why's it still recording?"

We all froze for a second, looking at the camera. Realization set in.

"Fuckballs," I said.

And that's when the surgical knife came sailing out of the dark tunnel besides Fountain and caught him right in the arm. He howled and dove away from Craig. I knew it had all been recorded clear as day, just as the killer had wanted it to be.

"James!" Katrin yelled, detaching herself from the wall and rushing to him. She stood over him and twirled, her blade ready.

Now all three of them were behind Craig's chair, all framed perfectly for whatever our killer wanted to capture on video. So instead of taking the bait I hung back, bit my lip, prayed Katrin would just get the hell out of there. When I realized she wasn't going to move I knew I had to draw fire away from her and onto me.

"I'm not running into your frame, asshole! So no matter what happens, you are still going to have to deal with me. Which means if you want that video tape you're gonna have to come out of the shadows to get it. And that's when I'll fucking kill you."

Katrin realized now what she'd done, and stepped away from Fountain.

"Get Craig out of the shot," I whispered.

"Right," she answered, and started to drag Craig out of the camera light. For a girl, she had some muscle; Craig wasn't made of clouds and flower petals. When she started to struggle Fountain limped behind her and tried to help, but his arm was gushing blood.

That's when a dark shadow came charging out of the passage behind Craig like a rogue gorilla and plowed into Fountain with the force of a freight train. My new benefactor went sailing through the air and hit the wall to my left with a crunch that spoke of a dislocated shoulder. He screamed in agony.

The man whirled, his shroud trailing behind him. I was up and moving instantly, but not fast enough to help Katrin, who was swinging her blade at the figure. Her knife caught the excess of the hood hiding his face, but the figure ducked to the right and came up swinging something long and hard. It was a sword.

Katrin ducked his swing, kicked out her leg and threw her shoulder into the move at the same time. The hooded attacker couldn't parry both maneuvers and caught the force of her weight in his chest. He went down hard, the sword sliding across the cement ground, and Katrin fell on top of him. She landed two punches to his face, knocking his hood off. I was a step away, trying to see his face, to see if I was right, when his elbow came up and got Katrin under the bridge of her nose. She grunted as blood shot up toward the ceiling from her nostrils. Then she was down for the count, rolling and moaning and trying to keep her nose bones in place.

"Katrin!" Craig yelled, trying desperately to break his binds.

I leapt up and over Craig and hit the guy as he was standing up. We went to the ground together and I felt his fist hitting my head. I saw stars for a minute but I knew I couldn't give into the pain. I'd been hit enough times by now to know that these punches weren't the worst I'd ever taken, and that I wasn't going to black out so long as I kept him from jogging my chin around. The skull is pretty damn formidable when you get right down to it. His blows hurt, especially when he found my own nose, which still wasn't healed well from my activities in San Diego, but I decided I would care later.

I slammed my fist into his mouth and felt a tooth break free. Damn I felt good inside when I heard it. As I slammed him again I saw his face, and I knew I'd been right. It was the barista. I was sort of glad I'd figured it out, because I might have been shocked otherwise. He grit his teeth as he took my next blow and I watched his eyebrow split and pump out blood.

I saw the sword nearby, reached out for it. I could feel him going limp beneath me and I figured I had him now.

What I wasn't counting on was the way he was able to buck me off him like some crazed bull at a rodeo. The guy had to be on methamphetamine. I also wasn't counting on the stun gun he hit me with in the groin. I spasmed, felt every muscle in my body seize up so tightly I thought my asshole might end up in my throat.

It passed in a second or two but the damage was done. I felt like a bull mastiff had made me its bitch.

Why does everyone here hate your balls, I heard Tooth say.

Then his boot caught my cheek and I was drifting toward blackness. Before I passed out I saw Craig struggling tirelessly against his binds, shouting, "Fight me, fucker! Fight me!"

He and Tooth would have been good friends.

Chapter 23

I awoke tied to a chair. He'd tied a burlap bag over my head like I was a scarecrow. My mouth was stuffed with a rag and bound in tape. I couldn't see shit. I could hear Katrin next to me, and next to her was Craig. I could discern the former because she was moaning, and I could discern the latter because he was laughing, crazed. He was gagged as well but I caught the gist of his words. "You're a fucking ponce! You dickless twat. Tie people to chairs and torture 'em, what a fucking sissy way to kill someone. C'mon, you arsehole, untie me. Give me a real go."

"Shut up." The killer's voice was low. Controlled. I heard Craig scream, though I couldn't tell why.

"You'll never sustain this madness," Fountain said. His voice was clear, and he was across the room from me. "We know who you are now. You work at the coffee shop. We've seen you. We'll get your name, your accounts, you'll never disappear from us."

"First, you don't know me. You only figured it out minutes ago so you have no leverage here. Second, if I wanted to disappear I would have been long gone. But I *want* to be here, to talk to you. I know you've been following me for some time and will just keep it up unless I stop it. You've become quite the thorn in my side, James."

I guessed it was no surprise this guy knew James' name. Still, it was shocking to hear him say it.

"It's your own fault," Fountain said. "You killed someone special to me."

"Special? That's funny. Are you saying that for the benefit of your friends here? She wasn't special in any way. Well, perhaps to me, to my clientele."

"Clientele implies human beings. Who you pander to are animals."

"And yet I'm considered a genius in some circles. Do you know how often I've been downloaded? It's in the millions. And your Angeline helped make that possible."

"You fucking twats are boring me to goddamn tears here," Craig said. "How about you two shut the fuck up and let's get back to me and the dickless cappuccino maker having our grudge match.

C'mon, you wanker, put up or shut up."

I heard Craig huffing, then what sounded like bone breaking. Then Craig was shouting himself hoarse. "Ah yeah! Fuck yeah! Do your worst you fucking dildo sucker. I got more where that came from!"

"Leave him alone!" Fountain yelled.

"Just sit back and watch the show, James. Watch me like you've been doing for so long. Now that you have a front row seat. An up close and personal ticket to my show."

"You are never going to live through this. You *will* die."

"No, I will kill your friends slowly, like I've done before, and then I'll go see Sydney. Or maybe Milan. They say it's the new hot spot for lovers. But I have no one to call my own. Perhaps I'll take you instead. After all, I feel like we've become good friends over the last few years."

"You have no friends."

"Rude."

"And when we kill you, you will die alone. But it will not be enough pain for you. I can only pray you suffer eternally when we're done."

"Amusing. But like I've said, the only one killing anyone here is me."

I heard him walk to his camera and position it, heard the little creaks and pops that accompany adjusting a tripod. "My coup de grâce. Four at once. I will be a legend."

"You'll be nothing," Craig said. "Not even a footnote. You'll be forgotten like my morning farts and no one will care. As soon as I get out of this chair and kill you."

"Yeah yeah, so you've said. I'm bored by your voice. Let's begin, shall we?"

After that I didn't hear his voice. Nor did I hear Fountain's. But I heard the sudden squeal of pain coming from Katrin beside me. Her squeal became a shriek and she convulsed in her chair. The metal legs banged against the concrete ground.

My gut wrenched and I felt blood flush throughout my body in terror. What was he doing to her! Was he cutting her nose off like in his videos? Was he cutting off her eyelids?

Again she screamed, and this time her mouth tape came loose, which meant it was probably slick with blood. Her terrified wail made my head swim. She was kicking and fighting with all her might, but if she was tied up like me she likely wasn't hitting him.

There was the sound of something ripping, like fabric, or skin. She cried out in pain, and I tried to shout her name but with the tape and rag gagging me it just sounded like noises.

Craig was screaming bloody murder. "Take me instead, you fucking fuck!"

Man oh man, we have seen this all before, ain't we, Roger. You know exactly what's going on. Sheeit, I feel like a kid again listening to all this death and destruction. Sure do wish Butch was here to listen with me. But you ruined that relationship, you dumb turtle dick.

And then Craig was breathing real heavy. He was sort of laughing and sort of crying all at once, and I knew it was bad because I could hear a bone breaking. Craig sucked in air and let out a roar.

What the hell was going on!

I shook to get my hood off, but it was on tight.

This is like your worst nightmare happening all over again, isn't it, Roger? Can't you just smell my basement? Smell all that good flesh that belonged to your sister. Something I never told you about her, about what I did to her. Wanna hear it? I shit on her. I stood over her and shit right on her tits. I think she liked it. Can you imagine that? Someone shitting on you as you bleed out, knowing your life is ending, but now you've got some guy's shit on your chest. Oh man that's the good stuff. But then she died, so that was the end of that fun.

"Fuck you," I screamed, thrashing my head around.

I heard Craig yelling something, and Katrin yelling now too. "You motherfucker!" Damn, she was as tough as they came. I think she was challenging the guy to a fight.

Then something happened. New voices entered the room, and there was even more yelling, and what sounded like a tussle. I heard fists hitting flesh, and bodies falling, and people grunting and struggling. I heard Fountain yell, "Don't let him get away!"

A gunshot rang out and I thought my ears might bleed. The sound echoed off the walls and hit me from every aural angle. There were running feet, and yelps of pain, and Craig was laughing again.

And then my hood was being pulled off and I struggled to make sense of the faces before me. Two men, one with a long white beard. He was fixing a fedora on his head, his nose bleeding. "Walter," I said. Behind him was Uri, untying Fountain. Uri's ear was a mound of red gore.

"Are you hurt?" he asked.

"Yes. He tasered my fucking balls. But I can fight."

"Better than us. We didn't expect him to have a gun. But then we didn't expect to find him so close to our work. We were ill prepared."

"Looks like you did good enough."

He held up some heavy bolt cutters. "These helped. Got in a good swing at him. Only brought them because we know a lot of these rooms down here are locked up."

"Why weren't you in the church earlier?"

"We were, but we left to check on a lead. It turned out to be nothing. When we returned we headed to the basement to get a ledger, saw blood inside. Found the bodies outside and the open grate. We didn't need to be Holmes and Watson to deduce the rest."

"You call the cops?"

"No. We handle some things on our own."

Now Fountain was free and he rushed over and yanked on Katrin's binds. I blushed at what I saw. Her shirt was ripped open and her breasts were exposed. Thin bloody slashes cut like vines across her chest from where the killer had cut her. I glimpsed both of her nipples, still intact, before Fountain closed her shirt for her and cut her binds with the bolt cutters. She moaned in pain and cried angry tears.

My hands were suddenly free and Walter motioned me to my feet, then moved off to free Craig. If Katrin's cuts had her hurting, then Craig must have been in hell. He was missing a couple fingers, and his cheeks were sliced open. One foot looked bent in the wrong direction. The very tip of his nose was nothing but a bloody stump. But he was lucid, and irate. "Hurry up, you fucking twit. Get this shit off me."

Fountain handed the cutters to Uri, who in turn cut the wire around Craig's bleeding hands. Walter was wrapping a portion of his shirt around Craig's fingers to staunch the bleeding. At least he and Brittany would have something in common.

Katrin was standing now. "Where is that fucker!"

We all knew who she meant, but as I looked around I didn't see the guy. He must have run off down one of the tunnels.

I worked quickly to unwind the wire at my feet and was free in thirty seconds. Just as I stood, Fountain appeared in front of me and whispered in my ear. "This moment here, Roger, right now, in this place, this is why you're here. He went down that tunnel there, to your left. Katrin and Craig will follow you, but they're hurt, even if they don't admit it. Me, I'd go but I can't even punch with this arm right now and Uri and Walter are not fighters, despite the commendable job they did here."

"And he as a gun," I said, realizing that I was probably the only person in the room to have survived a gun fight before.

"Indeed he does."

"I'm fucking coming," Katrin said, standing up and picking her blade up off the floor. But she stopped short and put a hand to her chest. She was in pain and was not going to be much help.

"Roger." I heard Fountain's voice again, saw his face hovering in front of me. "He's getting away."

For the briefest of moments I almost asked, *So?* Then Tooth was before me. *You've got this, man. I've got a six-pack of New England's finest craft beer riding on you winning this fight. Do your superhero shit and make him pay. And shit, if you do lose, then you get to hang out with me all the time. So get off your pussy ass already, that hot chick is watching.*

I looked at Katrin once more as she hugged herself and bled down the front of her shirt. I looked at Craig as he gnashed his teeth in anger and picked up his severed fingers from the ground, fumbling with them like they were hot coals. I looked at Uri and Walter, each bleeding and battered. Without further ado, I stood and walked into the tunnel our perp had escaped down. It was cold and black and I was on auto-pilot.

My footfalls echoed off the walls like the staccato beat of my own heart. With each step, I fought internally with myself. Just turn back, I thought, and get on a plane and go back home. Go all the way to New Hampshire and curl up in your mom's lap and go to sleep. Isn't that what you really want? To feel safe again? To be where no one can harm you?

The other side of me had different plans. Hurry up, it said, this guy is getting away. Hit him with everything you've got. Make him pay for Christa and Katrin and Craig and Brittany. Make him pay for every woman on those tapes.

For Jamie.

I guess that side won the argument, because I kept going.

I could barely see. My eyes were adjusting too slowly and I knew he could be anywhere, even right beside me. Instinctively I felt for my phone in my pocket and was stunned to find it still there. The guy had never taken it from me. There were no bars down here, but that wasn't what I was after. The flashlight app lit up the scene before me and I almost wished I hadn't turned it on. Everything around me reminded me of being in Skinny Man's basement again. The dankness, the rot, the dirt, the concrete, the rusted hardware. The walls arced overhead with green slime and brown mineral deposits that dripped down on my head. A thin trail of yellow goo lined the floor like the emergency aisle lights in a movie theater. It even seemed to glow. Up ahead a rat ran out of some hole in the wall, stopped to take a dump, then disappeared into the shadows.

Another thirty feet and the tunnel hit a wall. "Shit," I muttered, then noticed that I could get beyond the wall by ducking low and crawling on my knees through a small opening that acted almost like a bilge hole. I did just that, feeling the slime and mold coat my hands.

I cursed at what lay beyond the barrier. This new tunnel was sunken down about three feet, and filled with brown water. "Shit fuck shit," I said, knowing I had little choice but to drop into it, hoping it wasn't ten feet deep.

I stepped lightly into the water and felt my foot hit bottom. The water came up to my knees; not deep, but still too deep considering what it must consist of. A steady stream of excrement and God knew what else. Thankfully it didn't smell like shit, more like trash and chemicals. I prayed it was just some kind of runoff from the river.

I sloshed through it, following the curve of the tunnel, and suddenly heard splashing ahead. I tried to move faster without picking up my legs, just pushing them forward in the muck. It made noise, but not as much as before.

And then I could hear him breathing, just up ahead. I tried to let my eyes adjust again but it was simply too dark to make out anything but blackness and even deeper blackness. I shined my light around and all I saw before me was a large wall grate, like prison bars, sealing off the rest of the tunnel.

Where the hell did he go, I wondered, my heart rate now frantic. He was here a second ago, which meant he was either still close or he'd found a way around the barrier. I moved the light around me, saw nothing but more slime and brown water. Then I looked up, saw some ladder rungs about two feet over my head. They led up to a manhole cover. The fucker had escaped after all!

"No!" I shouted. I knew there was no way I'd find him now, not out in the streets. He was long gone. I'd had him just inches from my fingertips and I'd let him get away. Everything I was trying to do—avenge the women, avenge my friends—it had been a waste. Sure, he might attack us again on another day, maybe soon, maybe years from now, but he might also disappear back into the underground and satiate his bloodlust on more unsuspecting women.

If he went up those rungs, Skinny Man whispered, *he's got the quietest feet I ever heard. And that manhole cover . . . it must be magical 'cause it was as silent as a woman's fart.*

He's right, Tooth said, *if he went up there I'll eat your skid-marked underwear.*

I spun around, playing the light off the cold stone walls, looking for some kind of sign I'd missed, something to tell me where he'd gone, but there was nothing. All I could hear was my own shallow breathing, the steady drip of water on the walls, and the sloshing of the water by my knees. I stood still, letting the water settle, noting how the sound felt dulled all around me, like canned laughter in a sitcom, only with ambient noise instead of chuckles. I could just feel something in my bones, something that said I wasn't alone.

He's under the water, I realized.

I didn't know if I should stay still or look for him, but not knowing where he was put me at a disadvantage. So I gave a few kicks but didn't feel him. Then I reached down and swirled my hand in the water, felt some hard things float against my forearm. Could have been anything really? Trash, wood, human excrement. There was several feet of tunnel leading back toward the grate, and I knew he could be anywhere. Was he using some kind of breathing apparatus? Could he just hold his breath for long periods?

The water went still around me and I tried to listen for bubbles, but I heard nothing. C'mon, you sonofabitch, I thought. Where are you? Just give me a sign.

The water exploded upwards like a geyser right in front of me and his entire body engulfed me. His arms went around my throat and his wet cape and hood slapped over my head. I was being yanked down, my knees caught up in his own legs. The water came over me and I was submerged, my throat being squeezed, a wet cloak tying up my arms.

I had no air in my lungs and I couldn't find my footing.

I was going to die.

Chapter 24

It was only a second later that I felt my sneakers find the floor. That was good, but panic was beginning to overtake me. I could not think, could not rationalize a plan, could only kick off the bottom out of sheer survival instinct. I had enough adrenaline coursing through me I could have lifted a car. As it was I lifted us both up out of the water, his fingers still squeezing my Adam's apple, and landed on top of him in the water again. We both went under, only this time I was on top of him, my back to his chest. He wouldn't let go of his stranglehold but now my hands were free and I found his thumbs and pulled them back, seeing spots before my eyes, knowing I had just seconds before I passed out. One of his hands came free and I thrust my head up, fighting for the surface, feeling the sludge break over my chin just as my body made one last desperate gulp for air. I inhaled almost as much water as oxygen, which tasted like shit and brine, but it was enough to keep me awake. I sucked in more before he pulled me under again and his arm went around my neck in a new choke hold. I went to throw my head back at his face but before I could I felt a sting in my side.

His blade went in beneath my ribs, gunning for my heart. The sudden pain shot up my head. Thankfully, with my clothing bunched up, and with his cloak around me, the blade didn't get very far. Had I not been poked, cut, stabbed, shot and had the shit kicked out of me before I might have started to cry, but I knew this was one of the tamer wounds in my résumé. I didn't bank on him twisting the blade though, and that hurt so much I couldn't help but scream under water, letting out my precious air.

Finally, I threw my head back and felt it connect with his face. He grunted underwater and his grip loosened. I was up and out of the water in a flash, gasping for air, my hands going to my side to feel for the wound.

I saw it before I touched it, a red gash with the scalpel still stuck in it. I yanked it out and watched my blood run out and mix with the brown water surrounding me, all of it eerily illuminated by my still-working submerged cell phone.

He stood up in front of me, his mouth running red, and said, "That's mine. I want it back."

With a sneer, I threw the scalpel into the water. "Oops. My bad."

He chuckled. Why do they always chuckle when they're trying to kill me? Do I look funny when I'm near death? "That's okay. I have *this*."

Fuck. I'd completely forgotten he had a gun. Why the hell had he even tried to drown me?

"It's crude," he said. "I prefer something more intimate. That's my thing, really, watching it all unfold, feeling your hot breath leak out over time as I explore your insides. It's got a divine power to it. But in a pinch, this will do."

Okay, question answered. He raised it and pointed it at me.

"It won't work," I said.

"Oh, I think my plan will pan out just fine."

"No, not your plan. The gun. It won't work."

"What? What won't work? The gun? It's been in water before. It'll fire. See . . . "

"Wait! No, I mean it won't kill me. Maybe hurt me. But it'll misfire, or buck so hard the bullet just grazes me, or something will make it jam. I dunno what will happen but something will go wrong for you."

He cocked his head like a dog hearing a far-off noise. "You've got quite the ego."

"I'm just saying . . . it'll happen. And when it happens, I'm going to rush you, and I'm going to kill you."

"I'll take the bet. Any last words?"

"Where's Christa?"

"Ah . . . her. Yeah, she's gone. I cut her into little bits and fed them to stray cats. Her bones are here and there, mostly ground up and sitting in a landfill somewhere. It's sort of my thing. Or did you never ask where any of the bodies went?"

He had me there. I had assumed they'd been found, but getting rid of them made more sense. It's why he hadn't been caught. All he needed was the tapes to keep reliving his dreams over and over, to go down in infamy.

"Anything else?" he asked.

"No. Well, yeah, maybe. Just answer me one thing because I'm going to need to feel justified in yelling at my boss after I kill you.

The girls, the one's from the foundation, they were sold to you without them even knowing it. Their whereabouts, their histories. Someone gave you easy prey. It was basically a slavery ring. Right?"

"Sure."

"Angeline Mathias supplied them to you?"

He said nothing. I took it as confirmation of my guess.

"Were you the only buyer?" I asked.

"No. But I don't know what those other guys did with their girls. Took them to Dubai and married them for all I know. Me, well, it's obvious."

"Why kill Angeline?"

"I'd almost think you really do believe you're going to live. Do you really need these answers before you die?"

"Yes. Why kill the person who was supplying you with your vice?"

"I don't feel like talking about this. My night has been ruined already."

"Because she cut you off, right? Why'd she cut you off?"

"Because she was a stupid whore! They all were. Now I have to go. G'night."

"Wait! Don't—tell me, had she been found out? Was she trying to cover her tracks, shut down her operation to avoid arrest? The police found out?"

"The cops didn't know about her. They didn't know shit. And besides, she'd eat the cops alive. The woman had power over others. No, the cunt cut me off because—"

He went rigid. His mouth worked like a marionette had gotten its strings tangled. Slowly he turned around to look behind himself. I saw the switchblade sticking out at the base of his skull, the point lodged in his brain stem. I hadn't even heard it being thrown.

Katrin and Craig stood there, each wet and bloodied, pissed and exhausted. When the hell had they arrived? And how had they been so silent in the water? The killer reached for the knife but Katrin drew another from her belt and overhanded it. It sang through the air and got him in the eye.

His guttural scream built like an approaching train. It grew so loud I thought the walls would crumble. His gun came up and barked. My ears rang. But his bullet went wide and struck nothing but cement.

"I don't need all my fingers for you," Craig said, yanking the gun from the guy's hands. "Told you I'd kill your ass."

Craig punched him in the face with his bandaged fist. The killer went down and Craig stepped on his head, held him under the water.

"Don't," I said. "Don't kill him."

Craig's face was a twisted mess of hatred and exhaustion. "Why not?"

"Well for one, can you live with it? It's not easy."

"Roger Roger, you're not the only one here with blood on their hands. Why do you think we're all working together?"

That kind of stunned me. I had never figured either Craig or Katrin as killers, but seeing the way Katrin had flung her blade made me second guess everything. When I looked at her she just frowned.

"If he dies . . . those girls . . . their friends and relatives . . . they get no satisfaction. Give them that at least."

The killer's arms started flailing in the water. He was panicking, suffocating, his heart about to burst.

"Fountain told us to put him down, not talk to him," Katrin said. "He'll just kill again, somehow, some way. It's not like he'll confess. I stuck a knife in the back of his brain for one thing, and if he doesn't end up brain damaged he'll just plead insanity."

"Let him up!" I yelled.

Reluctantly, Craig took his foot off the killer's neck and the man raised up out of the water, the knife still in the back of his neck.

He was holding the gun. How'd he'd gotten it was beyond me. Even Craig looked stunned, but then I realized Craig didn't have any feeling in his ruined hands and must have dropped it in the water during their struggle.

He aimed it at me and pulled the trigger. I saw the orange flash, felt my shoulder go hot and wet. Lord God it hurt so bad. My right side went numb. I half-expected to see my arm fall into the water near my knees. He spun and pointed the gun at Katrin's head. I heard the shot, saw Katrin fall to the water. Craig screamed, swinging a bloodied half-fingerless fist at him. I was running, jumping, catching him around the waist and taking him down, punching him. And then all I saw was Skinny Man, swimming into my vision.

Bloodlust, Roger. Oooh yeah, boy, you got it. Swing that fist. Feel them teeth smash out. Feel that nose break. Might as well rip off an ear and gouge out an eye. That's it! Get a finger in that eye and yank and pull. Feel that gristle? That's the good stuff, Roger boy. Grab his hair and smash his face on the cement wall. Go on, do it! Yeah, that's the thing. See that blood. Man oh man, I feel like getting naked and dancing. That's it, keep smashing that skull in, feel it start to crack, see the brains coming out. Look! His eyeball just popped out. You should fuck the socket, like that old joke. Or was it a movie line? Who cares, just fuck his open skull hole! Or keep smashing. That works too! Jesus Christ, son, you are a natural at this. Me and you, we coulda been a team. But fuck, I don't do teams, less it's a team of Jamie clones all tied up and begging for my knife. Hey, you listening to me? I'm trying to tell you something and you just keep smashing away at that guy's head. Jesus his brains are going everywhere. He ain't even moving no more. You did it! Look at that blood, look at how his eyes are dangling out. Hey, Roger . . .

Then another voice I felt safer listening too.

Roger, enough, buddy. You're entering Sith territory.

And then a third:

"Roger! Roger, enough!"

I fell back, felt Katrin's arms around my neck. She was breathing hard, pulling at me. She was alive!

"It's okay," she said. "Stop screaming. Just breathe."

I stopped moving, looked at the malformed, gore-covered face before me, the one I still held up by the collar of its shirt. The killer's eye was gone, and his mouth was nothing but jagged little white points poking through red ichor. His cheekbones were split plums, bits of pearl white jutting through wet skin.

"I think he's dead, Roger," she whispered.

Jesus Christ. I let the body drop, realizing what I'd done. I looked into her eyes and wanted to cry. "I thought he shot you. I can't see anyone else I care about die. I just can't . . . "

"You fucking lost it, dude," Craig said, cradling his hand against his stomach. "You went berserker. It was a little bit awesome. But gross. But you know, awesome too."

I stood up and looked at the dead body floating before me. Jesus, what had I done? Killed. Again. And this time literally with my bare hands.

I started to shake, felt cold inside.

"Hey," Katrin said, spinning me around and meeting my eyes. "He missed. I threw myself down as fast as I could. He missed."

"And I killed him with my bare hands."

"He woulda killed me when I stood up. Or he woulda killed Craig. And then James. And then gone out and kept doing it. Let it go. How's your shoulder?"

"Hurts. Can't feel much."

"He took a chunk out of the top, but the bullet went high. Some stitches and bandages and you'll live. I don't think he was much good with guns. You're lucky."

"So I'm told. What do we . . . do with his body?" I asked.

"Let it stay and rot," Craig suggested. "Let the fucking rats eat it. I need to get to a hospital, try to get these fingers reattached. I'm heading back."

I stared at the body a little while longer. I didn't even know the guy's name. But I'd never forget the videos he'd put online, the way he'd butchered so many. And Christa . . . would they ever find her body? She was dead because of me, because of who I was, and I didn't really feel any better knowing I'd beaten her murderer to death.

"I'm taking it to the police," I said. "This will exonerate Fountain."

"No it won't. It'll make him a stronger suspect. Craig's right for once. Just leave the fucker for the rats. This water washes out to the river. It'll dissipate for a while and then someone will track the smell and find him. Just another idiot trying to explore the sewers who slipped and fell." She went over and yanked the knives out of his body, hid them back on her person.

"Yeah. Sure. Fuck it."

And so we left him there, dead, in the water. Like a piece of trash.

We made our way back to the hub. Fountain, Uri and Walter were taking down the recording equipment; I knew they were going to bring it back to the church and study it.

Fountain saw my bruised face, put a hand on my shoulder. "Craig filled me in. I knew it, Roger. I knew you would succeed."

"I wouldn't call it a rousing success. He's dead."

"It was necessary. And your shoulder . . . do you need medical attention?"

"Probably. I don't care. I just killed a man with my bare hands. Is this why you brought me here? Is this the special ability you want me to have? Answer me!"

"Roger, you did a great service tonight."

"Something about all of this stinks, Fountain. But I'm too tired to care. I'm going home to sleep. At the apartment."

I stormed past him, out the door that was still adorned with Piotr's and Oscar's heads, and eventually found my way back to my room. Katrin followed silently, and at some point came into my room and got in bed with me.

Chapter 25

I soon found myself inside her, and she was biting my lip and saying thank you to me, but for what I was unclear. We slept through the morning and into the afternoon. When I awoke and went to the kitchen I saw Fountain at the table.

"Roger—"

"Let's talk," I said, pulling up a chair next to him.

"I think you should rest more."

"Fuck you. You lied. And I had a lot to think about this morning as I laid in bed with my shoulder throbbing. Jesus, I'm getting real tired of getting shot."

"You should have gone to the hospital."

"They would have just bandaged it, same as Katrin did. It's mostly a cut. He missed his shot."

"I knew he would."

"It's scary that you still think I have some kind of power."

"And you don't think you do?"

"No. Although I did try to scare him with the possibility of it. No, I think he was a knife guy and never did any target shooting. He didn't know the buck of his own gun, whether it kicked right or left. He figured he could just point it straight and fire. That's why I'm alive. Not magic."

"You're wrong. You're alive because it's your power. You survive."

"Whatever, we're ahead of things here. Why didn't you tell us the truth? Why keep it a secret about Angeline, that she wasn't your wife?"

He paused, then: "Because I was told to."

"And you listen to everything they say?"

"Most of it. I'm here because of them."

"Or you lied because we'd be more sympathetic to the cause if we thought she was your wife?"

"If you like."

"I think maybe they told you to lie but you knew it was a good way to get help on your side so you went with it. Does that work?"

"I loved her, Roger."

"Did you really?"

"Yes. I wanted her to be my wife. Isn't that enough?"

I believed him. I could see real pain in his face when he thought
of her. I tried to steer the conversation to another point. "I thought
maybe this guy—"

"Alec."

"What?"

"That's his name," Fountain explained. "We tracked his place of
employment. That's the name he went by there, so for now, we call
him Alec. I doubt it's his real name. We'll find out eventually. We will
have his place of residence soon enough."

"Okay. I thought maybe Alec was just lucky, using the Soaring
Skies Foundation, spying on teenage homeless girls, lucky to have
found a source of victims. But to then kill the women heading it .
. . it's sort of like cutting off your supply. Why risk shutting down
the charity? Why risk halting the company's work for an investigation? Unless . . . "

He was stone-faced now. I could tell I was on the right track.

"You knew she was helping him. You knew she was selling
girls."

There was a pause so long I thought I might qualify for the sen-
ior discount at the diner down the street by the time it ended. Then
Fountain's eyes got a little more wet, more red, angry and embarrassed at once. "Yes, she was helping him. But I didn't know—"

"You didn't know?"

"Of course not. Not when I had fallen in love with her."

"Then when . . . "

"I started to see her lifestyle. The clothing, the jewelry, the
apartment she moved to overlooking Central Park. I don't know
why I became suspicious, but I did. I knew the people that were
funding Soaring Skies. I knew the money was enough to get the
girls medical treatment, feed them and get them started on life
again. I knew most of the funds came from donations. So where
was she getting the money for the lavish lifestyle?"

"So you started snooping?"

"I did. I found she had several hidden email accounts, as well
as some offshore bank accounts."

"How'd you find this out?"

"The church helped. They have people in place. It behooved
them to find out what was going on."

"Churches hate to lose face. Hurts their tithes, their livelihood, their exemption from the rules of governmental law."

"They also simply don't like when people they're helping are being murdered."

"Bullshit. They helped fund Soaring Skies. Right? They were one of the founding organizations."

"One thing does not breed the other." He sounded a little angry with me, but I guess I deserved it, insulting his family and all. But shit, I still didn't trust anyone in organized religion, especially not here.

"Sorry. Continue."

"I found her email communiqués with a person she only referred to as Cable. I thought it was her cable service at first."

"A cable service that shows very select films."

"Indeed. Through these, I learned she was revealing the locations of girls Soaring Skies had relocated. Not all of them, mind you, just select ones. Easy targets. And after each reveal, she received a payment."

"And your people were able to uncover the amounts?"

"Some of our people are in banking, yes. We found some figures."

"So . . . lots of money?"

"Plenty. And then a few days later a video would appear online of a girl Soaring Skies had saved being butchered alive."

"What a cunt."

"I didn't want to believe it at first. It made no sense. Why would she do it? I asked myself over and over. But it didn't change the fact she was helping this person, this Cable."

"Money moves people. It's a sad fact."

"As I said, I didn't want to believe it."

"You think Cable is Alec?"

"Right now, yes. But I can't confirm it till we dig some more."

"So what went wrong? Why'd he kill her?"

"Honestly, I don't know. Except we found one email conversation . . . she mentioned getting out."

"Out of what?"

"Out of the business, is my guess."

"Out of human trafficking? And you think he got pissed? By

leaving, she was cutting off his supply?"

"I think she was happy with the money he'd paid her for the information. She was set for life. So she was opting out. I think he pleaded with her to stay on, and she said no. She could be stubborn."

"And so he killed her. She cut off his supply and if he couldn't have the girls, he'd have her instead. I'm surprised she didn't cave once he had her with a knife to her throat."

He steepled his fingers, rested his chin on them. "She must have argued, angered him. Perhaps he was too far consumed by his sudden hatred of her. I can only think she kept telling him no."

"Please tell me you don't think she developed a conscience."

"I'd like to think so, but it wouldn't change my view of her now."

"So in the end, the church is just covering up its own mess. They hire Angeline, she offers the girls to Alec, Cable, whoever, and if word ever gets out the church is fucked. They'll look like accomplices, never receive another donation. It's quite the fucking scandal."

He didn't say anything but I knew I was right.

"I should have been more honest with you, Roger. I'm sorry. But like I said, it wasn't my choice."

"I might have still helped had you just told me the church wanted me to kill someone."

"First off, the church does not condone killing. I make those decisions and I bear the guilt."

"Yeah, but the church doesn't exactly stop you," I said.

"Secondly, *would* you have?"

"I might have thought twice about things. But, honestly, when you showed me the video . . . I probably would have stayed. Alec deserved to die."

"I hope he is suffering eternal hell."

We paused, let the exchange soak in for a second.

"So what now?" I asked. "Now that the church is free of shame."

"Free? This hunt is far from over."

"How so? Alec is dead."

"But his peers are not. You remember the man you helped me

apprehend?"

"The shithead shooting up little girls. How can I forget? Wait, you mean he and Alec knew each other? Angeline supplied him as well?"

"It seems Angeline supplied information to an underground world you can only dare to imagine. Alec took girls to satisfy his demented bloodlust. Others took them for sex slavery. Others for drug muling. Some engaged in human sacrifices, to control darker forces that I am not in the mood to explain. They don't all know each other in person, but they know each other. Their deeds are whispered of in the shadows and like fingerprints, are recognizable to those who know what they're looking for. But when we catch one of these vile men, we get a lead on another. And then another. And it takes us to all manner of places. They are everywhere, still thriving."

Something clicked in place in my head. "Like San Diego. That's why you were really in Marshall Aldritch's mansion. You were look-ing for the girls he'd kidnapped."

"Oh, I was there for you too, Roger, as I said before. It is part of my job to recognize abilities such as yours and Katrin's and Craig's. But I admit it was opportunistic. I was also there to find the girl you watched get eaten alive. Her name was Heather. I arrived too late to save her, and so my attention was turned to you, because if I couldn't save her, I could sway you to help me save others. And you have."

"Because you think I have powers. Which is stupid."

"I think you have a gift. It's different. And I think you know it now. I think you looked at that little girl you saved in that apart-ment and you knew you were meant to be here, to put an end to Alec's spree. It was no mistake that you came to us."

"Says you. If I'd known how crazy you were before I arrived, things could be different."

"We're not crazy. But we are fighting something that takes a cer-tain mindset. And you have it."

"What I have are broken bones and gunshot wounds."

"Wounds heal."

"Yeah, but they become scars."

He pointed at my chest. "Your scars are merely a reminder of trials you've endured and survived. They are your story, written on your body, your temple. They are medals of victory and badges of triumph. You earned them so that others may live. Never forget that each scar you've earned is a person whose life you've saved."

"Saved? I don't know that I'm saving anyone. Everyone I save ends up broken."

"But with a second chance. Think about it."

"What I think is that you're crazy. But I repeat, what now?"

He leaned back, and for the first time he seemed a little happier, more relaxed. "Well, that depends. There is a man in Rio feeding children to pythons for sport. A man in Auvers sur Oise who grinds women's heads into dust to use in a Satanic conjuring ritual—complete with reports of a cloven-hoofed man running in the fields. We've received reports of a married couple in Sydney raping and murdering hikers in the outback then selling their body parts as cattle feed. I've got files and files of this type of thing."

"Let me guess. They're stored in the church undercroft?"

"Yes. And then there is the news item on the girl in Kingston who got stabbed in a mugging. Twelve times in the neck. She was rushed to a hospital only to awake in the morning with not a single scratch on her."

"Accelerated healing?"

"Won't know for sure until we look into it."

"You're gonna go talk to her?"

"At some point, yes."

Just then my phone buzzed. It was a text message from Teddy. I didn't even know he knew how to text. It read, *Are you alive? Come Home. Tooth's dad.*

"What is your gut telling you?" he asked.

"It's telling me I need a moment to think about things." With that, I got up and left.

Chapter 26

I found Katrin in her bedroom, waiting for me. The cuts on her face were more swollen than before. Probably by tomorrow they'd start to go down.

"What'd he say," she asked.

"Lots. Nothing. Depends on what you believe."

"He say anything about Angeline?"

I filled her in briefly on what I now knew. She seemed pissed, but didn't we all.

"So what are you gonna do?" she asked.

"I didn't know. But I have to ask, you and me, this whole thing . . . was it okay?"

"God, you're a fucking asshole, you know that."

"Sorry, I'm just real bad with girls. You've seen what happens."

"Yeah, it was okay. Do you want me to grade you?"

"No, no, that's not what I mean. I mean . . . are we okay? Are we . . . look, I think I sort of like you."

"What're we in fucking high school?"

"No. Sorry. Fuck it." I got up and paced for a minute.

"It's okay," she said. "I'm acting mean. I'm annoyed. What're you doing?"

"Thinking."

"About what?"

"About whether I'm going to keep this up. Go to Sydney or Kingston or the fucking moon, chasing sickos. It's a shitty life. I thought I could atone for things, but I feel like things are just more nuts here. That's not what I want, even if Fountain is right about my . . . ability."

"What ability? The one where a bunch of dead people follow you around?"

I stopped pacing. "Can you really see people around me? Truthfully?"

"I told you I can."

I wanted so badly to believe her now, because if that was real, maybe Fountain's assessment of me was real too. But how could I ever know for sure? Maybe she was just a tad crazy. I don't know that it bothered me, to be honest.

My phone buzzed again. I looked at the screen. Another message from Teddy. *Very serious. Come home. Tooth's dad.*

I texted back: *What about Tooth's dad?*

"Who's that?" Katrin asked.

"An old friend."

"What do they want?"

Teddy's reply came. *Murdered. Come home if you can.*

"Oh my god," I whispered.

Katrin got up, put her arms around me. "What?"

"I have to go."

"Go where?"

I looked into her eyes, smelled the dirt on her forehead. I could hear Fountain on the phone in the other room, talking to someone about shipping containers. Craig still wasn't back from the hospital; I had no idea if the doctors had been able to reattach his fingers. Over Katrin's shoulder, out the window, the Brandenburg Gate loomed in the distance, a golden motif of victory in motion.

I looked at her lips, dipped my head and kissed her. "Life isn't about what you get, it's about what you leave behind."

"The fuck does that mean?"

"It means I have to go home."

I went back to my room to pack.

AUTHOR BIO

Ryan C. Thomas is the author of many novels and novellas, including the cult classic, *The Summer I Died*. He lives in San Diego with his wife, son, and two dogs. When he is not writing, he is playing guitar in the bars or watching really bad B-movies.

Visit him online at www.ryancthomas.com

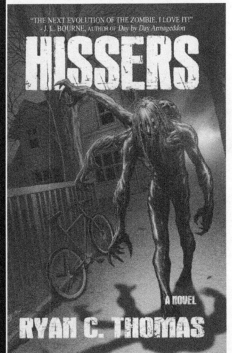

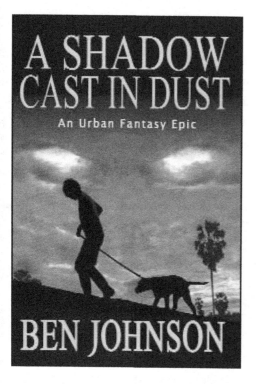

PLENTIFUL POISON

by Kyle Lybeck

Denver was ground zero. At the time no one knew what they truly had. It was too late once they had a grasp. A killing machine unlike any other: fast, adaptive, and brutally blood-thirsty.

A quiet morning starts for the Baker family, until the news stories start to flood in. The complete absurdity of them seems impossible. That is, until they meet their first rager.

Nobody is safe. Everyone is at risk. All you can do is avoid the poison.

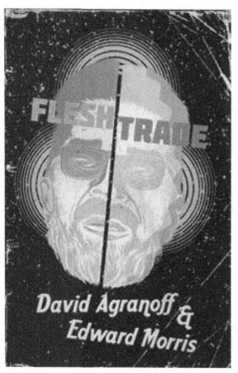

For more Grand Mal Press titles
please visit us online at
www.grandmalpress.com

Made in the USA
Monee, IL
02 October 2022